PRAISE FOR THE NOVELS OF
LAUREN BARATZ-LOGSTED

THE THIN PINK LINE

"Wonderfully funny debut with a fine sense of the absurd and a flair for comic characterization."
—*Kirkus* starred review

"Hilarious and original." —*Publishers Weekly*

"This is amusing, light fun." —*Booklist*

CROSSING THE LINE

"Baratz-Logsted has a great voice." —*RT Book Reviews*

"Even better than the first book!" —*Booklist*

THE BRO-MAGNET

"There are so many memorable moments in this book that I could spend page after page quoting them."
—*USA Today*

ISN'T IT BRO-MANTIC

"Will have readers experiencing major belly laughs."
—*RT Book Reviews*

## THE SISTERS CLUB

"Who doesn't need a sister? That's the question at the heart of the charming novel, *The Sisters Club*. With her deft touch and sure eye for character, Lauren Baratz-Logsted lovingly evokes the lives of four ordinary women who become each other's surrogate families. A warm, wise, and witty tale. You will love it!"

—Elizabeth Letts, bestselling author
of *The Eighty-Dollar Champion*


## FALLING FOR PRINCE CHARLES

"Strong characterization, eyebrow-raising situations and quirky dialogue will leave you cheering for this decidedly unusual couple who, against all odds, find love."

—*RT Book Reviews*

"Daisy's madcap adventure is more comedy than romance, and her most unusual and unlikely relationship with Prince Charles will appeal to readers looking for lots of giggles."

—*Publishers Weekly*

"Lauren Baratz-Logsted has mastered the real-life fairy tale in her explosive and hilarious *Falling for Prince Charles*. It's all here, lovelorn Daisy Silverman flush with cash and high hopes, Prince Charles who can't resist her, and London in all its splendor. Curl up and get ready to laugh long into the foggy night."

—Adriana Trigiani, *New York Times*
bestselling author of *The Shoemaker's Wife*

# the *other* brother

## LAUREN BARATZ-LOGSTED

**DIVERSION
BOOKS**

**Also by Lauren Baratz-Logsted**

*Falling for Prince Charles*
*The Sister's Club*

Jane Taylor Novels    Johnny Smith Novels
*The Thin Pink Line*      *The Bro-Magnet*
*Crossing the Line*      *Isn't is Bromantic?*

Diversion Books
A Division of Diversion Publishing Corp.
443 Park Avenue South, Suite 1008
New York, New York 10016
www.DiversionBooks.com

For more information, email info@diversionbooks.com

First Diversion Books edition August 2018.
Paperback ISBN: 978-1-63576-042-2
eBook ISBN: 978-1-63576-041-5

LSIDB/1808

For my sister-in-law,
Kathleen Baratz,
sister and friend.

# PART I

## *London*

HE SUCKED ALL THE AIR OUT OF THE ROOM.

Jack's dad had asked about the agency, and Jack had replied about how well things were going. He'd even started to tell about our exciting plans for the summer when Denny cut him off, launching into a tale about some gig he'd done in Malaysia the week before. As Denny went on, and on and on, I saw Jack's face fall. Well, who can beat a gig in Malaysia?

We were in the sitting room at my in-laws' house, having pre-dinner drinks. My husband and his father, Burt, were side by side on the sofa. Burt's a big-bellied, burly man with muttonchops, a look he's favored the whole time I've known him, the muttonchops having long since gone white; bowlegged, Burt always looks like he just climbed off a Harley. My boys were pretending to play something on the floor not too far from Denny's swinging foot. There was so much pent-up energy in that swinging foot.

Of course Denny was seated in the best chair in the

room, by the fireplace. Me, I was standing with my drink next to the occasional table, the one with family photos blanketing it. There were several pictures of my sons, one for each year from womb until now, and several of Jack, including our wedding portrait. I'm sorry to say I look like a giant confection in it; blame the dress on the Princess Di fervor that had still been going on two years after her own wedding, which was when mine took place—I'd choose differently now if I could. As for Denny, the only pictures of him on display were from when he was a small child. Really, on the entire lower level of the house, there was no other evidence that he had ever lived there, which had been part of the problem once upon a time.

I suppose *he'd* say that it wasn't his fault, strictly speaking, that the air went out of the room whenever he spoke. *He'd* say that the room was too small to hold him, that he was more used to arenas, and sometimes even those weren't big enough! And if he said that? The world would agree with him. Not many people can get the whole entire world to agree with them on a single thing, perhaps because most people aren't known by pretty much every living person on the planet, but my brother-in-law can and was, simply because my brother-in-law was Denny Springer, lead singer for the greatest rock-and-roll band in the world; or, as it's usually printed in mags: The Greatest Rock-and-Roll Band In The World, like it's an official title they've earned or an award won, like the Booker or the Nobel.

Even in remote parts of the planet, people knew who Denny Springer was. Why, I read a story once, in one of those same mags, about one time when Denny was contributing to that charity album that was supposed to save the rainforest; they helicoptered him in and some woman came out of the bush or whatever it's called—as a travel agent, you'd think I'd know these things—and even though her tribe had supposedly never had contact with civilization before, after her initial shock at seeing him, she'd launched into an off-key rendition of "Frustration," his signature song, after which she had him autograph her bra, which, if I remember correctly, was made out of polished gourds.

It's safe to say that the world has cut Denny some slack at every turn.

It's even safer to say that I never have.

Thankfully, Edith called us all in to Easter dinner then. Physically, Edith often reminds me of the main character from *Keeping Up Appearances,* only much shorter and minus the faux plummy accent. She always wears dresses, and there's almost always a belt high up that only serves to accentuate the firm ball of tweed-covered belly below. Edith is also frequently hysterical, but not in a funny way. At least, though, as she loudly shrieked for us to come in to dinner, she was saving us from hearing more about Malaysia. Or so I thought.

Not that my sons needed it; saving, that is. The way they'd stared at their uncle, like he was some sort of celebrity or something. Well, who could blame them? They'd seen him on the news or on the covers of magazines countless times. But in person? Hardly half a dozen.

In the dining room, without thinking, without even asking Edith where *she* wanted us all to sit, Denny immediately settled into the seat at the head of the table. I saw Burt open his mouth, preparatory to objecting—it was his seat, after all, his house—but then Edith jabbed him in the ribs with an elbow as she set the platter with the lamb at the foot of the table instead, giving her husband an amused eye-roll and a jerk of the head in the general direction of their eldest son. Despite the condescension in that jerking head and those rolling eyes, I knew that Edith didn't look down on her son, necessarily. It was more like both she and Burt were eternally puzzled by Denny and not a little frightened of him too.

Once, while watching a televised program of one of his concerts with them, Burt shook his head in confusion throughout and Edith was heard to mutter, "I thought he was going to be a maths teacher..."

Now the man who'd been meant to be a maths teacher was opening a case he'd kept close by since arriving earlier in the day and removing a large device, from which there came a ringing sound.

"I've been expecting a call," Denny said importantly, punching a button on the device and placing it to his ear.

"What's that?" Burt asked.

"It's a mobile phone," Denny said, covering the speaker with one hand.

Of course there were smaller mobiles available by then, but Denny would have to have one that looked more ornate, like something the Queen might use. Or Batman.

"A phone?" Burt said. "Look at that contraption. A phone in its own little suitcase?" He snorted. "I can't see those ever catching on."

Looking annoyed, Denny rose from his chair and exited the room to continue his call in private, stopping only long enough to snag a hot cross bun from the basket Edith had put out earlier.

My boys' eyes followed him like he was God.

And at the table: silence.

The only noises were the sounds of Denny talking and laughing his end of the conversation in the living room.

After a full ten minutes, the realization dawning on all of us that Denny wouldn't be returning anytime soon, Jack offered, "I suppose we might as well go ahead and eat then."

"We can't eat Easter dinner without your brother," Edith said stridently.

"Why?" Jack said. "We've been eating Easter dinner without him for twenty years or more."

"And that's the point," Edith said. Strident as she might naturally be, it was rare for her to say no to Jack. She loved him. Really, she did. "He hasn't been here in so long, it wouldn't be right." A firm nod of the head. "We'll wait."

All this talk about how long it'd been since Denny was home, coupled with him not even bothering to remain at the table, did make me wonder: just why had Denny come home?

Even if Jack hadn't persuaded Edith that we could start eating, by speaking up he had broken the ice, so he and Burt went back to talking about the travel agency again. They'd gotten as far as rehashing what had already been said—business very good; booming, really!—and Jack was once again on the verge of sharing our summer plans, when Denny returned.

Without so much as an apology, he reseated himself at the head of the table, crossing one skinny leg over the other as he lounged back in his chair. "Where were we?" he wondered. And then, not waiting for an answer: "Ah, right—Malaysia!"

Burt finally carved up the lamb, then my eldest handed a plate to Denny, my eldest's hands shaking like he were making an offering to a god who might smite him if displeased. I worried Denny might say something rude or mocking, but to his credit, he steadied the plate with his own hands, all the while giving my son a high-wattage smile of reassurance. That is the thing about my brother-in-law: a total asswipe, but then there are these glimpses of blinding block-out-the-sun charisma, and in those instances you see exactly what the whole world sees, why there are women who would—and have—walked on broken glass to have one of those smiles directed at them.

And a moment later: "Lamb's cold," Denny announced.

Well, for fuck's sake, what did the man expect?

I can't say he used a complaining tone—it was more like he was making an empirical observation—but still.

He pushed the plate slightly away from himself, only half-heartedly picking at the potatoes and veg as he took us on a whirlwind tour of his recent experiences in the East, near and Far. I winced at some of the "sex, drugs" parts of his "sex, drugs, and rock and roll" anecdotes, but there was no stopping him once he got going, and I could only hope my boys didn't know their hookers from their hookahs just yet. Perhaps it was all gobbledygook to them?

"You should eat more," Edith said when Denny paused for breath. "You always were a skinny lad, but you're a grown man now. It's time you put some meat on you."

Oh, he was grown all right. How old was Denny now? I did the numbers in my head. If I was thirty-three, Denny was forty-two; for quite some time, like a moon attached to a planet, I'd always known what my age was in relation to Denny.

To his credit, again, Denny ate some more of the lamb, which really was dreadfully cold, before pushing the plate aside for good.

When Edith tried to protest, again, he put her off with a wave of the hand. "I'm not really that hungry today," he said, immediately belying the words by grabbing another hot cross bun.

This he only picked at, fingering off the sticky icing and popping his glistening forefinger into his mouth in a way that, under other circumstances, could only be deemed sexual.

It did occur to me, as it must have to Edith, that a man like Denny must almost always be hungry for something; he simply wasn't hungry for mum-made lamb with potatoes and a proper veg on the side. I felt bad for Edith then. As my boys got increasingly older and independent—or as independent as they could be at nine and seven—some days I felt all I could do for them as each step in life took them further from my womb, further from my home, was to provide a good meal for them and love them. But poor Edith. Denny, his taste buds long since grown accustomed to the most exotic cuisines and the finest chefs in the world, couldn't, or wouldn't, let her do that.

Hell, the man had his own personal world-class chef. Everyone who read the mags knew that.

There are times, I must confess, that I do believe I spend too much time surreptitiously reading the mags or trying deliberately not to.

The main course finished, I helped Edith clear the table

15

for dessert. She'd just brought the pudding in when Denny reached into his inside jacket pocket, drawing out a packet of French cigarettes. He had one out and between his lips, a gold lighter flicking in his other hand—that lighter probably weighing more in solid gold than everything in my jewelry box combined—when Edith shouted, "You can't smoke that in here!"

Denny was so startled he nearly dropped his unlit smoke.

"I can't?" he said dumbly.

Edith pointed with vehemence at a sign on the sideboard: *Thank You For Not Smoking.*

I knew that sign. Edith had similar signs, which she'd put out the year before, in every room in the house. Honestly, it was impossible to believe that Denny had missed them.

"Christ," Denny muttered. "It's worse than America."

Edith ignored that. "If you must smoke that," she said, "you may do so outside. Pudding can wait a bit."

Why not? We'd waited for the lamb for a half hour. At least the pudding couldn't go cold since it already was.

"Your dad and Jack can have an after-dinner drink while we wait for you," Edith added. "And if you're going, you can take the dog with you for a walk." She paused before yelling, "Digger!"

The previously unseen Digger, a spaniel, came scampering out. You'd think he'd have been around earlier, but Digger often hides when we come to visit. The boys have a tendency to carry him around by his armpits, as a result of which he has the tendency to play dead without anyone asking him to.

Dumbfounded, Denny dropped to one knee and gave

the dog a good scratch on the head and belly. "I can't believe you still have Digger," he said.

Honestly. The man really was a prat. Did he really think this was the same Digger from when he was a child growing up in this house? If so, the dog would be over two hundred years old in dog years! In the time I'd known the Springers, I'd seen at least one Digger come and go.

"Dennis." Edith laughed as though surely her son must be joking while I was equally certain that, surely, he was not.

The scratching hands stopped mid-scratch as he stiffened at that *Dennis*. For over two decades now he'd only ever been *Denny* or *Den*, and that old familiar must have rankled with its reminder that he wasn't always the stuff of groupie wet dreams; that, once upon a time, even he had been a silly little boy, capable of saying extraordinarily foolish things.

The front door of the Springer house, which is not a particularly large house, is in full view of the dining room table, and Denny was just turning the knob as I rose.

"I think I'll join you," I called.

I felt more than saw Jack glare at me. Jack hated it when I smoked.

But screw that. I hated how hard it was to stay slim after having two kids.

When I first met Jack Springer, twelve years prior to that Easter dinner, I had no idea who he was. Or, maybe it would be more proper to say, I had no idea whose brother he was.

We met in a pub, which, I believe, is every young girl's dream, to be able to one day tell her children, "Your father and I met in a pub. We were both fairly wasted at the time."

I was there with my best friends, Stella and Bria. Back then, we called ourselves The Three A's because of the final vowel sound in all of our names. Well, we thought we were clever.

It was Karaoke Night and we'd already had our go at it with "Every Breath You Take," complete with hand gestures like shading our eyes visor-like and telescoping our heads every time we sang "I'll be watching you"—nothing like a little stalker music. Stella and Bria had met two guys to while away the night with, and so I was on my own at the bar, finishing up the bottom of a G&T, when I noticed the man on the stool next to me watching me. For all I knew, he could have just got there or he could have been there for the last hour. That's the thing about Jack, as opposed to his brother: you can't miss Denny, while Jack takes a lot longer to show up on the radar. It's not that Jack's bad to look at—far from it. It's more like his looks sneak up on you, one of those all-around average types who start to look better and better the longer you know them.

But you'd never peg him as being related to someone possessed of one of the most famous faces on the planet. For one thing, even leaving off the height discrepancy, they don't look a thing alike. Jack has close-cropped, sandy-colored hair that starts to spring back into curls the instant he steps from the shower; kind, brown eyes, as opposed to Denny's sea-glass eyes that have only a few flecks of brown; a smile that's more reassuring than Denny's hundred-watt grin, Denny's mouth when he laughs so wide it looks like he could eat the world; and in addition to being tall, unlike his slight older brother, Jack is sturdy and strong. If you had to guess his profession on first sight, you'd likely guess copper, and not one of the corrupt ones either.

So, as I say, there's no reason, if you didn't already know, for anyone to connect the two men. And so I didn't.

"Can I buy you another one of those?" he asked with a chin nod toward my empty glass.

I looked him over again. Already he looked better, if only by the barest of increments, than the first time I'd glanced at him. I could certainly do worse, I finally concluded, and in fact, many times I had.

"Sure," I said, raising my eyebrows expectantly, hoping he'd guess what I was searching for.

He did. "Jack," he filled in for me, and nothing more.

Well, it wasn't like I needed to know his last name. We'd probably converse for exactly the amount of time it took me to down my fresh G&T, and that would be that. It's not like I'd need to know his whole name for my Christmas list or anything. It's not like we were going to be picking out His and Hers towels the next day.

Of course, as it turned out, we wound up talking through several rounds of drinks. Well, mostly I talked, at least in the beginning. That's the thing about Jack. Unlike Denny, who can only be depended upon to talk about what *he's* doing and what interests *him*, as though he expects the whole world to be waiting for every utterance, hanging on every last word—which, I suppose, to be fair, they do— and unlike any other man I'd ever met, Jack was all about finding out what interested me.

So I told him how I was at loose ends; how I'd recently graduated from university and, having gone to school to study one thing only to realize near the end that it no longer suited, I was killing time working in a book shop until the right idea for what to do with my life came along.

That may not sound like much to tell another person, but you'd be surprised how much time you can consume talking about how adrift you're feeling when you're drifting on the effects of about a half-dozen or so G&Ts. So basically, I just nattered on while Jack mostly listened. Except he didn't just listen. My recollection of events in the days to follow and right up to now, is that he interjected with meaningful comments at appropriate points and with humor in the few moments when I grew maudlin over my own sorry state. As for that humor, it wasn't like he was laughing at me—although eventually I started laughing at myself—and it wasn't over-the-top hilarious; it was just nice, and gentle, like him.

In fact, I was just thinking about how surprisingly nice this all was—this man, this talking thing—that it was the most pleasant evening I'd enjoyed in I didn't even know how long, when some guy doing the karaoke launched into "Frustration."

And that's when Jack rolled his eyes, accompanied by an inexplicably sad shake of the head.

Before I could ask him about that, he changed his own subject.

"I heard you and your friends earlier," he said, "singing. You weren't half bad."

"Pfft." I shrugged off the compliment. "Anyone can sing along with the bouncing ball. What about you?" I gestured with my head toward the D.J. "Do you sing?"

"I do, actually." He spoke the words with great care. "But not like this."

I did wonder what that could mean, but I also wondered where the barman was with my fresh drink, and the latter wondering took precedence over the former.

It's funny how you can go out with your friends several weekends in a row and meet various different guys, potential love interests, none of them clicking, and then you meet one who does. Before long, Jack and I were doing that giddy "we just met and now we're comparing interests" thing; you know the one, in which somehow it magically turns out you both have a lot in common, as though it might be an omen of something deeper, or at least you manage to manipulate things so that it would appear so.

Typically, it's fairly obvious stuff: you both think J.M.W. Turner is the greatest British artist ever and you're in agreement that John Cleese is the best Python.

"What's your favorite color?"

"Blue."

"You love blue? *Me too!*"

"I like breathing."

"This is *so* amazing—*me too!*"

It was like that.

And then of course our talk turned to books, TV, and film, followed by, inevitably, music.

Even there, it would appear we thought as one; well, mostly. As he reeled off names of bands and individual artists, we were in surprising synch. The only thing we differed on was Bon Jovi; they were brand spanking new on the scene, and while he foresaw a great future, at the time all I could see was hair, and not in a good way. But since his own was more conservatively cropped, I got the impression that my thoughts on the band from the wrong Jersey were as much a relief to him as anything else. And, thankfully, he was wise enough not to ask if I was Beatles or Led Zeppelin. It's my experience that that's a debate best not had upon just meeting a new man because while some people can be both Beatles and Led Zeppelin, that's by no means always the case and it's just too much of a risk.

"What do you think of them?" he asked with a head gesture toward the latest karaoke singer, who was murdering "Frustration" even worse than the guy who'd attempted it a half hour earlier.

"You mean the guy singing karaoke?" He'd said 'them,' but there was only one person singing. Perhaps he'd drunk too much and was seeing double? Or maybe I'd drunk too much and was only seeing one where there should be two? No, it was definitely just one singer.

"No." He spoke in an even voice. "The band who originally recorded the song."

I tried to figure out what he was looking for, in that way you sometimes do with a new man you've just met when you think you're still playing the "we just met and now we're comparing interests" game; we'd been getting on so well, I didn't want to louse things up. And I'd already crossed him once, on Bon Jovi, I didn't want to run the risk of crossing him twice. Unfortunately, his face was neutral, a bloody Switzerland of uselessness. Then I remembered that eye-roll from earlier, which it appeared, might be a clue.

"Well," I proceeded cautiously, "I suppose they are a bit overrated."

"A bit over…" He barked a laugh. "Yes. I'd say that's exactly right."

"You're not a fan, then?"

"You might say that."

Then he launched into a laundry-list critique of everything wrong with Denny and his band: the exaggerated dance moves that ran the risk of overflowing into self-caricature; the occasional overeagerness to pump out a hit single attached to the latest music craze, like disco nearly a half-decade ago, almost sure to cause embarrassment later on in a career, not even fit enough for a greatest hits album, even if "Disco Balls to You" had charted at #1 in 1978—what self-respecting rock-and-roll band would commit such a musical faux pas? And what about that label, The

Greatest Rock-and-Roll Band In The World—could such a thing be empirically proven, and if not, why claim it?

I found myself nodding in agreement with what he said because everything he said was technically true.

"So, really?" he said at one point, stopping his own tirade long enough to solicit my opinion. "You're really not a fan?"

"Not in the slightest," I reassured him.

It wasn't even until our second date—well, our first if you don't count the drunken meeting in the pub as a date, per se—that I learned his last name was Springer too, just like the lead singer for the band he wasn't a fan of.

I STEPPED OUTSIDE, PULLING THE DOOR SHUT BEHIND ME.

Denny was already on the front stoop, a lit cigarette dangling from his fingers. On the edges of the concrete, not much bigger than a postage stamp, stood two bodyguards dressed in suits. And in front of the house was parked a long, white limousine, the liveried driver leaning against the front of the car enjoying his own cigarette break. A chauffeur and two bodyguards—Denny had needed all this just to visit his parents for the holiday. What did he need the bodyguards for? In the city, I could understand it, maybe, but here? What did he think was going to happen, that old Mrs. Parker across the way was going to maul him for an autograph? Instead of revering him, she was more likely to pity his parents. "Poor Edith," I could hear her saying. "At least my Darren comes to see me every week, but when's the last time that one was around? Oh, I wish for her sake he'd get a proper job, give up all that nonsense."

"Mona," Denny said with what could only be described

as a slight leer. "Did you come out here for some alone time with me?"

I regarded my brother-in-law from my height, even in flats, of one inch taller than him. Only five-seven to Jack's six feet—Denny'd gotten his mom's height while Jack got their dad's—it was always a surprise to see Denny in person, to stand so close to him like this and realize how slight he was, when on stage he always towered larger than life. And yet somehow, no room was big enough for him, no room could contain him.

I ignored his question as I lit a cigarette, squinting at him through the smoke and gesturing with my chin. "What's with the sunglasses? It's not *that* bright out."

In truth, the sun was shining, but it was a late-March shine, not a July one, and the day was brisk. His hair looked amazing—exactly as it did in all the recent pictures—that brown shaggy cut with hints of gold and even silver and bronze glimmering through; honestly, if you got rid of the brown bits and braided up the rest, it'd look like that tricolored jewelry that was so trendy in the shops. But that long scarf around his neck and those sunglasses—was this supposed to be him traveling incognito? Because if that was the case, he should have ditched the bodyguards, the scarf, and the sunglasses in the suburbs in March, and no one would be the wiser for his presence here.

"They're prescription," he said, sounding wounded. "I have light-sensitive eyes."

Yeah, right. First I'd heard of that.

"Let's walk," I said, stepping off the stoop. "If any smoke gets in the window crevices, your mum'll have a cow."

Despite my words, I loved Denny's mum. But I didn't

want her to have another cow because as far as I could tell, she'd already had one: him.

"Worse than the Americans," he muttered again, which I guessed was currently the worst epithet he could think of.

Still, despite his grumbling, he followed my lead. He stole a concerned glance at the empty street—I suspect he was wary of the hordes that would no doubt descend demanding autographs should he step out into it—so I took pity on him, instead circling the house on the small patch of grass surrounding it, Digger nipping at our heels, the bodyguards trailing close behind us *just in case*.

I don't know about him, but I felt ridiculous.

"You know," I said, after the silence became unbearable, feeling an unaccountable flash of real anger, "you could try spending more time with your brother."

"Why?" he said, startled. Was that a spark of concern for someone else? "Is he dying?"

Now that anger was more than a flash. "No, he's not *dying*!" God, what a prat.

"Then what then? Is it about money? Because, if so, you know how I feel about—"

"It's not about money either—God! Yes, I do know how you feel about that."

Not that he'd ever told me directly, but anyone who read the mags knew how Denny Springer felt about giving "handouts" to family. He said other people could do what they liked with their money, but it wasn't his job to support every relative that crawled out of the woodwork, that each individual had to earn his own way, just as he had had to earn his. Even his two eldest children—Shadow, twenty-two; and Pipe, twenty-one (I know if you read the mags, you already know this, but just in case you don't, his third child was, indeed, named Dream)—although he was willing to pay their way at university, once finished, they were expected to get proper jobs and not rely on Daddy for constant support and handouts. Not that "Daddy" had been around for support other than financial in their formative years, at least not according to the mags.

Of course, it wasn't strictly true to say that Denny refused to financially assist any family members in over-the-top fashion. He'd tried to buy his parents the big house. In fact, he went ahead and *bought* his parents the big house, without bothering to ask first. But when Edith saw it, it was her turn to refuse him. "What do I need with all that space?" she reportedly told him. "I'd have to get cleaning help in with all those rooms. I don't want strangers touching my things!"

So he had tried to help, exactly once, and had been refused.

Still, that wasn't what I was after, and I reiterated as much.

"We don't want your money. Is that all you think most people want from you?"

He shrugged, not bothered, a shrug that said, 'That. Plus proximity to power, influence, and success, and sex beyond your wildest dreams.'

Well, when a person put it in a shrug like that, another person could maybe see the appeal.

"If Jack's not dying," Denny said, "and he doesn't need a handout, then what is it you want from me?"

"I just think you should spend more time with your brother."

"Because...?"

"Because he *is* your brother."

Denny still looked puzzled by my logic.

"Look," I said, feeling no small measure of vexation. Then I proceeded to explain our plans for the summer, the plans Jack had tried to explain to Burt twice before being interrupted by Denny's need to go on and on about Malaysia. I scowled at the Springer family home. For all I knew, Jack was in there still trying to explain and had yet to get the whole thing out. "Things have gone very well for us with the agency."

"The agency?"

I was a step away from tearing my hair out. Or his.

"The agency," I said. "The *agency*. You do know we're travel agents, don't you?"

"Right, right," he said hurriedly, but I hardly felt reassured.

"Anyway, things have been going so well, we've decided to go away for the summer. We're taking a house in the States—coastal Connecticut, to be exact." I didn't bother adding what we planned to do there, how Jack was going to work on his songwriting and guitar playing. Denny didn't need to know that.

"Coastal Connecticut? That sounds rather...*provincial.*"

*Ignore, Mona, ignore.*

"And seeing you here, I got to thinking..."

"That it would be good for me to visit? So I could 'spend more time with Jack,' as you say?"

"That was the general idea. With all the time you spend surrounded by yes-men"—*not to mention yes-women, I* thought—"it would do you good to spend time with real people, with family, specifically your brother—"

"I think you've firmly established that by now, that Jack is, in fact, my brother—"

"—whom you've hardly spent any time with at all in over two decades. Plus, wouldn't you like to get to know William and Harry?"

He physically pulled back at that. "You mean the princes?"

"Not the bloody princes!" And this time, I couldn't stop myself from adding, "You prat. Your *nephews*, William and Harry."

"You know," he huffed, "if you didn't want people to confuse them, you might have thought to pick out different names."

"What's telling is that you have two nephews, your only nephews, who've been on this planet for a combined total of sixteen years, and you only just this minute learned what their names are."

He opened his mouth in outraged protest, but no words came out. I suspect even he saw that he didn't have a leg to stand on. "Huh," was all he finally said.

It felt like a minor victory.

"Well, I suppose you're a very busy man," I said.

"Oh, yes. Always busy."

"So I don't imagine you can get away this summer, not even part of it. You're probably going to be on tour or something."

"Actually, no. We just finished up a world tour in Malaysia. Did I tell you about—"

"Yes," I cut him off, "I'm almost certain you did."

"Well, then, look. I'll think about it, OK?"

I supposed it was as good as I was going to get. But I knew what would happen. He'd think about it for maybe five minutes, and then he'd forget what he'd been thinking. Ah, well. At least I'd tried.

Later, I'd wonder why I was so specifically focused on him spending more time with Jack as opposed to, say, his parents. But then I'd remind myself that he did at least see his parents occasionally—every once in a while he'd persuade Burt and Edith to let him fly them to one of his many houses for a visit—while for twenty years his relationship with Jack had been virtually nonexistent. If one were lucky enough to have a sibling, something I lacked, shouldn't there be more of a relationship? I was doing this for Jack.

We'd circled back round to the front of the house again. Honestly, we'd circled so many times in the same direction, I felt myself going dizzy as I stepped onto the stoop. Placing my hand on the doorknob, I heard him clear his throat. When I turned, he was still on the lawn.

"Say my goodbyes," he said, "won't you?"

"You're leaving?"

"Yes."

"Not stopping the night?"

"I hardly think so. I've booked a room at a hotel nearby."

I was about to protest the idiocy of this, not to mention the insensitivity, but then I tried to picture him—Denny Springer—sleeping in the bedroom he'd grown up in, and the picture didn't work. I'd seen that room before, of course, unchanged since he'd left it over twenty years ago to try to make it big, which he had. That room with its posters of Einstein and Robert Johnson, twin evidence of where his mathematical/musical aspirations lay; the impossibly narrow bed. A few times since moving out of my own parents' house, I'd had cause to sleep in my childhood bed and had never minded, despite the strangeness. But the idea of Denny Springer doing the same—it was beyond incongruous. He had a point, but I hated conceding it to him.

"Why did you even bother coming here today anyway, *Dennis?*" I asked.

He winced at that last, and it occurred to me that maybe I should start calling him that on a regular basis, but he recovered quickly.

"Well, I broke up with my girlfriend, didn't I?"

I couldn't say I was sorry to hear that. Not that I had anything against the girl, his latest long-term squeeze, a high-fashion model named Lalaina LaLani; Lalaina LaLani—a name that's almost impossible to say without sounding like you're stuttering.

So even the great Denny Springer, on the heels of a breakup, sometimes needed the comforts of family and home, even if he couldn't be bothered to learn the details of the lives of the former, even if he'd never sleep in the latter again.

"Did you not know I broke up with my girlfriend?" he pressed. "Don't you people read the magazines?"

It's not accurate to say I didn't know who Jack Springer's brother was when I first met Jack. Of course I did. I just didn't know he was Jack Springer's brother.

I first fell in love with Denny Springer in the summer of 1975, the year I turned thirteen. Well, me and every other girl in England, followed shortly by every other girl in the world. Actually, it was probably more like ninety percent of the girls and ten percent of the boys, if you make mathematical adjustments to allow for the guestimated population of gay people, and I see no reason not to. After all, I wouldn't want to overestimate his appeal.

• • •

They say you can tell a lot about a person by looking at the friends they have, the company they keep. I've some-times thought that looking at my lifelong circle—Stella,

Bria, and me—what it says about us is that we're lazy and perhaps watch too much TV. Roll back the clock just a bit further, to 1968. There's us, our first day at school. Everyone else, after briefly checking each other out, is pairing off or forming small groups of instantaneous best friendship. Some of these won't last the week, some might not even last the day, but at least they're all making the effort, choosing. Now, look at Stella, Bria, and me. We're hanging back, watching what the others do, in my case waiting—hoping—someone will pick me. But before long, everyone else is matched up and there remains the three of us. Stella gravitates over toward Bria and for a moment I'm left all alone. Thankfully, it's not for long. Soon, they drift over to me and we all look each other over.

If there could have been a microphone attached to each of our brains at that point, I've always imagined the output would read something like: *Yeah. We can make this work.*

And we did, I think in part because we'd all been watching the same TV shows.

Here's the thing: Stella is tall, has blonde hair and blue eyes. Bria is short, with curly red hair and green eyes. Me, I'm dark hair, dark eyes. Back then, TV shows and movies were always throwing together three girls with those coloring combinations. You know, three actresses trying to make it in the city or three stewardesses who share a flat? There was that one show in particular, the famous one we all watched, where the girls were all sisters, as if that made any kind of genetic sense. But of course we didn't think about that at the time. What kid ever does?

Not having anyone else pick us first was what we had in common. That show was what we had in common.

When you're young, you live inside TV shows. This meant, in our case, that we playacted what we saw on the screen. As we got more creative, we'd come up with our own episodes. But by then, what we saw had formed who we were, perhaps as much as any genetics of our own or things we'd learned from watching our parents. Stella, like the blonde on TV, became the vain, loopy one. Bria, true to her prototype, became the crazy tomboy. And me? I was the smart, practical one, like the dark-haired girls always are.

Honestly, there were times, looking around the classroom, considering how some of the other groups had re-formed, I'd count myself lucky that Stella and Bria hadn't swapped me out for one of the other dark-haired girls. After all, my type was the most common, the easiest to replace. Perhaps, I thought, they were lazy too. It took me years to accept the fact that no matter our initial reasons for forming our triangular relationship, they'd come to love and value me all the same.

If kids start out living inside TV programs, before too many years pass, they find themselves living inside music instead. You graduate from fantasizing about an episode in which—surprisingly—your dark-haired character for once gets the man instead of your blonde sister, to doing the math on the age difference between yourself and famous rock stars. *Only nine years' difference? OK, maybe not today then, not when I'm still thirteen, but, in time,* you think, *this could still work. I mean,* you tell yourself, *it's not like I've got a thing for someone really old, like Sinatra. It's not like I'm effing crazy.*

So yeah, by the time we were thirteen, we were still together but had traded our celluloid fantasies for vinyl ones. And somewhere along the way, as friends will do, we'd abbreviated our names. I think, sometimes, that people do this to be cool, nicknames being a badge to prove to others how super close you all are. It certainly can't be for the verbal savings of a syllable here and there, the time saved in not having to write out a few extra letters. Somehow, if you have a nickname, it makes a person feel more special, it makes a person feel less lonely in the world.

Unless of course that nickname is something derogatory.

So Stella had become Stel. Bria was Bri. And me? I became Mon. I loved this when I'd see it written out, when we passed notes in class: *Mon*—it made me sound like I might have a hidden Rasta side to my practical personality, like on holiday you might find me jamming with Bob Marley in Jamaica or something, even though I couldn't play an instrument or even sing particularly well.

This all went along fine when we stuck to using our nicknames in private notes, but when we started verbalizing, that's when the trouble started. You can see what would have happened, can't you? Stella and Bria's nicknames—written or verbal—were exactly the same. But what's the first syllable of Mona sound like when you say it out loud? Right. It's Moan, isn't it? Picture being thirteen years old, feeling pretty cool, and then one of your two best friends shouts down the hall something that sounds like, "Hey, Moan, you coming to lunch or what?"

Well, of *course* the group of boys standing next to you starts to snicker. Of *course* you start getting the rep of being a bit of a whinger, even though you most emphatically are not. And just when you think the fuss is finally dying down, you get your first real kiss in a closet during some basement kissing game at a party and the kisser—Peter Prawn, the prat—christens you "Moaning Mona" to all who will listen and you're back to square one all over again, only worse, because instead of a whinger now you're too loudly hot to trot.

I can take a lot, but that was a bit much even for me. I yanked Stella and Bria aside and told them if I couldn't be Mon pronounced in the Rasta fashion, I wouldn't answer when they called me and I'd go back to using their full names, and then where would we all be? Immature, I know, but you try being Moaning Mona for a week when you're thirteen and then we can talk about fair tactics.

So yeah, we were thirteen and living inside music. And the best place to do that? Stella's basement. Bria and I had basements too, of course, but not like Stella's. Bria's dad had a shop and mine worked in the law. Stella's did something indefinable in the business world by day, but that wasn't the good part. Her parents were both heavily into music themselves, among other things, so their basement was kitted out like a rock star's dream, or at least a thirteen-year-old's version of a rock star's dream. Everything was red and black, there was a special organ on which you could do whole songs because it had buttons for other instruments as well, a massive sound system, giant pillows everywhere, and the whole place was soundproofed. Oh, and it also had a huge wine closet. Always well stocked, and the Bradfords *never* counted the bottles.

Here's the thing about the Bradfords, Mr. and Mrs.: even though it was 1975, they were still going through their "groovy" phase. When Mr. Bradford would come home from work, he'd rip off his tie, change into moccasins, and he and his wife would practice transcendental meditation as a smoky haze settled over whichever room they were in. By this point, Stella was getting high on a regular basis. Mrs. B used to say it broke her heart. But she'd never ground Stella or yell at her. Instead, each time Stella got busted with dope in her room, Mrs. B would get all sad and give her the "I'm so disappointed" speech, which probably would have been more effective if it wasn't Mrs. B's purse and Mr. B's sock drawer that Stella was always getting her dope from.

Still, those speeches always got to Stella, who could be quite sensitive in her loopy kind of way. She'd break down; she and Mrs. B would have a good cry in each other's arms, both promising to do better. Then Saturday night would roll around, and Bria and I would both be back down for a night in the basement, music blaring, wine bottles open, the occasional spliff to draw on, and no worries of having our little slice of heaven disturbed. After all, the Bradfords didn't believe in intruding on children's privacy, did they?

• • •

We were lying on our stomachs on the floor in Stella's basement, listening to the new album by our favorite band while religiously studying the album cover, which was what people did with a new album back then. I can't imagine how kids do it with CDs now—that must totally suck. Anyway, it wasn't destined to be the band's best album, not by a long shot. In fact, for years people would make fun of it for its too-psychedelic music and the fey costumes they all had on. But still, even their worst album was better than most bands' best. Plus, this was before all that criticism started, and we didn't care.

It was my album—my mum had taken me to the shops earlier that cold Saturday afternoon—so I was situated in the middle.

We were playing one of our favorite games, a game we'd be red-faced embarrassed if anyone else ever caught us out at: which one do you most want to end up with?

"Lex," Stella said right away. Well, we all knew she was going to say that, didn't we?

The Bradfords had gone on holiday to Switzerland two months previous. The Glasses—Bria's family—and my own tended more towards holidays in Dover, or perhaps the Cotswolds if our parents were feeling really exotic. The Bradfords tended to stray further afield, and Mr. B had heard tell of some sort of Swiss maharajah he was hoping to confer with about his om. Anyway, one afternoon, Mr. and Mrs. B were doing that, leaving Stella to her own devices, which in this case entailed Stella wandering the streets of Zurich alone.

And that's where she saw him: Lex, lead guitarist for our favorite band, just walking down the street like anyone else. She said she went into hysterics so bad when she saw him, she couldn't speak, the tears just rolling down her face; she said she was surprised she didn't outright pee herself and that she wasn't entirely sure she didn't, at least a little bit.

Considering Lex's reputation, he was very kind to her. Believe me, having seen Stella in hysterics before, I wouldn't have blamed him one bit if he'd just kept walking right on past her as fast as he could. But Lex didn't do that. Instead, in big, looping handwriting, he scrawled a personalized autograph for her on a scrap of notebook paper on which he'd apparently crossed out some lyrics that failed to please him: *To Crying Girl, from Lex: Rock on.* He also gave her a guitar pick that was chewed off on one end. Apparently, he'd been using it to clean his teeth. We would have doubted her story. She had no witnesses, after all. But she did have that chewed-off guitar pick. We all knew about Lex, his teeth, and his guitar picks.

And of course the note and the pick were now framed behind glass, adding one more layer of cool to Stella's already cool basement. So really, she had to say Lex, didn't she?

I could see Bria's eyes staring at Denny, so I was sure that's who she was going to say—in fact I was sure Stella would have wanted to say that too, if only the pick hadn't made her say otherwise—but the name that came out of her mouth was: "8."

8 was the drummer. Diehard fans of the band knew that his real name was the all-too-common Jimmy Jones, but no one had called him that in years, instead referring to the enigmatic number he'd chosen to go with his enigmatic persona.

The other two looked at me: my turn.

Why hadn't Bria said Denny? I wondered. It was the obvious choice. And if she'd done so, it would have made my decision so much easier: we could have both gone with Denny, leaving Stella her chewed-up pick. And Bria should have said Denny, for so many reasons, like the fact that her cousin, while holidaying with her parents in Rome, had seen Denny in a bar. Supposedly, he was nice too, although he hadn't given away any chewed-up items as proof.

So my friends, or in some cases at least the cousins of my

friends, had gotten to meet members of the band. But not me. Not when I was thirteen.

If only out of family loyalty, then, Bria should have chosen Denny. Plus, he was the best one. Even my mum could see that.

When we'd gotten home from the shops earlier in the day, my mum had demanded to see my purchase. She was like that with my albums, inspecting the outsides to make sure there wasn't anything subversive to corrupt my forming mind. I could have told her she had to actually listen to the words to get to that part, but she didn't ask me, did she?

"I just want to see what all the fuss is about," she'd said, grabbing the album out of my hands when I tried to balk. Then we sat down side by side on the sofa, since I was even more eager than she was to study that cover.

"Huh," she snorted at the costumes they wore. "They look ridiculous."

I, in turn, silently rolled my eyes at her snorting. She just didn't get it, did she?

But then her finger came to rest near Denny's face, so tiny on the cover, as though she were caressing his cheek. "That one," she said, tapping her finger, and a sigh came out of her then. I don't think I'd ever heard my mother make that exact sound before. If I'd had words for it at the time, I suppose those words would have been *wistful, desire, wanting.* "That one really has *something*," she said, "doesn't he?"

I felt a surge of strange pride then that, in that moment, even my mother could see the legitimacy of what I felt.

It would be many years before I'd return the favor. Having spent most of my life laughing at her fascination with Frank

Sinatra, one time I was helping her clean out the attic when she came across her own old albums. She put one on for a listen and made me look at the cover with her, as we'd done with mine so many years before. I listened and looked at the cover. For the first time, I saw what she was seeing, heard what she was hearing. This wasn't the pathetic Frank, it wasn't the Frank with bad hair plugs. It was peak Sinatra, with all the idiosyncratic phrasing that name implies.

People talk about "Can you separate the singer from the song?" but that's not really it, is it? It's that some people, some very few people, have *something*. They have an *it* that no one else has. At university, I'd studied charismatic authorities: Kennedy, Martin Luther King, Hitler. That's the problem with charismatic authorities: you don't know what they're going to use it for, only that they have something no one else has. When they talk, it's not a speech; it's truth. When they sing, there's nothing else like it. It's not an exaggeration to say that there are a million voices in the world that are technically better than Denny Springer's, and yet he's where he is. Where are they?

Charisma.

I've never been a religious person, but if I had to pick one thing I think is close to being a miracle, it's charisma. It can't be bought, it can't be learned, it can't be practiced into being. It just is.

It's what Denny Springer has and Jack Springer does not.

• • •

"Trey," I said back down in Stella's basement.

"Trey?" Stella and Bria laughed, with Bria adding,

"How can you possibly pick the creepy bass player? No one picks him!"

I just shrugged. I mean, I hadn't had any choice, had I? If they were both insistent on picking anyone but Denny, I had to do the same. But we all knew the truth, and I knew they knew it too:

Denny was the best one.

In so very many ways, Denny was the only one.

DENNY LOOKED DOWN WITH A MIXTURE OF SHOCK AND puzzlement at the restraining hand on his forearm. It was my hand. I had to admit, I was shocked too. In the twelve years since becoming his sister-in-law, it would be reasonable to assume that in that time we'd have had some physical contact, however minimal. Kisses on the cheek in greeting? Perhaps a hug? At the very least a handshake the first time Jack introduced us? But none of that had ever happened. It was the first time in the twelve years since I'd met Jack that I'd touched Denny.

It occurred to me then that I'd never seen the others touch him either. Not his parents. Not Jack. Sure, fans were always trying to get a touch in, hence the two bodyguards. But his own family? The people who presumably knew him best? It was like there was a no-fly zone around him.

And something else occurred to me in that instant: the way his forearm felt beneath my hand, even in spite of the clothes he was wearing, separating his skin from mine.

Looking at him in person, it was each time surprising anew that someone who was so large in the public consciousness should be so slight. And yet, touching him, expecting fragility—no, it turned out he didn't feel fragile at all. More like there was an indomitable strength there.

"Can I do something for you, Mona?" he said at last, tearing his gaze from the offending hand.

"Wait," I said a second time, my voice more controlled than it had been the first time I said that word to him.

Flash back two minutes before: me standing on the stoop watching as, across the lawn, Denny was about to climb into the back of his white stretch limo.

"Wait!" I called after him, striding purposefully across the lawn, Digger in hot pursuit at my heels.

Denny stopped in front of the open door, and that's when I landed beside him, placing my hand on his arm, which brings us back to the second "Wait."

"Hold up, Jeeves," Denny said to his chauffeur.

"Is his name really Jeeves?" I asked, stunned.

"Of course not," Denny said, snorting as though I might be daft. "It's just what I call him."

"Why?"

"Because I can."

I opened my mouth to object to this imperious insensitivity on his part, but I was stopped by the sound of someone else speaking.

"What's all this fuss about?" a grating voice said.

I looked over the top of the limo to find Mrs. Parker from across the way; Nosy Parker, more like it.

"Good afternoon, Mrs. Parker," I said. "Lovely day, isn't it?"

"What was all that screaming?" she persisted.

"It was only one scream," I said, tamping down the sigh that was fighting to get out of me. It had hardly been a scream anyway. If it had been, wouldn't Jack and his parents have heard us from inside and come running? Mrs. Parker had no doubt been observing us from between her curtains, as was her habit, and had come out just in time to hear my mildly raised "Wait."

"Just one?" She was aghast. "I thought someone was being *murdered* out here." She squinted her eyes, straining up on tiptoe. "Who's that you've got with you?"

Not waiting for an answer, she trundled over to our side of the limo. "Dennis Springer!" She placed a hand to her chest. "As I live and breathe!"

"If you're alive, Mrs. Parker," Denny said cheerfully enough, "I certainly hope you're breathing."

"You always did have a sense of humor." She swatted in the general direction of his arm, which I realized I was still holding on to. Immediately, I let him go.

Mrs. Parker's eyes narrowed. "You know, you should visit your mum more often."

"Yes, ma'am," he said gravely.

"Well, then." She looked around as though expecting to find something. But then, not finding whatever it was she sought, she added a disappointed, "I guess if no one's being *murdered*..." and trundled back around the limo and toward her house.

Denny stood almost like a soldier at attention, watching her go until she was safely inside. That's when he burst out laughing. I couldn't stop myself from joining in.

"'If no one's being *murdered*,'" he gasped out between

laughs in what I must admit was a credible imitation of Mrs. Parker.

"Like that's where the bar is set for conversing with the neighbors!" I gasped back, peeling off into another laugh.

When people go off into hysterical laughter together like that, it likely strikes others that the effect is disproportionate to the cause. After all, what can be so funny as to inspire all that? Especially given the subjective nature of humor, with two totally disparate people rarely finding the same things funny. But try telling that to the two people laughing their arses off?

I was nearly doubled over as I reached out and laid my hand on Denny's forearm for support. This time, neither of us displayed shock. If anything, for the briefest of seconds it felt like the most natural thing in the world.

But then Denny said, "If you weren't going to murder me, then what did you want?" and the moment was broken.

"Right," I said, sobering up. "You can't just leave without saying a proper goodbye to your mother."

Denny climbed into the limo before regarding me once more. "Kind of defeats the purpose of having you do it, doesn't it?"

"You can't be that insensitive!" I cried as Digger let out a little yip.

"Hey," Denny said, and I could almost see his eyes lighting up behind his dark sunglasses.

*Thank you*, I thought. *He's finally seeing the light.*

"I don't suppose I could take Digger with me," he said hopefully.

"What?"

"It's only, I could really use a dog."

I scooped Digger up protectively in my arms. "No, you can't have your parents' *dog*!"

"Right, then. What about you?"

"What about me?"

"Would you care to come with me?" Not waiting for an answer, he added, "You did say I should spend more time with my family…"

I thought about it for a moment. Was he mad? Then:

"I'm not coming with you!" I was outraged, even more so when he said:

"The joke's never as funny if you're not the one making it, is it, Mona?"

Then, before I could say anything else, he tapped the interior roof of the limo sharply twice. "Onward, Jeeves."

• • •

"Well, that was a long smoke," Jack observed when I reentered the house, Digger still in my arms.

"Where's Denny?" Edith asked, craning to look over my shoulder, as though he might be hiding back there.

"He had to leave," I said. *Had to*, not *wanted to* or *decided to*. I couldn't tell Edith that leaving was something he'd done by choice, I couldn't hurt her that way, so instead I embellished the lie. "He was called away on some urgent business."

"Huh," Burt said. "But how is that possible?" He indicated an object on the sideboard. "He left his phone here." Not waiting for an answer, Burt shrugged his own question away. Burt was never one to be bothered by the great mysteries of the universe. "Well, so long as it's here…" He picked up the phone with a smile, studied the buttons on it. "Perhaps we should call a few people?"

"WILL YOU MARRY ME?"

That was what Jack had asked me that day in the travel agency.

When we'd first met on Karaoke Night at the bar, I'd told him I was working in a book shop until the right thing came along. Then, on our first real date, after kissing me goodnight at the door, he asked if I'd like to come work with him in the travel agency he'd just opened while I tried to figure out what I wanted to do. He said he was only doing that himself until the right thing came along. Of course, in his case, he already knew what that was: he wanted to be a professional musician, and he figured it was only a matter of time before he'd get his big break.

I said I wasn't sure if working together while dating each other was such a good idea. What if one didn't work out? What kind of impact would failure to mesh in one area have on the other?

He kissed me again and said to just think about it.

He'd been working the agency alone since opening it and thought having me there with him could be fun.

On our next date, he made dinner for me at his flat. It was a proper dinner too, none of this "Look, I cooked for you! I broiled a steak!" nonsense that guys usually try to palm off, at least in my experience up to that point. It was a lasagna with vegetables and a red cream sauce that looked as though it took hours to prepare, and I knew he'd made it himself because when he excused himself to the lav at one point, I took the liberty of peeking in his trash bin. The lasagna had tasted so perfect, just the right combination of crunchy vegetables and velvety sauce, I was sure he'd bought takeaway from some restaurant and then reheated it. But my detection efforts, rather than yielding the takeaway container I was sure I'd find, instead showed the heels of a zucchini, an eggplant, and an onion, an empty container of heavy cream, and a large empty tin of whole tomatoes. OK, so maybe his recycling habits left something to be desired, but one thing was certain: the man could really cook. Or, at the very least, he could make one killer lasagna.

By the time he returned, I was back in my seat, having poured us each another glass of wine from the lovely Barolo he'd opened.

As he cleared away the dishes he informed me, "I'm afraid I have a confession to make about tonight's meal."

*Here it comes*, I thought. *He'll tell me his mum or an aunt came by in the afternoon and made the lasagna for him to pass off as his own doing.*

"The thing is," he went on, "I can't make pudding for shit. I don't know what it is, but even with a clear and detailed recipe, it never comes out looking like the picture.

Of course, I did think about buying something at a fancy bakery to impress you and then passing it off as my own, but then I rejected that plan. I mean, we've only just started seeing one another. Shouldn't I begin as I mean to go on? And if I begin with dishonesty, even a seemingly innocent deception, where does that leave us in terms of the potential future, so..."

At this point, he flung open the freezer and removed a pint carton. "How do you feel about store-bought ice cream?" He took off the lid, revealing that a few tablespoons of the ice cream had already been consumed by someone. "I had to try it when I got it home," he said. "I mean, I did have to make sure it was going to be good enough, didn't I?"

A few seconds ago, he'd asked me how I felt. Of course, he'd been talking about store-bought ice cream, but how I felt right then was, well, if someone asked me to compare myself to a food item—you know, "What kind of food are you?" being something along the lines of the time someone asked Katharine Hepburn, "What kind of tree are you?"— I'd have to say I was a perfect lasagna: all crisp cleanness and velvety warmth in just the right places. Because the thing was, as I saw then, not only was this handsome man I'd met at karaoke an incredibly good cook, but he was also honest and funny.

I couldn't quite believe my good fortune in having met him.

So when, not long after we finished off the ice cream, he pulled out an acoustic guitar, I fought and actually won the battle in terms of not letting my dismay show on my face. The thing was, over the years at school and then university,

I'd dated more than one guy who fancied himself The Next Great Thing in the music department. They were all just waiting for their big break. And you know what the only other thing they all had in common was? None of them were anywhere near being great, unless you counted what was going on in their own minds. Some were downright awful, with the best of the bunch just being shades of OK.

So of course when Jack pulled out his acoustic, naturally my inward sigh said, *Oh, no, here comes more of the same.* As he tuned it, I resolved to suffer through however many painful songs I might be subjected to with a smile that didn't look desperate and tried to plan ahead to encouraging things to say about it at the end—"You play a *very* nice C chord!"—but then I remembered what he'd said about honesty, about how he wanted to begin this thing with us as he meant to go on, and I wondered, only mildly starting to panic: *How does* that *work? Do I tell him he sucks? That he's not very good? Not to give up the travel agency just yet?*

I was still trying to work this all out in my head when it hit me that he'd stopped tuning his guitar and was actually playing a song. It wasn't anything I'd ever heard before— later I'd learn he wrote it himself—and as he started to sing, it was as though a lake of relief spread out inside of me, and I started to smile, so widely I fear I may have looked demented. But, in the moment, I didn't care how I looked because, get this: Jack Springer was good!

Oh, it wasn't like he was a candidate for The Next Great Thing. I mean, in 1983, it would have to be electric, no? But the song he played was good, even better than good, and the same could be said of his voice. Honestly, if Bob Dylan could sing and hadn't already existed, Jack Springer could have been him. Well, and if it had been twenty years earlier.

So when he finished playing, it positively thrilled me that I could say, in all honesty, that I had liked what I heard. A few minutes later, it thrilled me to go into his bedroom with him. And the next morning, it thrilled me to say, feeling absolutely no caution about it at all anymore, that yes, I'd give it a try. Even though we were dating, I'd come work with him in his new travel agency, and I wouldn't think any more about how one might affect the other.

• • •

"Will you marry me?"

So there we were in the office.

Turn the clock back three hours.

It was nine a.m., Jack had just put the key in the door and I'd followed him inside. It was a Thursday, which meant that no sooner had I slung my bag over the back of my chair than Mrs. Stevens came doddering in. Mrs. Stevens was a blue-haired pensioner with an enormous black leather purse that she clutched to her chest as though it might contain all the money she had in the world, which, sometimes, I suspected it did.

"I'm thinking of taking a trip," she announced. "I've been saving up for it my whole life. Do you think you might help me, dear?"

"Of course, Mrs. Stevens," I said. "Why don't you have a seat?"

I made her a cup of tea and we began with the brochures.

First, we went through local possibilities: Dover, Bath, the Cotswolds.

"These are all so lovely," Mrs. Stevens said, "but I do think I'd like to leave the country. You know I've never done that?"

I did know.

Ireland. Scotland. Wales.

"Oh, Wales!" She jiggled her purse on her knees in her excitement. "I hear they have *wonderful* bookstores there!"

Having been a bookseller, however briefly, I'd heard that too.

"But you know," she said, looking a bit dismayed, "it's still just the U.K. Do you have anything for the Continent?"

Rome. Paris. Berlin.

"Oh, I just couldn't go to Germany," she said. "I know it's been years, and one shouldn't hold a grudge, but, you know—" and here she lowered her voice to a whisper, even though Jack was the only other person in the room; for some reason, Thursday mornings were always slow "—*the war.*"

Prague. Bonn. Vienna.

"Oh, I do love a good Viennese torte! But I was thinking, perhaps somewhere tropical?"

The Bahamas. Bermuda. Bimini.

Might as well work the B's all at once.

"Can you imagine me?" She put a hand to her chest. "In my bikini in Bimini?" She pronounced *Bimini* so that it rhymed with *bikini.* "What would the neighbors say when I showed them the snapshots?"

I could only guess.

"Oh, so hard to choose," she said. "And, of course, nice

as beaches are, I mean, it's only a beach, right? I do think, if I'm going to take a trip, it should be more exotic."

Easter Island. The Seychelles. Queensland.

That last I threw in just because I knew from past experience she liked the idea of there being a place called Queensland.

"Gives a girl hope, doesn't it?" she liked to say.

I didn't think that her hopes were the same as mine, but I kind of felt as though I knew what she meant.

"But these are all with tour buses," she said, as though such a thing might be beneath her. "Do you have something more adventurous?"

African safari. A trip down the Amazon. Pony rides in Iceland.

"How about Mount Everest?" I offered. "You could do an assisted climb. You know, you might not make it all the way to the top, but it's still there, right?"

Climbing Mount Everest was always the last resort. I could never think of anything more exotic, more adventurous, more *not-England* than the prospect of climbing Mount Everest.

Apparently, Mrs. Stevens couldn't think of anything more all of those things than Everest either. We always stopped at Everest.

Which was a good thing. By that point, I was always out of brochures.

"So much to think about," Mrs. Stevens said. "So hard to decide."

"Well," I said, gathering up the brochures now strewn across my desk and offering them out to her like a magician displaying a deck of cards for her to choose from, "perhaps you'd like to take a few of these home with you, give it a think?"

"Oh, could I?" she said, hopefully, gratefully.

"Of course."

She wound up taking one of everything I had away with her in her purse. I pictured her at home, going over them all, taking great care to decide on a trip I somehow knew she'd never take. In the choice between grand adventure and the money she'd saved up, she'd always choose the safety of the cash in her purse.

And next Thursday? She'd be back at my desk again. Of course she would, since I'd inherited her from Jack when I first started working for him.

As the bell on the door signaled her safe exit, I placed my hands behind my neck. "Well, there's three hours of my life I'll never get back again." Then I laughed. "But so what? She's so sweet. And anyway, she always compliments my tea. You do realize, don't you, that I'm the only woman in England who can't make a proper cup of tea? I used to wonder why that is. How is it that I somehow manage to burn it? You would think that—"

"Will you marry me?"

"What?"

"I know it's crazy," he said, "and we haven't known each other for very long, but I've never been in love before. I mean, I've loved other women, sure, but I've never been *in* love, not in my entire life, and now I am. With you."

That's when I told him that I'd never been in love before meeting him either, which wasn't strictly true. I'd been in love exactly once before, but that hadn't counted. Of course, I didn't tell him that part. Why bring up something that doesn't count? Something that amounted to no more than a mere schoolgirl crush?

And then I told him yes. A choice between the safety of what we had and the grand adventure we might have? Of course I said yes.

• • •

"But you've only known him three months!" my father said. He said this after Jack asked him for my hand in marriage, to which my father replied that there'd be no hand handing over until he and my mother had discussed it with me first. "What do you think this is," my father demanded of Jack, "the Middle Ages?"

If my father had asked me what I thought Jack was thinking, I would have said I thought he thought he was doing the right thing, which was just Jack's way, in all things. As for me, I thought it was damn sweet. Honestly. It's not like I had fantasies of some caveman Neanderthal—I'd have said no to a man like that—but decent manners and asking my dad for my hand? Like I said, sweet.

But apparently my dad didn't see any of it the same as me, which was why he was freezing Jack out as he demanded, "What can you possibly know about each other?" Followed by, "I mean, do you even really know this man?" Which led right onto my mother adding, "You're not pregnant, are you?"

Leave it to a mum. But of course, being a mum, she had to ask that, didn't she?

"No!" I laughed, too happy with Jack to even be indignant.

"Then I don't see what the rush is," my mother said, eyes still narrowed. "You're giving me *how* much time to plan this wedding?"

We told her.

"I can't help it," Jack said. "I've never loved anyone like this in my whole life, and I want to spend as many minutes as possible of the rest of my life making Mona happy as her husband."

"Oh, Christ," my dad said, "we're not even at the wedding yet and already he's doing his vows."

My dad's voice may have been gruff, but I didn't miss the slight hitch in it, and I certainly didn't miss the tears in his eyes or my mother's. Two minutes ago they'd been ready to interrogate us, and now they were completely on board with us.

My parents had always been hopelessly middle class and had only ever wanted my happiness, and I loved them for it.

"Well," my mother said, sniffling into a tissue, "with such little notice, the only dress we'll be able to find will be off the rack…"

• • •

Like I said earlier, for my wedding gown, I went for the Princess Di knockoff. As I believe I also mentioned earlier, I'd choose differently now. But at the time? I loved it. And it being two years since she'd married Charles, the initial fervor for the dress had worn off, so I'd gotten my copy damn cheap.

It was my wedding day!

We were in the bride's room at the church. Stel and Bri

were there in their purple gowns, my twin Maids of Honor. Over the course of our long friendship, we'd discussed what to do when each of us got married. The plan had always been that we'd switch off so that each of us got a turn at being the next most important person to the bride—well, except for the groom—and no one got left out. But when it came down to it, and me being the first in the group to leap for marriage, I just couldn't do it. I couldn't decide on which one to bestow the honor, and so I'd plumped for two Maids of Honor. But that was OK since, to balance everything out, Jack had agreed to pick two Best Men.

My mother was there too. As Stel and Bri fussed with the hem of my dress, my mother nervously played with my bouquet.

"Did you ever wonder why they call it Baby's Breath?" she asked. "I don't know. Something about that always strikes me as being barbaric."

That's when the knock came at the door.

Since this wasn't *Jane Eyre*, that knock didn't herald the news that there was a madwoman, another wife, living in the attic. But it did come with its own doom.

My mother answered the door, stuck her head out. "Yes?" she said.

*Mumble, mumble* came the voice she was speaking to.

"No, you can't talk to her right now," my mother said, sounding indignant. "It's simply bad luck to see her in her dress before the wedding."

"Is that Jack?" I asked.

Based on her words, it had to be.

Was he having a case of the pre-wedding jitters? I wondered. I couldn't blame him if he was. The past few weeks had been so whirlwind. And if he wanted to chuck the whole thing? Perhaps simply go on the great honeymoon we had planned and not bother with the service? I'd agree to that. I loved him that much.

The one thing I couldn't bear to do, though, was let him remain standing on the other side of the door, jittering alone. I had to do whatever I could to make him feel better, to let him know that no matter what happened, everything would be OK.

Hiking up my voluminous skirts, I made for the door.

"What do you think you're doing?" my mother practically shrieked at me.

"I'm just going to talk to him around the edge of the door." It was all I could do not to roll my eyes at her silly superstitions. "I promise, I will not let him see the dress."

And then my head was poking through the door, I was seeing him in his tux, and he was seeing the small part of me that could be seen.

My first glimpse of his face revealed a man who was very upset—in fact, I don't think I'd ever seen Jack looking like that up to that point; Jack is simply not an upset sort of person—but as soon as I said, "Hey, you," softly, his own expression softened.

"Hey, you," he said back. "You look gorgeous. Well, the tiny part of you that I can see."

"You're not looking too shabby yourself," I said, thinking about how blazingly handsome he looked. *Honestly*, I thought, *it's a shame people can't just go through life in gowns and tuxes, because a girl could get used to this.*

I shushed my mum, who was making anxious mum noises behind me, before turning back to him. But when he didn't speak again, instead looking at me with those happy eyes—I knew then where the phrase "moony eyed" came from because I was feeling the same way myself, like I was so happy it was like I was on another planet; or, you know, the moon—I felt the need to prompt him.

"So," I said, "what's up that couldn't wait until after the service? Is there some sort of problem I should know about?"

"Oh. Right." And with that, he was back down to earth. From the expression on his face, it was a glum earth. "My brother can't make it."

"Oh no!" I said, all sympathy.

Jack had originally asked his dad, Burt, to be his Best Man. He said his dad was his best friend anyway, which I thought was sweet almost to the point of making me cry, and plus, Burt would get such a kick out of it. But then, when I decided to go with two Maids of Honor, Jack decided to ask his brother to be his second, so that everything would be even. For a while he'd debated—perhaps he should ask one of his friends?—but then his mother, Edith, piped up with, "What about your brother? It was one thing when it was just Burt. But now that it's going to be Burt plus someone else, don't you think that someone else should be your own brother? I'd hate for your brother to feel offended at not being picked."

And so Jack had. Picked his brother, that is. And now it turned out Jack's brother couldn't make it. Still, I thought, there were worse things that could happen on a person's wedding day. And that's when it struck me how insensitive I was being. Jack had said his brother couldn't make it.

"Oh no!" I said again. "I hope everything's all right! There hasn't been an...*accident*, has there?"

"No, oh God no," Jack said hurriedly. "I'm sorry. Instead of saying my brother *can't* make it, I should have said he *won't* make it."

I must have looked perplexed at what the significance might be in this slight change of wording, because Jack produced a telegram, which he handed to me.

*Can't shake the paparazzi. STOP. The show must go on without me. STOP. Don't want to make your Big Day all about me. STOP. Present to follow. STOP. Love, Den*

If anything, I was even more perplexed now than I had been before. Why would Jack's brother have trouble shaking the paparazzi?

And then, finally, it hit me.

People will say I must have known all along. People will say that, *somehow*, I must have suspected. But let me state for the record here: No, I did not. And, in my defense, when I later on made clear what I'd learned to Stel and Bri and my parents, it turned out that none of them had suspected either. Perhaps we only see what we want to see.

Sure, Jack had told me he had a brother. Of course he had a brother—that brother was supposed to be in our wedding party! And Jack had even told me about that brother, at least a little bit. He'd said his brother was five years older than him by way of an explanation for why they'd never been particularly close. They'd always been at different stages in their development, and then his brother had struck out on his own when Jack was just thirteen. Sure, I thought it a bit strange I hadn't met the brother prior to our wedding day. I suppose, though, I just chalked it up to the older brother being busy with his own life and Jack's and my courtship being such a whirlwind.

But in the days and weeks and even years afterward, any time I tried to review the events and conversations during the three months we were dating and the fourth month when we were planning our wedding, I couldn't for the life of me ever recall Jack referring to his sibling as anything other than "my brother." Even Edith and Burt, when they spoke of him, it was always "Jack's brother," without a name. They were like three versions of Cordelia from *King Lear*, all focusing on the blood bond rather than any emotion attached to the relationship. And if I had heard a name mentioned at all? It would have been Dennis, and I hadn't made the connection.

Perhaps if they had even once referred to him as Denny. But Dennis Springer?

What were the odds? There must have been a million Dennis Springers in England. Or at least a few dozen. There was no reason for me to think it was the same person.

And yet, as it turned out, it was.

No, I hadn't made the connection before this. But who would? Who, outside of immediate family, would ever think of Paul McCartney as James, which is his real first name? Who, meeting someone named Michael McCartney, would assume he happens to have an older brother who just happens to be one of the most famous musical artists in the world? You just don't think like that, not unless you're told. And Jack, Burt, and Edith—no one had told me. I mean, you'd think someone would have said, right? If there was a word bigger than gobsmacked, that's what I was feeling.

"So what do you think I should do?" Jack asked.

"Do?" I echoed dumbly, still reeling.

"You know," he said, "about only having one Best Man when you have two Maids of Honor?"

"Don't worry about it," I said, still numb. "Just go with Burt. Everything doesn't have to be perfect, everything doesn't have to be symmetrical, and Burt's enough man for two."

• • •

For the first, and probably only, time in their lives together, Denny had taken the high road, done the unselfish thing: He'd sought to make Jack's Big Day be not all about him.

But of course, it was, in the end.

For, as I stood at the top of the aisle, on the arm of my father, looking ahead toward my husband-to-be, all I could think was:

*Oh my God.*

*I'm about to marry Denny Springer's brother.*

# PART II

## *Connecticut*

WHEN JACK AND I WERE FIRST MARRIED, AND BEFORE WE had our first son, travel together was so easy. As business at the agency picked up, sometimes we'd take organized tour groups to various places, leaving behind in the office the women we'd hired to help out. At first, I would make detailed lists, starting a few weeks before a trip. I love making lists. In fact, Jack would laugh at me about this trait. "You know," he'd say, "if you're ever under psychiatric observation, the first thing they're going to write in your file is: *frequently engages in strange list-making activity.*" Well, he could laugh. But who wants to find themselves in a strange country, only to realize something vital has been left behind? Still, Jack is so laid back, about almost everything, soon I learned to grow to be more like him, at least in this one regard. Before I knew it, I too was capable of jetting off to places with the knowledge that, so long as I had my passport and one good credit card with me, anything I might have forgotten could be replaced.

But all that changes after you have kids.

Kids. In a way, they're like dolls in that they're not quite the same, not ever fully complete, without all their accessories. They just *need* so much. Whatever they do—school, sports, games—they need the right gear. And then, if you take them on a trip, particularly a trip that will end with them living in another country for almost three months, well…

There was just no way I could get us all across the Atlantic without a lot of stuff. The boys wouldn't let me. I tried to pass on to them Jack's philosophy of travel—"You've each got your passports, and your father and I have credit cards, so we're good to go!"—but they weren't having any of that.

"But what if they don't carry my brand of toothpaste there?" William asked, worried.

"Well," I answered without thinking about it first, "they probably don't."

"They *don't*?" Harry asked. Now he was worried too.

"Of course not," I said. "It's a whole different country. They'll have their own products in terms of probably anything you can think of."

My mistake. Now the boys were horrified.

I know. It's odd for two boys under the age of ten to worry first about whether they'll have the proper gear to brush their teeth. What can I say? I trained them well: dental hygiene first. I suppose the extremity of their reaction may have stemmed from the fact that I told them that if they didn't brush at least twice a day, all their teeth would fall out, or, at best, they'd wind up with the rotten teeth of Lex, Denny's lead guitarist. Extreme? Perhaps. But you try getting two small boys to brush their teeth on any kind of a regular basis. Given any sort of option at all, they'll forego it completely.

But now, my parenting brilliance had come back to bite me on the arse. I was going to need to make sure they had enough of their special brand of toothpaste, and anything else they deemed essential, to last until they got acclimated enough to their new surroundings that maybe they could start to accept a little bit of change. And so…

Hello again, Strange List-Making Behavior!

● ● ●

So you get to the airport, you know you've got everything on the lists, and you think: *Yea! Home free!* Right?

Wrong.

One of the curious features of transatlantic travel is that when a person flies from the Northeastern United States to England, they land approximately twelve hours later due to the time difference. But when traveling in the opposite direction, also due to the time difference, you arrive at approximately the same time you departed. The boys loved this bit of trivia. They wondered: "If we just keep flying to the west forever, will we never age?" I didn't love it quite so much because here's the thing: no matter how you slice it, no matter which way you're going or what time it is, you're still going to be in the air for six hours.

Six hours in a confined space with two boys, boys who are wound up with excitement: "We are going to a new place!"; "We will have adventures!"—it was wonderful in its own way, seeing them like that. As with the toothpaste, William can be a bit fearful, and then Harry, who is normally less so, has a tendency to fall into line with that. So it was really great that they were finally both getting on board with the adventure of the whole thing. But then, six hours of two boys winding themselves up into practically manic levels of excitement, well, it is a bit much. I mean, they're good boys, but you can't expect them just to read quietly for a whole long flight. Of course, that's what I wanted to do—read quietly. I had some books I'd brought along, but also, in the airport while Jack was off getting coffee, I'd picked up some mags, one of which had a featured article on Denny. From the headlines on the cover, it appeared he might have a new girlfriend, with whom he'd replaced Lalaina LaLani. I thought maybe I could take it out of my bag and read it if Jack fell asleep, as he often did while flying.

But there was going to be no rest for anybody, not with William and Harry bouncing off the walls, threatening to disturb everyone around us. To be fair, none of the other passengers seemed to mind, not too much. No one even glared at them over their repeated trips to the lav to investigate. But then, when the cabin lights dimmed and people started to pull down their shades in preparation for the in-flight movie, I got the distinct impression that if they kept popping up and down, we might have a mutiny on our hands. So what else could I do? I promised the boys they could watch too, even if the film was rated more mature than they were accustomed. I glanced quickly at the movie listing in the in-flight magazine. Not going to the cinema much myself, the title didn't mean anything to me, but this sounded like a horror film. Still, if they were showing it on the plane, how bad could it be?

• • •

What could the airline people possibly have been thinking of?

You can't show a film like that to people on a *plane*!

Perhaps the airline had made the same mistake I had, glancing at it quickly and assuming it was one thing, only to have it turn out to be something else entirely?

Turned out, *Alive* wasn't a horror film, not in the conventional sense, but rather, it was the cinematic adaptation of a nonfiction book about a Uruguayan rugby team whose plane crashes in the Andes. Lots of people die, but some live, and then when things start getting really bad, they have to, you know, eat each other. I mean, they only eat those who've already died, but still.

As the credits rolled, the boys stared at the screen, agog. Well, we all did. And then, as the lights in the cabin came back on, the questions started.

"That's not going to happen to us, is it?" William was outraged, and being very loud about it.

"Oh, I don't think so," Jack said in an almost frustratingly mild tone of voice. "After all, that happened in the Andes. We won't be flying over South America. So whatever might happen to us, it can't *exactly* be that."

I may have been frustrated with Jack's tone, but the boys immediately calmed down. That's Jack all over. I was ready to sue the airline, while he was taking the whole thing in intellectual stride. If Jack had been the one to give the boys reason for brushing their teeth, it wouldn't have been my elaborate fear-based approach. Rather, he'd have simply said, "Because I said so, right?" and they'd have said, "OK."

"But if it did happen," William persisted, "would we get eaten?"

"Tell you what," Jack said. "We can continue this discussion if you like, but only if you can keep your voices down to a whisper." He cast a glance around us. "Because I can't imagine everyone else appreciates this topic quite as much as you do."

"Fine," William whispered. "Would we get eaten?"

"Well, that all depends, doesn't it," Jack said.

"On what?" Harry asked.

"On what else is available," Jack said.

I couldn't help it. As my menfolk looked around the cabin, sizing up the other passengers, I did too.

"No," Jack concluded. "You're the smallest ones here, so you'd be safe until the very end."

"What about Mummy?" William wanted to know.

Jack eyed me. Then: "Have you lost weight?"

I had actually. In preparation for the trip, I'd been watching what I ate. Sometimes being hungry made me a bitch, but I was hoping it would be worth it once I hit the beach in the new bikini I had packed away.

"Maybe just a bit," I admitted.

"You look fantastic." Jack smiled. "But then, you looked fantastic before too." He turned back to the boys. "No, I think Mummy's safe. Honestly, in our family, I'm the only one in danger. I'm the only one a group of people could make a decent meal out of."

I expected the boys to be upset at hearing this, but Jack said the words with such equanimity, they were more curious than anything else.

"But wouldn't that bother you?" William asked.

"Hardly." Jack laughed. "I am dead in this scenario, right? So why in the world would it bother me? I give you my express permission right now: if it ever becomes necessary, you can eat me. In fact, I insist."

"Jack!" That was me of course.

"What?" he said. "I'm only trying to keep you all from feeling any guilt afterward."

• • •

Having survived the flight, with a little help from a cannibalism discussion, it turned out that JFK was not as close to coastal Connecticut as it might've been most helpful for it to be. Of course, we'd known this in advance. But flying to a closer airport would've necessitated a nondirect flight with a layover in somewhere like Atlanta, which would have kind of defeated the purpose.

"When are we going to get there?" William whinged.

"This is taking *for-e-ver*," Harry supplied, holding up his end of the whinging bargain.

I can't say I blamed them for feeling fractious. I was feeling that way too.

It didn't help that the AC in the leased car was on the fritz. It didn't help that Jack was having trouble "driving on the wrong side of the road," as he put it. And it really didn't help when we got stuck in a godawful mess of stopped traffic.

Then the boys really started complaining, so of course, I put my foot down.

"You know what I remind myself," I said, "when I'm stuck in traffic and start feeling upset about it?"

"What?" Looking in the vanity mirror, I could see the sullen expression on William's face.

"I tell myself that, chances are, whoever's at the front of the traffic jam is having a far worse time of it than I am, that what is a mere inconvenience for me is likely a real tragedy for someone else, and I just hope they'll be OK."

I can't say that my pronouncement magically transformed the boys into paragons of patience, but they did let up a bit, and for that I was grateful. That's the thing about kids: if you let yourself get carried away, you can come up with a whole laundry list of things you'd like for them in this world. But the truth of the matter is, if I could get them to just occasionally think of someone other than themselves, I'd consider the war mostly won.

Speaking of lists...

"While we're stuck here," I said, "why don't we start making a list of things we'd like from the shops? You know, once we get to the house, we'll need to find a market so we have something for dinner tonight and breakfast in the morning."

So that's what we did, made up a list containing the things we liked most (bread and jam, which I suspected we would find, and Ricicles cereal, with its reassuring picture of astronaut Captain Rik on the box, which I suspected we would not) while entertaining ourselves by adding things we'd never want to eat in a million years—the boys' fancies were utterly captured when Jack suggested vultures' legs—and before we knew it traffic was moving again.

• • •

Some might think coastal Connecticut to be provincial, but what's wrong with a little bit of quaint?

As multilane congested highway gave way to tree-lined two-lane parkway, and that in turn gave way to increasingly less traveled roads, the smell of salt water coming through the rolled-down windows, I thought we could do a lot worse than quaint.

Since Jack was doing the piloting of the car, in addition to keeping the boys entertained, it had been my job to function as navigator, which is one of those things that sounds far more fun in theory than in practice. But as we pulled into the dirt road of what I was already thinking of as our street, all aggravation fell away.

"Is this one ours?" William asked eagerly as we passed an incredibly long fence, over the top of which we could glimpse what could only be described as a mansion.

"Nope," I said serenely.

"What about that one?" Harry asked of the next mansion.

"Nope," I said, still serene.

And so it went on until we came to the next to the last house and drove through the gap in yet another tall fence. And there it was: our house.

"It's a bit small." William's tone was skeptical.

"It's larger than our house at home," I snapped.

OK, so maybe I wasn't completely relaxed yet. But I'd get there.

"It only looks on the small side," I went on more gently, "because it's sandwiched between two monster-sized houses. But really, it's a good size, surely big enough for just the four of us."

And it was.

Unlike the surrounding houses, which were all some shade of natural-stained wood with white trim, ours was a dark forest green with cream trim. The others looked like they could have been banged up rather recently, while ours looked as though it had been standing on that spot, withstanding hurricanes, for decades upon decades.

Retrieving the key from the place the owners said we'd find it, we pulled open the outer door, with its heavy wooden frame and screen barely held together, and let ourselves in.

Of course the real reason Jack had picked the Roone house was because of its basement. Apparently, at one point the elderly owners we were renting from had had a son who was a jazzman, and they'd soundproofed the basement because not everyone in the neighborhood appreciated hearing him play his sax at his preferred jam session time, which was three a.m.

Another reason we'd picked the Roone house? They'd given us a fabulous deal on it, some sentiment over Jack being a musician like their son had been. As well as we did financially, we'd normally not be able to afford a house for the whole summer, but we hadn't really done any traveling since the boys were born and what with the fabulous price the Roones had given us…

Just inside the back door was a small mudroom and, beyond that, an ancient kitchen looking almost as small. The flooring was narrow wooden slats throughout, and there was a dusting of sand over all of it, with greater piles gathered in the corners.

"You'd think they'd have cleaned the place before we came," I said, eyeing a straw broom in the corner.

"I'm sure they did," Jack said. "I think the beach just does that."

"Does what?"

"Finds its way into everything."

On the wood-board wall in the narrow dark hallway connecting the back of the lower level to the front, I could barely glimpse a small painting. The gilt frame was dusty, and as I peered closer, I saw it was an oil painting of a little girl.

"It looks like a Renoir," I said.

"I highly doubt that," Jack snorted.

"Mummy! Can we go swimming? Can we go swimming?"

The boys had raced ahead of us to the front of the house. We found them in a living area, a small dining table off to one side, the living area itself all overstuffed cushions and wicker, with double-hung windows surrounding the half-hexagon shape. There was a door to the side, I presumed leading onto the porch, and beyond all those windows was the beach and the water.

"Can we go swimming? Can we go swimming?"

"Of course not," I said. "We need to broom out this place, make it livable. We have to find our rooms and unpack our things. Above all, when we're finished with all that, we need to find the local market. You do want to eat tonight, don't you?"

Usually the idea of food took precedence over everything. Growing boys, as I'd come to learn, need almost constant nourishment, like grazing horses or cattle.

And yet William and Harry just groaned.

"But that will all take *for-e-ver*," said William.

"And *e-ver*," Harry added helpfully.

"Don't give your mum a hard time," Jack said, placing a hand behind each boy's neck and steering them around. "Let's go find our rooms."

I followed them up the winding stairs—more narrow darkness, more wood—to the second story. Up there, for the first time I realized that none of the floors were level. That, combined with the narrow passageways and the smell of dampness that hung in the air even with the windows closed, gave the whole the feeling of being on a ship.

Upstairs, there were two small bedrooms, one on each side of the house, and a larger one, clearly the master bedroom, at the back. I counted one tiny bathroom, and it occurred to me that I hadn't seen another downstairs. Were we really going to subsist with just one bathroom? All four of us?

"I want this room!" I heard Harry shout.

Jack and I found him in one of the side bedrooms, bouncing on an overly springy mattress.

William hung back against the wall, looking at his feet. "I think I want this one," he said.

"OK," Harry said, cheerfully enough. "Then I'll take the other one." He raced past all of us, around the back landing and past the master bedroom to the second small bedroom on the other side.

William pushed off the wall to go follow his brother, and Jack and I followed William.

"I think I want this one instead," William said, back to talking to his feet again.

"OK," Harry said, still agreeable. "Then I'll take the other one."

"Come to think of it…" William started to say.

"Why don't you pick the one you want first," Harry suggested, "and then I'll just take the other?"

"Or," William suggested to his feet, and yet sounding more hopeful, "you could pick first…and then I could sleep there too?"

Back home, the boys were accustomed to sharing a room. Both Jack and I had been convinced that they'd each be so happy here with their own spaces, their own independence. What I hadn't taken into account was the fact that the prospect of turning double digits—William would be ten in July—weighed heavily on William. A part of him wanted to grow up, be mature, be the big brother, knew he should want to spend more time on his own. But another part, currently a larger part, was having trouble with the notion of sleeping without his brother. What can I say? Some kids had teddy bears or pacifiers. William had Harry.

"*Or,*" Harry countersuggested, his eyes lighting up, "we can switch off, swapping rooms whenever we like, making it all one big adventure. *And,*" he added, "we can pop in and visit one another whenever we like without waking anyone else."

"But of course we'd wake them," William objected half-heartedly. It was only half-hearted because, in spite of his fears of independence, I could see that the novelty of Harry's scheme appealed to him, plus the part that involved regular visits. "We'd be tramping by their bedroom all the time."

"No we wouldn't," Harry insisted. "Didn't anyone else see this?"

He got off the bed and went to a door on the right. In the other bedroom there'd been a door mirroring this one on the left. I had assumed them to be closets, but as Harry flung this one open, I saw they were connecting doors. And the space between the connections? It was a single long room running the front of the house, the only furniture in it a daybed. Opposite that daybed? An entire wall of old-fashioned windows, many of which had been left ajar, causing lacy panel curtains to billow into the room. And the view from that daybed? The sand and the water, only that.

Where the hell was my suitcase?

I barely registered their voices—William: "This could work"; Harry: "Wait. Where's she going?"—as I raced back down the stairs and out to the car, hauled out my suitcase, rummaged until I found what I wanted. Then, figuring the high back fence provided all the privacy I needed, I hurried out of my travel clothes and into my bateau bikini and sarong. When I'd bought the items, bateau and sarong, I'd fancied myself *quite* international.

Now I raced back through the house and out the front door, the sound of my menfolk hurrying behind me, stubbing my toe on a grill I hadn't noticed on the porch. But that didn't stop me. I didn't stop until I'd crossed the sand, the edges close to the water sharp with shells, and plunged into the water, surfacing to tilt my head up to the sun. In that moment, I wasn't a travel agent, I wasn't a wife, I wasn't a mother. I was just me.

"What's she *doing?*" I dimly heard William's voice.

"*I* thought she said we had to go to the market first," came Harry.

"Never mind that now," Jack said. "I think Mummy just found her bliss."

I'D FALLEN ASLEEP ON THE SAND AND WOKE TO A MOSQUITO biting me, smoke in the air, and the smell of something delicious on the breeze. As I hauled myself toward the porch, in the gathering twilight I glimpsed more than just the three bodies I expected to find there. Apparently the boys had made friends while I slept, and those friends came equipped with parents.

Despite my awkwardness at making friends initially in grade school, there's something different for kids outside of school. Unlike adults, who feel the need to go through what almost amounts to an interview stage, as though vetting someone for a position, children can make friends almost instantly, anytime, anywhere. My mother used to think that it was just me, being an only child, the way I'd go up to another kid while waiting for the elevator at a department store and say, "Hey, wanna play?" I think she secretly suspected I was some kind of lonely freak, and for a long time, hearing her tell those stories, I suspected it too. But then I had my own kids and started seeing the boys do the same thing. And even though they'd been a bit hesitant about taking this trip—"But we won't know anyone!"; "We're leaving all our friends behind!"—they'd already achieved that while I was sleeping. Like I said, anytime, anywhere.

"Ah! She's awake!" Jack said, in the midst of the act of flipping a burger, which is one thing I'd never seen my husband do.

Normally, I pride myself on my manners—if nothing else, you can't be successful in business without them—but I was still too groggy to exercise mine.

"What's all this?" I said, yawning.

"I am *barbecuing*," Jack said proudly, flipping another burger. "While you were sleeping, the boys and I found the market." He dropped his voice, whispering behind his spatula. "Just so you know, they do *not* have Captain Rik around here, but I'm hoping Tony the Tiger will win them over in time." And back to normal speaking voice: "Then we unpacked everything and they had a swim. They even had time to make some new friends."

"Aren't you lot exhausted?" I said. I was exhausted just hearing about it. "You haven't slept in forever."

"Not really." Jack shrugged. "I must've gotten my second wind. Anyway, when we were done swimming, I could smell the most marvelous smells coming from all the houses around us—did you know people around here barbecue all the time in the summer?—but frankly, I couldn't figure out how this thing works…"

His second wind? My husband sounded like he was on speed!

"…and that's when Biff offered to show me."

That's when one of the two adults sitting on my porch rose, offering me his hand for a shake. The man attached to the hand looked about our age, only more expensive somehow, and even more expensive looking yet was the woman next to him, who he introduced as his wife. I believed she said her name was Marsha.

"Your grill's a bit primitive compared to mine," Biff said, "but I was able to help Jack figure it out."

"Is that charcoal you're using?" I asked, unable to help myself from adding, "Isn't that supposed to be unhealthy?"

"Well, yeah, but you can't get cancer on the beach." Jack shrugged. "That's what Biff said."

"What can I do to help?" I offered Jack.

"I don't know. There's not much that really needs doing. Perhaps grab some drinks for everybody from the fridge?"

I was about to go do that, but Biff was already on his feet. "Let me get something from my place. I've got the perfect thing to drink with that."

Marsha rolled her eyes at this. And when he returned with a sterling champagne bucket filled with bottles of Budweiser, she rolled her eyes again.

"What?" he said. "No, you don't get it. It's so what it is, it allows the flavor of the meat to really shine."

It made no sense to me when he said it, but as I ate my burger, alternating with sips from my bottle of Budweiser, I kind of saw what he meant. The Budweiser didn't add anything, but it certainly didn't take anything away. Plus, the buzz I was catching from it was somehow wiping away the cobwebs of having essentially just woken up and the disorientation of immediately being thrust into a social situation.

The boys—our two and Biff and Marsha's, Billy and Tommy—dispensed with their food as quickly as was humanly possible—and headed back to whatever game they were playing in the sand.

"You know," Jack said, leaning close to me and lowering his voice a bit but not enough for the other couple not to overhear him, "Biff recognized me right away." From the bright light in Jack's eyes, I got the impression there'd been some pre-dinner drinking while I slept and that he had his own buzz going on.

"What do you mean he recognized you?"

"It's true," Biff supplied before Jack could answer. "I mean, he's Jack Springer, right? I have all of his albums."

"Even *Stirred Not Shaken*," Jack added, raising his eyebrows at the impressiveness of it all. "And you know almost no one has that."

This was true. *Stirred Not Shaken* had been released before Jack met me, and there were two albums since. Of course, almost no one had those either.

It struck me as odd. After all, Jack wasn't famous. But a total stranger met randomly on the beach in America was a fan? How bizarre. And yet Jack looked so thrilled—it was the kind of thing that almost never happened to him, being recognized for his music—I couldn't say anything to take away from that.

The men talked about Jack's music for a time while I listened to Marsha talk at me about the impossibility of finding an au pair who didn't ever want any time off, but then I heard Biff say something that caused me to turn from Marsha to see my husband's reaction.

"What's it like," Biff had just asked, "having Denny Springer for a brother?"

*Oh, no*, I thought. *Here it comes.* Jack almost never talked about his brother, and he never had any patience for people he deemed as using him to gain access to or information about Denny. *Now*, I thought, *Jack will see Biff as the user he probably is, and the bonhomie they've just shared will pass into distant memory.*

"About what you'd expect," Jack said tersely, which is what I'd about expected him to say, closing the case. But then, to my surprise, he laughed. And, having laughed, he expanded. "Think about other really famous people— presidents, actors, the Queen of England. Now think of those people's siblings. It's that. It's living your life in the biggest shadow you can possibly imagine. And that shadow is so all-encompassing. In the beginning, you think, 'This is kind of great.' And then after a while you think, 'I hate this.' And then, after another while you realize that the only way to stay sane is to simply ignore it. But what's it really *like*? I don't know. When I figure it out, I'll let you know. And anyway, it does come with its perks."

"Which are?" Biff asked.

"I don't know." Jack laughed again. "But it must, right? So I'll let you know when I figure that one out too."

I think it was the most I'd ever heard Jack say in one sitting about his brother, about what it was like being Denny's brother. And, like the Budweiser with the burger, his vagueness made no sense except that it did.

• • •

Guests gone, the boys asleep in their new rooms, I joined my husband in bed. I expected to find him asleep, but he was sitting up against the headboard, his chest naked, and the once-over he gave me as I climbed in next to him could only be described as salacious.

"You're kidding me, right?" I said.

He lifted the blanket, revealing that, no, he wasn't kidding in the slightest.

"But aren't you exhausted?"

"Ask me again afterward," he said, lowering his lips to my neck.

It's a funny thing about married sex. In the beginning, it's all every-chance-we-can-get sex, rip-each-other's-clothes-off-do-it-in-the-supply-room-at-work sex. But that's not sustainable. Particularly after you have kids, it's more like if-we-can-find-the-time-and-we're-both-not-completely-knackered sex. But that hadn't bothered me, even if it had bothered my friends when similar attrition had happened in their own marriages.

A few years after Jack and I were married, Stel and Bri both had weddings and, as soon as the glow had worn off, began fretting about it. They'd bring women's mags to our hen nights and take the ridiculous quizzes in them: "Are You Getting It As Often As You Should?" and "Is The Reason You're Not Getting Enough Bangs Because You Haven't Been Spending Enough Bucks?" They'd compare themselves to the national averages, feeling smug elation when they beat the averages or at least met them, worrying they were headed for divorce court when they did not. Me,

I didn't bother with the quizzes. I knew that what Jack and I had was good. Sure, we'd go through dry spells. There'd be times we were too busy with the agency, too busy being parents. Sometimes those dry spells would go on for weeks, like it just had; we'd both been so wrapped up planning the trip. But then we'd come together again and it would be some version of spectacular: spectacularly funny or spectacularly energetic or even spectacularly sad, as it had been after Jack's favorite aunt died too young.

The sex we had that night was spectacularly nice in its laziness.

Afterward, I snuggled into Jack's arms, but before I could drift off to sleep, I felt him disengage himself from me and rise from the bed.

"Where are you going?" I asked.

"To work," he said. "I thought of a new idea for a song."

"At this hour?" I said, at that point not even knowing anymore which hour this hour was. "Can't it wait until morning?"

"Well, I did come here to make a new album..."

Which was true. Jack normally put out an album at the rate of one every five years or so. His goal for the summer was to complete in three months what normally took him a half-decade. It was the real reason we were here.

I felt him kiss me on the forehead as I closed my eyes on a day that had seemingly gone on forever.

• • •

Talk about beginning as you mean to go on.

That first day set the template for the summer.

The boys would get up shockingly early, fly through breakfast, and then they were off, the beachside door slamming behind them as they raced to find the friends they would run with all day long until after dark, only returning at midday when hunger drove them to seek sustenance.

At first, I was a little concerned about this arrangement, being accustomed at home to knowing where they were every second. But Jack allayed those concerns. "It's not like that here, is it?" he said. "There's just the beach people, the boys know what the rules are—like no swimming alone— and there's so many of them in their pack now, I can't help but think there is safety in those numbers."

It was true. The boys had increased their circle of beach friends, and now they ran with girls as well as boys, including one older girl, Roberta, whom I suspected William had a crush on.

Jack referred to Roberta as "The Terminator," out of the boys' hearing of course.

"Look at the arms on her!" he told me. "I don't think you need worry about the boys' safety, not so long as Roberta's around."

Jack and I had increased our circle of beach friends as well. Most nights we were invited to barbecues at other people's houses or we had people to ours. We took a few trips into town to look at the shops or have a rare meal in a restaurant or even see a play, but mostly we stayed where we were.

So the boys ran all day and Jack worked on his music every night. Before long, he had two songs he was happy with.

If Jack had increased his production, the pace of our sex life had increased as well. Without discussing it, we'd somehow found ourselves back to that early-marriage pace of things, finding somewhere new in the house to do it almost every day. Sometimes, it'd be right after the boys thundered out for the morning. Sometimes, it'd be right before Jack went for his nightly sessions in the basement, or after he returned, triumphant. It was always good.

And what else did I do? The boys didn't really need much from me, other than food. So I was left to read on the beach or on the daybed in my favorite room of the house, listening to the beach sounds outside. Sometimes, I would tell myself I should want more from my days, that I should have a bigger purpose. But I didn't, not really.

We lived in that cocoon of peace for two weeks.

And then, one night, late, there came a knock at the door.

• • •

At first, I thought the pounding was a part of my dream. But as it went on, without ceasing, I swam up to consciousness. I waited for Jack to do something about it, but opening my eyes, I saw the vacant space beside me in bed. The clock on the night table said it was after three a.m., and still the knocking persisted. Realizing that Jack must still be working in the basement and would be unable to hear anything due to the soundproofing, I hauled myself out of bed and across the floor.

I couldn't imagine who it might be. Perhaps Marsha was having trouble again with her latest au pair? But surely even she wouldn't be inconsiderate enough to wake me up for that. Perhaps one of the other wives had had a fight with one of the other husbands then, a fight that had seemed more monumental and world ending due to a night of too much drinking? Surely it was something benign like that.

But as I arrived at the bottom of the staircase and turned into the kitchen, I thought: What if it wasn't something benign? What if it was some sort of dangerous intruder? Albeit, an incredibly well-mannered dangerous intruder if he was knocking to be let in, but still...

I cast about the kitchen, looking for something that might threaten the intruder away. It seemed all that Biff and the other men in this country ever talked about was baseball, and yet, where was a baseball bat when you needed one? Oh, and golf. They talked about that a lot too. A club would come in handy right now, but no such luck. And that broom, missing half its straw, would hardly do the job. At last, I settled on a cast-iron skillet, thinking it would have to do.

I flung open the door, skillet at the ready, unsure if I would be facing friend or foe.

And there he was, leaning against my doorjamb, fist still raised as though he'd been caught mid-pound.

"Oh, hello!" my brother-in-law said. "You know I had the damnedest time finding this place?"

DENNY SASHAYED PAST ME, FOLLOWED BY TWO TALL MEN, burly in their black suits and white shirts. All three of them toted similar mini suitcases, which I recognized as being the kind of case that had contained Denny's mobile phone when I'd last seen him back at Easter. Denny also wore a suit, only in his case it was cutting edge: gray silk with an eggplant-colored shirt and black skinny tie, wingtips on his feet, no socks. On his head was a Panama hat.

"Did you bring your whole entourage with you?" I asked peevishly, eyeing the men in black.

"Are you going to hit me with that if I say yes?"

It was only then I realized I was still gripping the handle of the frying pan. Naturally, I instantly felt foolish. And naturally, feeling foolish made me feel instantly more peeved.

"What are you—"

"Doing here?" my husband said.

Where had Jack come from?

Without waiting for an answer, Jack bent down and

kissed me on the cheek, whispering in my ear, "It was a really good night. I made an insane amount of progress on that new song."

If I hadn't had my sleep so rudely interrupted, it might have struck me then how strange it was for Jack to be doing and saying such things at that moment, like a cat spraying his spot.

"Aren't you happy to see me?" Denny asked.

"Of course I'm not *unhappy* about it," Jack said, sounding as though my peevishness had influenced him. "I'm just perplexed, that's all. What are you doing here? And how did you know where to find us?"

"As to the latter," Denny said—in that precise way he had of speaking sometimes, as if to say, "You know I could have been a teacher, right?"—"I called up our parents and they told me. As to the former, is it so surprising that I'd want to come hang out with my kid brother?"

Denny glanced at me briefly, as though checking to see if he had my approval. And then: "I thought maybe we could bond."

At this last, Denny reached up from his lesser height, encircling Jack in a hug that could only be called awkward.

If Jack had merely said he was perplexed before, he fully looked the picture now.

● ● ●

"Where are we going to put them all?" I practically hissed at Jack.

I'm never at my best when I first wake up. Add to that having been woken in the middle of the night from a sound sleep by the arrival of my brother-in-law, plus his two body-guards, and I was on the verge of being an outright bitch.

While Denny and the bodyguards made themselves comfortable at the front of the house, Jack and I busied ourselves making coffee in the kitchen. Well, I busied myself. Jack just kept me company.

"Look at that!" I heard Denny's pleased voice. "It's a little Renoir!"

"I don't think so," Jack snorted. "Can you imagine stuffing a Renoir in the dark hallway of a tip like this?"

'A tip like this'? I loved that house. I thought Jack did too. Was he trying to impress his brother?

"Perhaps you can't," Denny said, "but I can and it is. All you have to do is look at the brushstrokes. It's from his Ingres period."

His 'Ingres' period? Christ, it was about four in the morning. If I'd wanted an art lesson…But that was the point: I didn't want one. Without Denny having done much, already I felt as though I'd been invaded.

"So it's real?" Jack said, having joined Denny in the hallway.

"I'd say so. Yes."

"So it's worth…"

"This house." Denny paused as though considering. "Plus the big house next door and the one next to that—somewhere in that range."

Jack whistled. "Why would someone put something so valuable on the wall of a rental?"

"If you could afford something like that," Denny said with a shrug, "why would you ever want to hide it away?" Pause. "So, is there a problem?"

"Problem?" Jack sounded so vague. I could only assume he was still musing over the little painting.

"Yes," Denny said. "I thought I heard Mona say something along the lines of, 'Where are we going to put them all?'"

Damn.

"I kind of got the impression," Denny went on, "that she was referring to us. Unless of course she meant you've got whole closets full of these little Renoirs you're trying to find places to hang."

"Ah, no." Now Jack sounded sheepish. "You had it right the first time. It's just that, well, there are only three bedrooms here, the master and two smaller…"

"Perfect!"

"Perfect?"

"Of course! One for you and Mona—the master, I would think—and one for me, and one for Matt and Walter to share."

"Matt and Walter?"

"My bodyguards."

"Right. But the thing is, we've got the boys too…"

"The boys? You mean, *you've* got bodyguards too?"

"No! William and Harry."

"William and Harry?"

"*Our sons!*" I practically shouted from the kitchen. I kept it to practically only because I didn't want to wake those two boys, still sleeping upstairs.

"Oh, right!" Denny laughed. "The princes!"

Prat.

His laugh had that reassuring quality, you know, the one that says, 'Of *course* I know who your sons are! I never forgot about them for a second!' When, really, I was quite sure, he'd forgotten about them entirely.

"Oh, never mind all that now," Denny said in a slightly distorted voice, as though stifling a yawn. "Why don't you and Mona go on to bed? We can get sleeping arrangements sorted in the morning. I mean, I suppose I could just go on to a hotel now, but that would kind of defeat the purpose of bonding with you, wouldn't it?"

Jack was silent for so long, I sensed that he was dumbfounded by this turn of events. After all these years, here was Denny, coming to Jack, wanting to spend time with him.

"But where will you and the boys sleep?" I called from the kitchen.

"We can flop in the living room. I'll be fine like that for one night. Me, Lex, 8, and Trey—we all lived together in a one-room apartment back when we first started, back in our 'salad days,' as it were."

It was almost as though I could picture the look on Jack's face as Denny spoke these words: eager, as though finally hearing a firsthand report about life on Mars. In the years I'd known Jack, the few times we'd been around Denny, all Denny could talk about was whatever great thing *he* was doing right now, in the moment. But he never spoke about the past, all the years and things Jack might have naturally heard about if they'd had a more normal relationship.

Or maybe I was completely wrong about things? Maybe I was just projecting what I was feeling, projecting my own eagerness for details onto Jack. Maybe, if I could see Jack's face, what I'd see there would be doubt: doubt that this was really happening; doubt about his brother's motives at all.

"But what about your driver?" I called.

Without even going outside, I knew there was a driver out there, waiting in the car, just as there had been when we'd been at Burt and Edith's back at Easter.

"You mean Jeeves?" Denny called.

"If that is really his name," I countered.

"Oh, you needn't worry about Jeeves. He prefers to stay with the car at all times. Well, except for when he needs the loo. He worries if he leaves it unattended, some fan might nick it for a great big souvenir."

WHO COULD SLEEP AFTER ALL THAT?

I certainly couldn't.

But Jack could, apparently. And so I lay there, propped up on an elbow, watching my husband's face, so peaceful in sleep, the slightest of smiles playing the corners of his mouth.

I wondered: What did he really make of all this, this being what I had already come to think of as The Advent of Denny? Did he take what Denny'd said at face value, that he was here simply to finally bond with his younger brother? Was he satisfied with that? Or was he suspicious? Maybe satisfyingly suspicious? Or suspiciously satisfied? For the life of me, I couldn't tell. I had no idea what was going on in his sleeping head.

But I knew one thing; two, actually: I wasn't satisfied. And I was suspicious.

I remained like that, thinking, until the light coming through the curtains began to heighten, midnight blue turning into purple and then a strip of gold, and there came the sounds of the boys pounding down the stairs. The boys could sleep through anything, but they could also wake anybody, only in this instance, they hadn't wakened Jack. They'd be wanting their breakfast soon, so they could take off on another day. They'd also no doubt be wondering why three men were sleeping in our living room. I hauled myself out of bed and to the bathroom, after which I threw on a robe and headed down.

• • •

I passed through the living area, in which Matt and Walter, still in their suits, had made themselves at home by shoving several wicker chairs with overstuffed cushions close together and were now snoring soundly. In the dining area beyond I saw a curious sight: my two boys, mouths all but gaping open in agogment, seated across the table from my brother-in-law. Like his bodyguards, Denny also still wore the same clothes he'd arrived in last night. He even still had on the hat. I wouldn't say he looked tired—far from it; he looked wide awake, his clothes improbably unrumpled—perhaps, like me, he hadn't slept.

As I approached, he inclined his head toward me and then spoke sotto voce: "Are they always like this? I swear, they haven't moved a muscle since they got here."

"They're probably just hungry," I said in a normal voice.

What was with this sotto voce nonsense? Did he think they were animals in the zoo behind glass? That they could neither hear nor understand us?

"Ah!" Denny said. Then: "I suppose I am too, now that you mention it."

If he was so flipping hungry, couldn't he have helped himself?

I gathered three glasses from the kitchen, along with a pitcher of milk.

"You're looking fetching this morning, Mona," Denny observed.

Without comment, I went back to the kitchen, grabbed the cereal box, and returned, slapping it on the table with little grace.

"Ah, Tony the Tiger!" Denny said when he saw what I'd placed in front of him.

He poured some into his bowl, set the box back down, and reached for his spoon. When neither boy reached for the box, he picked it up a second time, waving it at them so I could hear the contents shaking around.

"What?" he said. "You don't like Tony the Tiger? I mean, he's no Captain Rik but…"

"*You* know who Captain Rik is?" this from Harry, breathless. I could be wrong, but I'm fairly certain that this was the first time one of my boys had ever addressed words directly to their uncle. Of course it would be Harry. He was always the bolder of the two. Bold or not, Harry's eyes were still practically bugging out at the idea of Denny knowing who Captain Rik was.

"Course," Denny answered mildly. "Doesn't everybody?"

When the boys continued to stare, Denny filled his spoon with a heaping mouthful of cereal, shoveled it in as though demonstrating that it wasn't poison, and commenced to chew, considering.

"You know," he said finally, "it'll never be Ricicles." He chewed some more, considered some more. "But it's got plenty of sugar, plenty of crunch." He shrugged. "I can't imagine asking more from a breakfast cereal."

"*You* eat Ricicles?" Harry again.

Denny snorted a laugh. "Doesn't everyone, mate? I mean, except when I'm in America of course. Then I eat this." He offered the box again. "Like I said, Tony the Tiger's no Captain Rik. But it'll do in a pinch."

This time Harry did take the box, breaking off in a peal of near-hysterical laughter as he did so. I could understand the feeling. Really? Denny Springer ate Ricicles? And he knew who Captain Rik was?

Harry poured himself a bowl, still giggling, before handing it to William, who began giggling as well.

Since Denny wasn't laughing, they quickly sobered up, commencing to eat their cereal, crunching whenever Denny crunched, though I noticed Denny's spoonfuls had gotten substantially smaller after the first heaping one. Then:

"So, are you staying here?" Harry asked.

"It would appear so," Denny said.

"But how *long* will you be staying?" Harry persisted.

For the first time, William spoke, only he didn't even look at Denny when he did so. Instead, he looked directly at his younger brother as he said in a hushed voice, "You can't ask him that question! Remember what Mummy always says? We're not to ask people how long they're ever staying, not even Grandma, because it makes people think we want them to leave." His voice going lower still, he added, "She says they think that even the times we don't mean it that way."

Denny glanced at me with a smile that was at risk of tipping over into a smirk, but he said nothing.

And neither did I. True, a part of me wanted to validate William, tell him that he was right, that I did always say that. But a far bigger part of me wanted to know the answer to Harry's question. Just how long was Denny planning on staying?

"No need to stand on ceremony," Denny informed the boys. "You can ask me anything. After all, I am your uncle, right?"

The boys looked startled at this last, as though registering the truth of it for the very first time. Somehow, one of the most famous people in the world also just happened to be their uncle.

"And you know," Denny went on, "it's not like I'm *Grandma*." He rolled his eyes at this, waggling his eyebrows in an exaggerated fashion.

The boys giggled again at this last, and I could tell that they were well and truly charmed by him. I couldn't help it. In the moment, I suppose I was too.

"As for the question of how long I'm going to stay?" Denny pondered. "I couldn't really say for certain. At least a bit, anyway."

*A bit?*

Was that the best he could do?

And back to being uncharmed.

"But where will you sleep?" Harry asked. "We only have three bedrooms."

"Last night," Denny said, "the boys and I slept here, in the living room. Well, the boys slept. I mostly just watched the light change over the water."

"*You* have boys?" Harry asked. For him, this must have seemed like even bigger riches than his uncle loving the same cereal, the idea that Denny might have boys like him and William. Perhaps, I could see the wheels in Harry's brain turning, Denny's boys—William and Harry's cousins—would be close to them in age and they could all play together today?

"Well, I do have some boys, but none of them are your ages nor are they here." Denny gave a sigh that was almost sad. "When I said, 'the boys,' I was referring to my bodyguards."

"Oh." Harry looked a little disappointed. But not much stops Harry for long. "You could have my room! And I could move in with William! William would like that!"

William didn't speak, but he did nod vigorously, and anyone looking at his eyes could plainly see: he would like that.

"*Thank* you!" Denny said. There was a long pause before he added triumphantly, "*Harry!*"

It was then I was sure that he hadn't known which boy was which until that moment.

"William." Denny, looking satisfied, regarded my eldest before turning to my youngest. "And Harry."

I would have bet anything that he still was unsure which was the oldest. He was probably thinking, *They always refer to them as "William and Harry." People have a tendency to name their children in descending order, and William is the slightly larger of the two. But then, I'm smaller than Jack even though I'm older, so size isn't always a reliable marker. And too, what if my brother and his wife are odd ducks who refer to their children in ascending order?*

Whatever was going on in his brain, after all these years if he didn't know which of his nephews were which, and who was older, I certainly wasn't going to help him.

"But wait," Denny said. "Are you sure I won't be putting you two out?"

"Oh, no. Even though William's two years older—he'll be ten soon—he doesn't mind rooming in with me," Harry supplied helpfully.

And thank you, Harry.

"But what about...the boys?" Harry asked. "Will they room in with you too?"

"Oh, I shouldn't think so," Denny said. "I prefer my own room if I can get it, and the boys prefer theirs. I think they rather like living rooms. Wouldn't be the first time."

Fantastic.

Two large shadows fell across the table, and there were the boys even as we spoke: Matt and Walter. They both looked a bit bleary eyed.

"Good morning, Boss," they said.

Back at the travel agency, I never liked it if one of the workers referred to me to my face as "Boss." There was just so much wrong with it—the idea that they were living in a subservient status; add to that the feeling that could never escape me that, perhaps, they were using the term ironically?

Denny, on the other hand, looked as though he wouldn't have it any other way.

Denny picked up the box of cereal again, waved it in their direction. "This. Apparently this is what we're all having for breakfast this morning."

One of the bodyguards, I believe it was Matt, took the

box, but then he looked around expectantly, so I went and retrieved more bowls and more glasses from the kitchen, placed them on the table.

Matt and Walter looked around the table, but there were only four chairs, three of which were taken up by Denny, William, and Harry. I remained standing.

The bodyguards just shrugged, poured cereal into their bowls, and commenced to eat standing up. I suppose they felt that, if only one of them could sit, then both of them must stand.

"William, Harry," I said, "shouldn't you be going? I'll bet your friends have been wondering where you are."

The boys did as I said, but they half backed their way out of the room, as though worried their uncle might be a chimera that would disappear while they were gone. But then the screen slammed. Matt and Walter were about to assume William and Harry's seats when Denny stopped them.

"Wait," he said. "Did you boys brush your teeth yet?"

Matt and Walter stared down at their feet, looking suitably embarrassed.

"Gross," Denny said. "Don't you know that if you don't brush your teeth regularly, they could all fall out? Or worse, you'll wind up looking like Lex?" Without waiting for a response, he added, "Do it now, please."

As Matt and Walter headed off to do his bidding, it occurred to me for the first time that if Denny stayed, keeping his entourage with him, there wouldn't just be five of us now sharing a single bathroom—which would be bad enough—but there would be seven. Plus the driver.

The driver!

I got another bowl and glass, filled them, headed out to

the driveway. When I got to the driver's side of the white stretch limo—what? Did Denny make sure to have one of these in any country he traveled in?—I made an impatient rolling-down-the-window gesture with one hand, spilling some cereal in the process.

"Ma'am?" the driver asked politely. "Can I do something for you?"

"Did you brush your teeth yet?" I demanded.

"Why, yes, ma'am. First thing when I get up and after every meal."

I shoved the glass of milk and bowl of cereal through the open window.

"Then here's your breakfast."

*  *  *

I reentered the back door to find Denny, in my kitchen, dumping the remainder of his cereal into the trash bin. Come to think of it, after the first few dramatic bites for William and Harry's sake, he'd only eaten a little more from the heaping bowl he'd poured himself.

"Not as hungry as you first thought you were?" I asked.

"I am, actually. But I can't eat that stuff. I prefer a Mediterranean diet. And I only eat organic."

Ooh. La-di-dah.

"I'll be sure to make a note of it," I said, "for the next time I'm at the shops."

"Please do," he said, and may I add, he said it without any irony whatsoever. Then: "But I wouldn't want you to go to any special trouble, not this very minute. I'll simply send the boys. Boys!"

He exited the kitchen, heading back to the dining area, and I followed him. Matt and Walter were at the table, eating. I could only assume they'd brushed their teeth.

"When you're done here," Denny announced, "I need you to go into town, find the finest organic market, get everything we need—you know, the usual staples. Also, I was thinking: a nice gazpacho for lunch and then, perhaps, Fontina-stuffed chicken for dinner?"

Fontina-stuffed...? Who did he think was going to make all this?

"We're at the *beach*," I pointed out. "We grill out, hamburgers and hot dogs mostly."

For once, I internally praised the Americans for their bizarre obsession with summer barbecuing.

"Right," Denny said to Matt and Walter. "Get some of those too. But be sure it's organic. None of that meat that has who-knows-what stuffed into it." He turned to me. "But surely, you can also grill an organic chicken on your grill, can't you? One stuffed with Fontina cheese, perhaps?" Not waiting for my answer, he turned back to the boys.

The boys. Gack! Now he had me doing it!

"We could also use some farm-fresh eggs for tomorrow's breakfast, and whatever vegetables are in season too."

This man really was the limit.

The boys moved to do his bidding, but he stopped them.

"Wait! How could I have forgotten?" He shot an embarrassed look my way. "We came away so quickly, it was all so spur of the moment, we didn't bring appropriate clothing. Really, we didn't bring anything at all except our toothbrushes, passports, and my credit cards." And back to the boys: "I'll need everything top to bottom: daywear;

eveningwear; something for bedtime too, I suppose. But, you know, as Mona has so helpfully pointed out, we are at the beach, so it should all be appropriately beachy. Lots of cotton and some linen. I'm thinking lots of neutral colors, definitely plenty of white. Specifically, I'd like a whole bunch of pristine white T-shirts, new of course, but they should also look as though I've worn them forever, so see what you can do about that."

"Right, Boss," Matt said.

"You did bring my size chart?" Denny asked.

"Always, Boss," Walter reassured him.

"What?" I rounded on Denny. "You're sending the boys to do your clothes shopping for you?"

"*And?*" He looked completely perplexed.

"Can't you even pick out clothes for yourself?"

"I can and have. Come to think of it, I just did. Did I not tell them exactly what I wanted?"

"Yes, but—"

"It's like this, Mona." He paused long enough to make a slight shooing motion at Matt and Walter.

I have to say: It *was* offensive.

"Oh, wait!" Denny called after them. "And don't forget to pick up whatever you might need for yourselves as well, Jeeves too." He made the shooing motion again.

With Matt and Walter off, Denny began once more.

"It's like this, Mona. I simply can't go shopping for my own clothes here, not in a town like Westport."

"Why ever not?"

"Well," he snorted, "I'd get mobbed, of course. I mean, *obviously.*"

I couldn't help it. I laughed.

"What's so funny?" he demanded.

"I just don't think it's like that here."

Now it was his turn to laugh. "It's like that *everywhere*, Mona. I think I should know."

"Maybe everywhere else. But not here."

"What's so special about here?"

"It's Westport."

"And?"

"A lot of famous people have lived in Westport."

"Like who?"

"Like Zelda and Scott Fitzgerald."

"Still around, are they?"

"Of course not. They're both *dead*."

"Well, then…"

"Bette Davis."

"Another dead one."

"That Martha Stewart person."

"Hardly rates."

"Look, I've actually seen them: Paul Newman, Robert Redford, Al Pacino—and no one was bothering them."

"I find that hard to believe."

"Well, it's true. I don't think they all live here—if the neighbors' account is to be trusted, many celebs just like to visit Westport, probably because they *don't* get bothered here. Even Diana Ross. Sure, people ogled her more than the usual celebrity—"

"I'd ogle Diana too. When it comes to other celebrities, Diana is highly oglable."

"—and I have to admit, I was tempted to trail her around for a bit, but no one bothered her."

"Where?"

"Excuse me?"

"Where is this nirvana where you saw all these famous people not being bothered?"

"In a bookstore in town."

"Huh. Must be some bookstore."

"It is. I even saw Patty Hearst there."

"Who?"

I explained about her being an American newspaper heiress who'd been kidnapped by a guerrilla group calling themselves the Symbionese Liberation Army, after which she renamed herself Tania for a time and helped out with a bank robbery before being arrested. She wound up serving two years and then went back to being wealthy.

"Oh. Well. If you're going to bring up *Tania*..."

"The point is, here is a notorious person, and while the bookstore clerk did make a crack after she left, something along the lines of, 'I neglected to ask her what life was like in the closet,' no one bothered her. As I said, I don't think it's like that here."

"Huh." Then: "See anyone else famous?"

"There was Linda Blair. You know, the girl whose head does a three-sixty in *The Exorcist*? In real life, she seems very nice and polite."

"Well, except for Diana Ross, none of the others you've mentioned are exactly hugely mobbable."

"Maybe so. But except for Jack, I haven't seen anyone even verbally acknowledge that they knew who a celebrity was, not to the celebrity's face."

"What do you mean, 'except for Jack'? Jack who?"

"Jack Springer? You know, your brother?"

"So, what? You're saying Jack's been accosting celebrities?" Denny considered this. "Doesn't really sound like the Jack I know." A shrug. "Not that I know him all that well."

"No, Jack doesn't accost celebrities! Someone else recognized *him*."

I went on to explain how our summer neighbor, Budweiser Biff, had recognized Jack right off the bat.

Denny regarded me as though I'd lost my mind. Which, considering the lack of sleep and the down-the-rabbit-hole conversation, I thought maybe I had. "Why on earth would anyone recognize Jack? Wait. Is it because I'm his brother?"

"No, you *prat*! Because of his own albums!"

"Really? Jack puts out albums?"

"Oh, come on. Surely, you must know that."

"Surely, I do not."

"How is that possible?"

"Because Burt and Edith never said?" He shrugged. "Certainly Jack never mentioned it. I'd have remembered if he did. I happen to have an excellent memory." Pause. "So. What exactly does Jack do on these albums?"

Through gritted teeth, I replied, "He sings and plays the guitar."

"How could I not have known this?" He seemed truly perplexed.

"I have no idea. You did grow up together."

"Not really. He was thirteen when I…moved out."

"And all this time, you never knew he was a musician too? You never jammed together?"

"No and no." Then: "Speaking of Jack, where is he now?"

"He works on his music all night in the basement, so he tends to sleep a good part of the day."

"Huh. I was once like that."

Deciding I'd had about as much of this as I could take, I moved to exit the room.

"Where are you going?" Denny asked.

"To start my day."

• • •

When I returned fifteen minutes later, in my bateau bikini and sarong, Denny was seated in a chair at the front of the living room, staring out at the water, his large mobile phone within reach.

"Going for a swim, are you?" he asked.

"It would appear so."

"Well, you look fetching, Mona."

It was the second time he'd used those words that morning. Did I feel flattered by it? Honestly, how could I not? If he even meant it. But he had annoyed me so much, with his sheer obliviousness of Jack's life, I couldn't really enjoy it.

"OK. Thanks," I said, pushing the screen door out. "Make yourself at home."

"You know," he stopped me, "it would never work."

"Excuse me?" What was he talking about?

"Even if what you say is true, even if the people in Westport don't bother celebrities, I can't just move around like other people can. If anyone saw me, word would get out, and then the press would get wind I'm staying here, and then we really would get mobbed. And that would spoil the whole point of me bonding with Jack, don't you think?"

When I returned hours later to make lunch for the boys, well, my boys, my brother-in-law was right where I'd left him: sitting in the living area, facing the water. Only now Matt and Walter had returned, all three of them were talking loudly on their mobile phones—I suspect so they could hear their own voices over the others—and everywhere I looked, there were boxes and shopping bags, so many there was barely space for me to walk. It looked like the shopping trip had been a smashing success. In theory, some of those boxes and bags must have contained things for the bodyguards and driver, but in practice, I guessed nearly all were for Denny. As he sat amongst all his things, he looked like a hotel guest who had arrived far too early for his reservation.

"Has Jack been down?" I asked when Denny got off the phone.

"Been and gone," he replied.

"How's that?"

"He came down, but then there was a knock on the door, and he told me he was going sailing with a friend."

That must have been Budweiser Biff.

"And he didn't invite you to go with them?"

"I'm sure he wanted to," Denny said, "but my new clothes hadn't arrived yet, and I'm not currently appropriately dressed for sailing, am I?" He didn't add, perhaps because he'd stressed the point so much already, that he also didn't want to be seen by people, didn't want anyone to know he was here.

"Yes, well, then," I said, "how about putting your things away? I hardly know where to walk."

"I would, but I wasn't sure which room was mine."

"Of the two smaller bedrooms, it's the one on the right-hand side facing the water."

For the first time it occurred to me that while my own boys could sleep through just about anything, having Denny plus his entourage around was definitely going to put a crimp in Jack's and my recent all-over-the-house sex life.

When he didn't move, I sought to prompt him along. "So, now you know which room is yours, you can go up now." I restrained myself from making the rude shooing motion I'd seen him use with his own boys, but only just.

"I would," he said, "but I did check the rooms out earlier, and it would appear that the boys have a game in progress."

Since there was now more than one version of "the boys" in my life, it took me a minute to realize that even though he usually meant his boys when he said it, the ones he was talking about now were mine.

"So?" I said. "Can't you just move them across the way? Or do you need Matt and Walter to do that for you too?"

He ignored my sarcasm. "I just don't think they'd like it very much if I moved things, not when they're in the middle of a game. They'll want to make certain everything's set up again exactly as they had it before."

You could have knocked me over. By far, this was the most sensitive thing I'd ever heard my brother-in-law say. And, of course, maddeningly, he was right.

"How did you...?" I started to ask.

"I know I haven't spent much time with my own," he said, "but I was a boy once."

That's the thing. It was always easy for me to picture Jack as a child, I could picture the continuity of it all. But Denny? It was impossible to picture him as a little person, with a little person's wants and needs; impossible to picture him as being anything but what he was, impossible to picture what makes someone go from being similar to my boys to being the man Denny was now.

"Right, then," I said.

There was the thunder of feet on the porch stairs, followed by, "Mum! Mum! What's for lunch?"

Then the sound of the screen yanking open and the boys nearly skidding into me. They must have seen that none of us could progress further into the room unless someone put some things away.

"Before that," I said, "how about you move your things around upstairs, help your uncle put away his stuff?"

"Oh, hey, Mrs. S.," Matt said. "Walter and I put all the groceries away. We hate intruding on someone else's kitchen, but you weren't around to ask. Hope you don't mind. We just didn't want the chicken to go bad."

• • •

I stood at the foot of the stairs, listening to the noises from above: the sounds of doors and closets opening and closing as Denny and my boys did whatever they were doing, of feet pattering back and forth between the bedroom on the right, through the dayroom, to the bedroom on the left. Occasionally, Matt and Walter would pass me, coming down empty handed only to head back up again with yet more parcels. I only caught the sound of voices rarely, always it sounded like Denny, and some laughter—also only Denny. Eventually, when the living area had been emptied of all the bags and boxes, William and Harry came back down, only this time without their usual thunder. For them, they were peculiarly subdued.

"Are we going to eat now?" William asked.

"In a minute," I said, heading up. "I want to check on your uncle."

When I got upstairs, I grabbed some towels from the linen closet. The door to the small bedroom on the right was open. Still, I tapped on it gently.

"Hello?" I poked my head in. If anything, the room looked more crammed with stuff now than the living room had downstairs. "Have you got everything you need?"

Denny looked around at all his clutter. "It would appear so."

"I thought you might like some towels," I said, offering what I was holding. "You know, for the bath."

"Oh, thank you!" he said. "I'll just put those…" He looked for a place on the dresser, but there wasn't any, so he just held them in his hand.

In truth, the towels were rather ratty looking—no doubt he was used to having everything plush and monogrammed in his various homes. Still, as we stood there awkwardly, he patted the top towel with one of his hands. "Very nice."

Then he started to remove his tie.

What? Was he going to undress right in front of me?

"Aren't you coming back down for lunch?" I asked.

"I think I'll have a little lie-down right now," he said, "if it's all the same to you. It has been a bit since I last slept."

Considering he hadn't slept at all the night before, it occurred to me that must be true.

"Right, then!" I said brightly. "I'll just leave you to it."

I was nearly gone when Denny's voice stopped me. "They're really good boys," he observed, "aren't they?"

For once, I knew exactly who he was talking about.

"Yes," I said, "they are. The best."

"They're so well-behaved."

"Sometimes."

"But they're also incredibly quiet. Are they always like that?"

*Only around you*, I wanted to respond but didn't.

Instead, I said, "Enjoy your rest," and gently closed the door behind me.

●  ●  ●

"Boss not coming down?" Walter asked.

"He said he wanted to sleep for a bit."

"Right."

I watched as Matt and Walter arranged the furniture as it had been when I first came down in the morning to find them sleeping.

"You don't want any lunch?" I said. "You're going to sleep in the middle of the day too?"

"We always sleep when Boss sleeps," Matt said.

"We like, whenever possible, to be awake whenever he's awake," Walter added. "You know, in case he needs us for anything."

It was like having a baby. I remembered, when I was pregnant with William, other mothers who had gone before me advised, "No matter what else you think needs doing, sleep when the baby sleeps. It'll never be as often as you'd like, and you'll need it."

Well, except for this morning, when Matt and Walter had been asleep but Denny not. Still, Walter had specified, "whenever possible"…

"What's for lunch?" Harry called.

I went to the kitchen. The counters were overflowing with whole-grain rolls and fruit, and when I opened the fridge, it was stocked full to overflowing too. At the front of the top shelf was a large plastic container with something green inside it.

"Looks like it's some form of gazpacho," I called back.

Well, at least I wouldn't have to heat it.

• • •

With the boys gone back to play with their friends, Jack off sailing, and Denny and the other boys sleeping, I found myself at loose ends. For the first time since coming to Westport, I felt restless, unsure what to do with myself. I couldn't go to the dayroom upstairs to read, as I did most afternoons, not with Denny in the next room; I wasn't comfortable reading in the living area with Matt and Walter snoring away; and I didn't want to go out in the sun—half a day outside each day was plenty. So I retired to the master bedroom with a book, feeling something of a prisoner in my own home.

The boys came thundering in about three p.m., looking for their mid-afternoon snack, but all the noise they made failed to rouse the slumbering bodyguards, nor did Denny come down. For snacks, I usually gave William and Harry whatever leftovers there were from the food the adults had eaten with cocktails the night before, but I found a package of whole-grain organic cookies on the counter. There was a sticky note attached, the handwriting all but illegible, but at last I made out the query: *Perhaps William and Harry would like these?* I figured Matt or Walter must have put that there when they were stowing the groceries away.

I expected the boys to balk at those cookies—they looked rather dry and unyielding to me—but Harry declared them, "The best chocolate chip cookies I've ever had!" and William added, "Can we always get these carob things?"

Jack returned at some point, looking newly sunburned after a day out on the water, but after a fast, if cheerfully buzzed, greeting, he retreated to the basement to work on a new song idea he'd had, something to do with a seagull.

As the sky began to darken, day thinking about turning to night, my own thoughts turned toward supper. I was on my way to the kitchen when there came a knock at the porch door. I found Budweiser Biff there, six-pack in hand.

"Marsha and I were wondering if you'd all like to come over for dinner?" he said. "We're having a few other people over."

"I'd love—" I started to say, thinking how nice it would be, after a day in which I felt as though I'd been mostly on my own, to enjoy some adult company and conversation. But Denny was still asleep. What if he awoke and we were all gone? Wouldn't that be rude? Particularly on his first full night here. As for the idea of bringing him with us, that was out. Hadn't Denny said he didn't want anyone to know he was here?

"I'd love to," I started again, "but could we have a rain check? We spend so many nights out late; not that we don't enjoy spending time with you and Marsha, but I do think we could all do with a quiet night in and early to bed."

"Oh. I see." Then, craning his neck as though trying to see into the room behind me: "Do you have company?"

Could he hear Matt and Walter snoring behind me?

"Why would you say that?" I asked.

"It's just that I saw the limo parked around back. I thought you might have a visitor."

He looked suspicious, and it occurred to me that Biff had spent the day with Jack. Hadn't Jack said anything about his brother being here? Denny had only spoken to me about not wanting to get mobbed by people, not Jack—Jack and Denny hadn't even seen each other since last night—and yet apparently Jack hadn't; said anything to Biff, that is.

"No," I said, not really feeling as though I were lying. After all, Denny wasn't a visitor, right? He was family.

"OK then, here." Biff handed me the six-pack he'd been carrying. It was Budweiser of course. "In case you get thirsty, you'll want these."

• • •

"What's this?" William asked, looking down at his plate.

The four of us had sat down to eat outside at the table on the porch. Even though Jack was the one who always operated the barbecue—just as it seemed that Americans loved to barbecue all summer long, I'd come to realize it was the American men who really liked to work the machinery, flipping food items right and left and acting hearty—I'd seen Jack do it enough times I'd been able to work it out for myself that night.

"It's Fontina-stuffed chicken," I said, sitting down with my own plate. "Is it not OK?"

While preparing the food for the grill, I'd briefly entertained the notion of asking Matt and Walter how to make it, if there was some special recipe I should be using. But then I figured, Fontina-stuffed chicken—that's about as self-explanatory as it gets, right?

William took a bite. "It's a bit oozy inside." He took another bite. "But yeah, it's OK."

Back home, I had friends with kids who were picky eaters. And God knows Biff and Marsha's boys were very picky. If I had money for every time I'd heard their youngest say something along the lines of, "The potato's touching the meat! Now I can't eat any of it!"—well…But my own two tended to be very good about food. Maybe it was that, me and Jack being travel agents and therefore always thinking about other cultures, we'd exposed them to a lot of culinary variety from a young age. I think part of it was that we mostly experimented in the comfort of our own home, so they always knew there were potential backups in the fridge, and another part was that we'd explained to them that there were people in the world that lived their lives in danger of literally starving to death every day, while the worst that might happen to them is that they'd have to wait for a few hours for the next meal to roll around.

"Well, it's what your uncle wanted for dinner," I said.

Jack raised an eyebrow at me, and then he laughed.

"It's ridiculous, isn't it?" I said, laughing too as I looked around the table with its marked absence of Denny.

Then I picked up my own knife and fork, cut into the chicken, took a bite. William was right. Definitely oozy.

• • •

I was nearly done with the cleanup from dinner when I heard footsteps approaching the kitchen doorway.

"Do you think we might have something to eat?" Matt asked tentatively.

"We did brush our teeth first," Walter added.

"Help yourselves to whatever you like," I said, thinking: How ridiculous! They shouldn't feel they had to ask me, not for food that their own boss had paid for.

"Oh, no," Walter said. "We couldn't possibly do that."

"It's your kitchen," Matt said. "It wouldn't be our place."

"But you were OK with putting the groceries away earlier," I pointed out.

"Oh, but that's completely different," Matt said.

"We couldn't just leave things out to spoil," Walter said. "That wouldn't be right."

"But it's your kitchen," Matt said again. "We can't just start making things whenever we feel like it."

I couldn't really see the distinction they were making, but at last I shrugged. Rather than continuing a circular argument, it was easier to get out more chicken, stuff it with cheese, and fire up the grill.

The chickens were almost done—and still no Denny in sight—when I remembered: *Shit! The driver!*

I kept forgetting about Jeeves.

• • •

With both hands full, I made the rolling-down-the-window motion again as best I could. Once the window was open, I handed the plate of chicken through, along with a cold can of Budweiser.

"Here you go," I said. "Dinner."

"Oh, thanks, ma'am." Jeeves smiled widely. "I was just starting to get a bit peckish."

"Well, I'm glad my timing's good. Enjoy."

I started to walk away and then stopped. True, the beach house was already filled near to overflowing. True, there were already seven people sharing one tiny bathroom. But what difference would one more make?

I turned back, gestured at the window again.

"I'm not quite done yet, ma'am. Would you like me

to leave the plate and bottle outside the back door when I'm finished?"

"Actually, I was wondering: wouldn't you prefer to come inside the house?"

"Oh no, ma'am, I couldn't do that."

"Of course you could. It would be more comfortable for you." I wondered where there was left for him to sleep. Not the basement—Jack worked there late at night or whenever the whim took him. And while I hated the idea of giving over the dayroom, it's not like I'd feel inclined to use it now, not with Denny next door. Perhaps the dining area? "Wherever you sleep in there, it has to be better than sleeping in the car."

"It's really thoughtful of you, ma'am, but no, I can't accept. I prefer to stay with the car. I like to be available with it as soon as Boss needs to go somewhere."

"But he hasn't gone anywhere all day. He hasn't gone anywhere in about eighteen hours by my reckoning."

"Ah, but eventually he will want to go somewhere again. And when he does, I'll be ready."

He smiled while he said all this, but there was some steel in that smile, and I could tell he wouldn't be budged.

"Very well then."

I started to walk away once more and stopped once more.

This was insanity.

"Still not done yet, ma'am. But if you'd like, I can hurry."

"That's not it," I said almost peevishly. "This is insanity."

"I'm sorry, ma'am, but I'm not following you here. What's insanity?"

"*This.*" I gestured at the limo. "*You.* You must hate your job. You're sitting out here, waiting on his whim—don't you *hate* this?"

Now he not only smiled, he laughed full out, practically in my face. It was like a laugh in a comic strip, so barkingly loud it could have knocked me off my feet.

"I'm sorry, ma'am," he said, controlling himself, "that must've come across as incredibly rude. But hate my job? I love my job! For starters, I get to drive, which is something I love. I've driven Boss in nearly every country in the world and on every continent. Did you know he once did a benefit concert on Antarctica? There were some scientists working on some sort of ecological stuff. Boss heard they were going stir crazy, and when there was a break in the schedule, he figured we'd all head down there, see if we could entertain them a bit while they were saving the planet. True, he did it indoors, but it was still Antarctica. I got to drive him in some sort of snow vehicle there. And someday? If more regular-type people get to go into space? I'll get to drive him on the Moon, or Mars even. Probably get to drive some sort of space vehicle."

The *Moon? Mars?* Had Jeeves been getting *stoned* out here?

"Oh, and did I tell you he pays me a fantastic salary? Fantastic salary—the boys too. And he's set up a pension fund for all of us. When we retire at age fifty, we'll be set for life. So yeah, maybe right now, sitting outside a quiet house on a quiet street, things are a bit dull. But things'll pick up again. They always do. Oh, and did I mention all the birds that throw themselves at me just because I drive him? Why, one time there was this girl who—"

"I get it, Jeeves, Denny's a saint." I waved a hand. "You

can bring the plate and bottle through to the kitchen when you're done. We leave the doors unlocked, it's that safe around here. Oh, and there's also a bathroom upstairs you can use for bathing and what have you, since Boss hasn't said how long he's staying."

• • •

Still no Denny.

If the whole point of Denny's visit was to finally spend some time with Jack, I couldn't see where that was happening. Jack had been asleep while Denny was awake, then Jack had gone sailing, and now that Jack was here, Denny was asleep. If things kept up like this, no matter how long Denny stayed—I still did wonder what "a bit" might mean—they'd never get any further with one another.

Jack did sit with me for a while in the living area, and we made the usual small talk about the boys and anything else that came into our heads. He really was being very sweet, and smiling often, but I could tell his mind wasn't really in it. So when he began to look antsy, surreptitiously casting glances at the door to the basement, I let him off the hook.

"Go on, then," I said. "Get back to your song."

"Are you sure you don't mind? Because if you do, I could just—"

"It's fine," I said. "I'll just sit up for a while."

With a grateful smile and a quick kiss on the forehead, he was gone.

William and Harry had found some old board games in a closet and pulled one out. When they read that it required two or more players, they thought more would be merrier and had invited the other boys, Matt and Walter, to join them. I'd tried to demur on behalf of the bodyguards, but they insisted they would find it enjoyable.

Now, as I sat in a wicker chair, looking out at the water, I heard their voices coming from the dining area.

"I'm not sure that's right," Matt said.

"I agree!" William said indignantly.

"Even though I was just in jail," Harry said, "shouldn't I still get two hundred dollars? After all, after being in prison, won't I need proper funds to start a new life?"

"Hang on," Walter said. "The rules are around here somewhere…"

I smiled to myself. The boys may have been bickering, but I could tell they were having fun, all four of them.

When I first had William and Harry, I was a fairly young mum. Sometimes I would chafe at it. Why was it no longer so easy to just get up and go whenever I wanted? Why, I sometimes thought, if I'm being honest, couldn't I simply go? Then I met another mother at the park, an older mum, who explained that as far as she was concerned, our children were simply on loan to us from the universe; that no matter how challenging we might find certain stages in their development, blink and those stages will have passed, never to return. There would come a time when my life would be my own again. And who knows? Maybe then I'd wish things back the way they had been before.

"And," she'd added, "was it really so great before?"

I thought about the years before the boys and, more specifically, the years before Jack—all that time at school, trying to fit in; all the years in the dating wilderness. There were definitely good things about before, but when I thought about it, I saw that even with the bad, there were so many better things after.

I'm not saying that conversation turned me into a perfect paragon of patient motherhood, but it did change the way I viewed things, at least whenever I thought to remind myself. Sometimes, it seemed now, the only requirement for my own happiness was that my own boys should be so.

So I just sat there for a long time, listening to their play, feeling content.

At one point, I heard the back door click open, and I figured it was Jeeves returning his dinner things. I knew I should go to the kitchen and do the washing up, but I was feeling too lazy. And when I heard the door click open again a short time later, I simply concluded it must be Jeeves leaving.

But then, as I stared out the front window, in my peripheral vision I saw a shadowy figure come around from the side of the house before beginning to move faster. It took me a while to realize what I was seeing.

With the waves glistening in the background, under the moonlit sky, my brother-in-law was running on the deserted beach, alone.

Since they'd stayed up so late the previous night with their board game, William and Harry were late coming down the next morning, and when their friends came round to see where they were, I went upstairs to rouse them.

Having done that, I proceeded through to the dayroom, figuring to have a look from my favorite window—it really was the best view in the house—while the boys brushed their teeth. As soon as I stepped into the room, though, I saw that I wasn't going to get to enjoy the view by myself.

Denny was already there. He was perched on the edge of the daybed, his posture ramrod straight, his naked feet crossed at the ankles. He was wearing sailor pants, low and loose on the hip, and the most pristinely white T-shirt I'd ever seen in my life, although, as requested, it somehow managed to look used.

Later, Matt and Walter would explain to me that after purchasing Denny's clothes but prior to bringing them to the house, they'd brought his dozen white T-shirts to a Laundromat, where they'd run them through the washer and dryer several times. Still later, I would wonder why they couldn't feel so liberal about availing themselves of the laundry facilities at the house.

"Good morning, Mona," Denny said, not taking his eyes from whatever he was looking at. "I'll bet you look fetching today."

"Er, thanks. Have you been sitting there long?"

"A few hours. Since the sun came up."

"What are you doing?" I asked, my own eyes focused on him rather than the view. Without dark glasses or makeup, and in the full light of day, for the first time in years I could fully see his face: the tracery of age; the lines carved around his eyes and mouth so deep, signatures of a life lived more fully than anyone else, the laughter always louder. Despite that his body, looking somehow vulnerable in his all-white clothing, could easily still pass for that of a teenage boy, for the first time Denny's face actually looked forty-two.

"Working," he said calmly. "Thinking."

"I see."

But I didn't. Not really.

"Will breakfast be ready soon? Only I haven't eaten in over twenty-four hours. Sometimes I go on fasts to clear my mind, but I prefer those fasts to be deliberate."

"If you were so hungry, why didn't you just go get yourself something to eat?"

"Oh, I couldn't do that. And intrude on your kitchen?"

It was similar to what Matt and Walter had said. I was beginning to suspect that's where they got it from.

I was already clear across the boys' bedroom when I heard his voice call after me:

"I think those eggs would be good this morning."

• • •

The way we'd spent the first day?

That was pretty much the pattern we settled into over the next two weeks: Me making everyone breakfast; William and Harry going off; Jack disappearing with Biff or one of the other men; me preparing all the other meals whenever anyone got hungry, because Denny and his entourage were all too polite to cook in my kitchen; Jack and Denny spending almost no time in one another's company. At night, we didn't accept invitations out because Denny didn't want others to know he was there—it would have felt rude to leave him behind—and we didn't have others over for the same reason. After dark, when everyone else was otherwise occupied, Denny would slip out for his quiet runs in the night.

The only big difference from the first day was that Denny and his boys, no longer suffering from jet lag, were awake in the afternoon, and all three of them spent most of their time in the living area, talking loudly into their large mobile phones. Except for the hours I spent on the beach, I felt as though my time and my life were no longer my own, but I couldn't spend all my time on the beach. And whenever I wanted to just go read in the dayroom, it seemed that Denny was always there in his white clothes, staring out the window, working and thinking.

There was one moment that was different from all the others.

One day, when Jack was off somewhere, Denny asked me if he might use the basement.

"You said there's a soundproofed music room down there that Jack uses, yes?" he said.

"Well, I don't think it's quite up to the standards you're used to..."

"I'm sure it'll be fine," he said, "so long as Jack doesn't need it himself right now."

He disappeared for a moment upstairs and then came running lightly straight back down with an acoustic guitar.

"Ready!" he said, sounding like William and Harry before embarking on a trip they wanted to take.

I switched on the light and led him down the rickety basement stairs.

"As you can see," I said, "it's pretty primitive..."

"It's fine," he said, only barely glancing at his surroundings as he sat down in a chair, placing his guitar on his knee.

I continued to stand there, and after a moment, he looked up, flashed me a wide smile. "Really, Mona, it's perfect. Thank you."

There was dismissal in those words. He had work to do and he was ready for me to be gone.

As I turned away, I saw him reach for a pad and pen that Jack had left out. I paused, wondering if this might bother Jack later, his things being disturbed. And now I began to regret letting Denny down there at all. But I had already let him in. It would be foolish now to try to take it back.

I started up the stairs, made it all the way to the top, turned the knob on the door, pushed the door open...

And then without walking through it, I pulled the door shut again so the click was audible, and, as silently as possible, I sat down on the stairs.

For the longest time, there was silence. I have to admit, after a few minutes, I started to get bored. Was this what creativity sounded like? Perhaps Denny wasn't as ready as he thought he was?

Then I heard the plink of a few notes, followed by a chord or two. Then came some humming, at which point I experienced an echoing hum inside myself. Even without any words at all, that humming was distinctive.

More silence. This time, I wasn't bored at all. Rather, I waited in anticipation for more sound. I knew it must be coming. In the wait, I pictured Denny doing what I'd seen Jack do on the rare occasions when I'd caught glimpses of him composing a song; Jack never really let me inside his creative process. The few times I'd seen him, Jack would stop every so often and make notes, changing a lyric to fit the tune or changing the tune to fit the lyric.

I knew from reading the mags that, usually, Denny wrote all the words and Lex wrote all the music. They didn't do this in any particular order. Rather, whenever inspiration struck one of them, that one would do whatever he wanted before tossing it over to the other guy to do his share, finding inspiration from inspiration. But sometimes, over the years, one or the other would do both; Lex more rarely, because Lex wasn't exactly strong on words, his interviews monosyllabic, punctuated by grunts. And in the beginning, when Denny did try to compose music, Lex would laugh at his efforts. Sometimes, the critics did too, even a few fans. But over time, Denny got better. No one was laughing anymore.

That—Denny creating a whole song on his own—that's what I was listening to.

And then, there it was, that voice: I hadn't heard that voice, not singing live like that, in eighteen years. I hadn't even heard it on tape very much, since Jack never played Denny's band's music and all our friends knew better than to. So the only times I heard his recorded voice were if I was absolutely alone in the car and a song came on the radio or, sometimes, in a department store if there was a knockoff version—true abominations, those. As for the last time I'd heard Denny sing live, it was when I was fifteen, at a concert I'd gone to with Stella and Bria.

But I couldn't think about that right now, didn't want to, because as I sat there, Denny was struggling over the phrasing of a line of lyrics. He'd get to the end—the last word was "it"—and each time he'd try it a different way. It seemed impossible to imagine, that there could be so many variations on "it," but there were. At last, he settled on the version that most conveyed wistful longing, turning a two-letter word into a multisyllable one, dragging the short "i" initially and then going up a few notes and hitting the full "it" hard. He sang the word the exact same way three times, and then he began at the beginning of the song, playing it straight through for the first time.

When he was finished, I could scarcely breathe. It would be impossible to describe the sensation of having music created so close. It was like I was in another time or as though time had completely stopped. When I looked at my watch, I saw that two hours had passed.

"Was that good?" his voice came up to me.

*How did he know I was here?*

"I could hear you breathing."

*From all the way over there?*

"I have extraordinary hearing. People always assume, because of the loud amplifiers and all the years of arena playing, that my hearing must be shot. But the truth of the matter is, I started out in life with such extra-extraordinary hearing, it used to be downright painful for me. Sometimes, it would get frustrating, trying to focus while being distracted by every little sound. And a poorly running appliance could drive me nearly mad. So I thank the heavens that music has wrecked my hearing because now it's merely exceptional." Pause. Then:

"So. Was it good?"

Briefly, I flirted with the idea of saying "no," of denying him. But Denny had known I was there. And still he had let me in in a way Jack never had.

"Yes," I said at last, again marveling at how much memory and meaning could be invested in one small word, "yes, it was good."

As I believe I may have mentioned, in two weeks, there was just one great moment. OK, maybe that moment lasted for two hours. But still.

Something had to give.

• • •

I'd had enough of the beach, enough of cooking meals for others at all hours, enough of having to find a place to simply *be* where others weren't. I wanted to take my book upstairs and spend the afternoon reading. So what if Denny was there, *working* and *thinking*? He could work and think somewhere else for a change. Whose house was it anyway?

I mounted the stairs fiercely, book in hand, determined to have my way for once. But as I climbed higher, I heard the sound of voices and female laughter coming from the front of the house. What was this? For the whole time we'd

135

been there, I was the only female in the house, and I certainly wasn't doing any laughing.

As far as I knew, Denny hadn't been out of the house, unless you counted him running on the beach at night, which I didn't. I always watched him when he ran, and I never saw him speak to anybody, probably because he went out so late, there was no one else there. So where had he commandeered a woman from then?

Entering the boys' bedroom, I saw that the door to the dayroom was wide open. How irresponsible! What if one of the boys had come back to get something from their bedroom, only to stumble upon their uncle and some woman having it off in the dayroom? Couldn't Denny have brought the woman to his own bedroom like a normal person and, you know, closed the door? I was so incensed I couldn't see straight. I couldn't even hear what Denny and the woman were saying, not over the roaring in my own head.

"Just what do you think you're doing?" I demanded without preamble as I burst into the room. I don't know what I'd expected to see exactly. Certainly something more gymnastic than what was on view.

As it was, Denny was seated on a white wicker chair he must've pulled into the room, a towel draped around his shoulders. Behind him stood the woman.

I think it's political correctness gone mad to say that *exotic* is a word that should no longer be used to describe a woman. *Exotic*, among other things, means "strikingly, excitingly, or mysteriously different or unusual," and this sensationally tall woman standing before me was certainly all that. As for one of the other definitions, "of or related to striptease, as in dancing," given her crotch-high short shorts and her baby T that was more bra than actual clothing, she had that covered too, if nothing else.

Their heads swiveled toward me as one, and they spoke at once too.

"I'm getting my hair cut," he said.

"I'm cutting his hair," she said.

There are times, when a person is angry about something but then becomes aware that things aren't what they thought, that anger gets defused and everyone has a good laugh. There are other times, though, that no matter how unreasonable—perhaps because it is unreasonable—the person instead forges forward, full steam ahead.

Which way was I going to go?

"This is just too much!" I yelled.

"Do you really think so?" Denny asked mildly. He held out his palm and the woman placed a hand mirror in it. Denny studied his reflection seriously from all sides. "But this is how much I always have her take off."

"Not the bloody haircut, you idiot!"

"What then?"

I was so exasperated. "Where did she come from?"

"England of course. I'm sorry! Where are my manners? Lulu, this is my sister-in-law, Mona. Mona, Lulu."

Lulu? His previous girlfriend had been named Lalaina LaLani. Didn't he know any women besides me whose names didn't begin with L?

Lulu shifted a pair of scissors to the hand that was already holding a comb and reached out the now free one toward me. It was a beautiful hand. And when she smiled, she could have lit up the silver screen. "Charmed," she said.

I had no choice but to shake her hand.

"Perhaps you'd like to get your hair cut too?" Denny suggested. "I'm sure Lulu wouldn't mind."

"Not at all," Lulu added.

"You look like you could use it," Denny said.

"My hair is fine the way it is!"

"OK, then, tell you what," Denny said. "It's becoming increasingly clear there's something on your mind. How about we let Lulu finish her job, and then I'll meet you downstairs, where we can discuss whatever that something is?"

Was I being *dismissed*?

I opened my mouth to protest but then stopped.

Did I really want to be having this fight with him in front of gorgeous Lulu?

Apparently, I did not.

"*Fine*," I said through gritted teeth.

• • •

Downstairs in the living area, I paced and fumed, fumed and paced.

The nerve of that man!

A part of me knew I was being unreasonably irate, knew it to my core, but what sort of person accepts an invitation for one only to bring a whole entourage and then adds a personal hairdresser to the mix? My brother-in-law, that's who. Not to mention, a big part of the part of me that knew I was being unreasonably irate suspected it was due to being upset about him bringing another woman here.

But I didn't want to think about that part.

Ten minutes later, I heard the sound of feet on the stairs accompanied by lots of male and female laughter.

"So, right," Denny said, "see you in two weeks?" There followed the bang of the back screen door slamming shut. A minute later, Denny joined me.

"Two weeks?" I asked. "You mean you're not moving her in here with all the rest of your entourage?"

"Of course not. Why would I do that? That would be excessive."

"So what do you do exactly? Every two weeks you just fly her to wherever you are in the world so she can keep your hair trimmed the perfect length?"

"Yes, that's exactly right."

"But that's insane!"

"Do you really think so? Because I think it would be insane for a person not to have perfect hair at all times if a person could afford it."

I tried to calculate what he must spend—the plane fares, other travel expenses, not to mention what he paid Lulu for what must be an enormous amount of time—just to get his hair cut. I simply couldn't fathom it.

Suddenly I was sure that, whatever this insane man was doing here, it had nothing to do with wanting to get closer to my husband.

"What are you doing here really?" I asked him tiredly, the fight having gone out of me.

"Excuse me?"

"Did you have a fight with Lex?"

"Why would you say that?"

"Because it's what you two do?"

"Again, why would you say that?"

All of a sudden, I saw things clearly: the reason Denny had come here at all, that song I'd heard him composing—Denny was working on a solo album.

Everyone knew the story of how the nexus of the band first formed. Lex beat Denny up on Denny's first day at school. While waiting to see the headmaster, they began physically fighting again, but then they cracked up laughing, began talking about what sort of music each liked. Before the headmaster came out to yell at them, they'd already worked out that Denny would be lead singer and Lex would play lead guitar. They'd even come up with the name of the band and the beginnings of their first song. That became the general pattern of what was to come. Fight, make up, get creative. They'd been together now for so long, they were more to each other than any romantic partner ever could be. Over time, though, the wash-rinse-repeat pattern of fight/make up/create had taken its toll. Sometimes, there was no make-up period at all, and instead they went off to create separately. They'd even each done a few solo albums—never nearly as successful as those done together. So that's what Denny was doing here. It was the only thing that made sense.

I knew all this from reading the mags, but of course I couldn't tell him that.

"Because it's the only thing that makes sense," I said finally. "Call it a lucky guess."

"*Guess? Sense?* Don't be daft! How many times do I have to tell you, I came here to spend time with my brother."

"Oh, really? And just how much time have you spent with Jack so far?"

He sighed. "Really, Mona. What's this really all about?"

And, just like that, the fight was back in me.

"*You*! You come here with your bodyguards and your drivers and your hairdressers—"

"Just one driver, just one hairdresser, and the hairdresser's already gone away."

"Do you have any idea how many meals I make a day? You all eat at different times, none of you can be bothered to make your own food—"

"We don't want to intrude on your kitchen. It wouldn't be right."

"Which is absolutely insane. Do you have any idea how many hours a day I'm spending in the kitchen?"

"I so wish you'd said something earlier. I'm happy to send for my personal chef. It'll take him the better part of the day and night to get here—first the private jet has to bring Lulu back before collecting him—but I assure you—"

"That's not the point!"

"Then what is?"

"Bringing your private chef here will be just one more person using the bathroom."

"Well, not exactly. I mean, he will reduce drastically the time you're spending in the kitchen, so he'll be doing much more than just using the loo…"

"But I don't want another person here! Gack! You and all your people—it's like dealing with King Lear!"

"At the risk of angering you further, I feel the need to point out: Aren't you exaggerating, just a tiny bit? After all, Lear arrived at his daughters' homes with one hundred men. So I hardly see where this qualifies—"

"*It's bloody close enough!*"

To his credit, he wasn't physically blown across the room

like a cartoon character by the foghorn quality with which I'd invested my voice. He didn't even flinch.

"I suppose, Mona, next you'll be quoting at me, 'What need you one?'"

"If the entourage fits…"

*Or doesn't*, I thought.

"Again," he said, in that maddeningly reasonable tone of voice, "I do wish you'd said something earlier instead of letting things fester."

"I'm saying something now."

"Yes, and I'm hearing you now. I just don't know why you didn't bring it up when things first started to bother you. I mean, you can't just expect other people to read your mind, can you?"

"I just wanted to have a peaceful summer. Is that too much to ask? It's fine that everyone else is having a good time, doing whatever they want, but is it too much to ask that I be allowed to do the same?"

"Of course not. I'll make arrangements to put the boys and Jeeves up at a nearby hotel. I'll only call them when I absolutely need them. Will that do?"

"I actually like them all." I was starting to feel guilty. But not much. "But they spend so much time in the bathroom!"

"Matt and Walter can be very vain that way."

"And the boys, *my* boys, enjoy playing board games with Matt and Walter at night."

"Then they can come for occasional visits. But no more taking over your living area. Will that do?"

I thought about it. Would that do?

I must have thought about it for too long because at last he said, "Unless of course you want me to leave too?"

And I thought about that even longer.

"No," I said at last, "you can stay."

. . .

"What's going on? I could hear you fighting from the beach! Well, mostly I heard you, Mona."

Denny had departed, presumably to give his workers their temporary walking papers, and now Jack was back, wanting to know what all the fuss had been about.

"Your brother." I tempered the impulse to speak the words in a raised tone since, apparently, my voice carried.

"What harm's he causing?"

"What harm?"

"Well, on the whole, I've found him to be surprisingly quiet. I mean, he doesn't really say very much, does he?"

Quiet? Jack only thought that because he was never around when Denny and his entourage were all jabbering at once on their mobile phones.

"So, as I said," Jack said, "what's the harm?"

Denny had destroyed the peace I'd initially found there, he'd completely disturbed the fabric of our time in Westport, changing every second of every day. That was the harm.

But I couldn't tell Jack. It was too much somehow, too big of an admission of the effect Denny had on me.

So I settled for a rehash of the things I'd told Denny: about being tired of cooking for everybody, about being tired of having so many people using one bathroom, about how I thought it only fair that I should get to enjoy a relaxing summer too. I got so caught up in my own rant that I stopped thinking about what I was saying, stopped choosing my words with care, which is how I ended up adding:

"I never should have invited him here in the first place."

"Wait. What? You invited him here? But I thought he came on his own steam."

Ah, crap.

I had no choice. I was forced to admit to having invited Denny back at Easter.

"How," Jack asked, "could you have neglected to tell me something like that?"

"I forgot."

"You forgot? That seems like a pretty big thing to forget."

"It's true, though. I issued the invitation and then I somehow forgot all about it." When Jack just continued to stare at me, I added, "Well, I never really thought he'd come, did I?"

A moment ago, Jack had looked as though he were growing angry. Now he merely looked a trifle sad, wounded.

"Then all that stuff about him coming here to spend time with me, to 'bond'"—he spoke the word scornfully—"that was just a load of malarkey?"

I could have pointed out that it wasn't as though Jack had exactly bent over backwards to spend time with Denny since he'd come either—Jack hadn't bent at all—but it didn't seem like the time, not when Jack looked so upset. Probably not the right time to point out what a ridiculous word I thought "malarkey" to be either.

"No," I said. "Your schedules just haven't meshed yet. I'm sure it'll be easier now that his entourage has gone." I explained how Matt and Walter and Jeeves would henceforth be staying at a local hotel. "But I'm sure he came for you. I'm positive."

I said the last even though I was not.

"When I invited him," I added, "I did say it was so you could bond. So, in showing up, that must've been what he wanted."

"Yes," Jack said, "but it wasn't his idea."

. . .

That night, for the first time since his arrival, Denny sat down with the family for dinner. The five of us ate at six because the boys had come home earlier than usual saying they were starving. Despite their initial bonding over pre-ferred cereal choices, the boys had not warmed up to Denny and were no more comfortable around him than they'd ever been. So conversation was limited and strained as we all sat on the porch, eating the burgers I'd asked Jack to barbecue. To Denny's credit, he didn't object to the fare, didn't ask if the beef was organic or the rolls whole grain. I wouldn't normally give credit to another adult for exhibiting basic good manners, but I figured that, having had my say earlier in the day, some exceptions did have to be made in his case.

If the usual festive dinnertime air was constrained by Denny's presence, he didn't appear to be aware of it. He simply ate his burger in peace, looking out at the water. It occurred to me that, with the exception of his late-night runs, this was the first time he'd been out of doors in over two weeks.

"So, Jack," he said at one point, "how's the songwriting going?"

It took a long moment before Jack answered. "In fits and starts."

"Yeah." Denny sighed, world weary. "It can be like that."

*Here's progress!* I thought. *They're having an actual exchange—it's even about music...sort of!*

"I used your basement a while back," Denny said. "That's quite a nice setup."

Jack looked startled.

"I hope you don't mind," Denny added.

"No," Jack said. "Any time. By all means."

But then silence returned to the table. And that, it would appear, was that.

• • •

To my surprise, when the boys picked up their empty plates to bring into the kitchen, Denny did as well. And when, once in the kitchen, the boys asked if I needed them to help with the cleanup and I told them to just go play, when Denny similarly asked if I needed help, I told him he was free to go too. I counted it a good thing, however shocking, that he was so contrite following our discussion. But it didn't mean I wanted him underfoot every second, trying to prove to me how wrong I'd been about him.

Besides, it was a really small kitchen.

As I turned on the water faucet, I nearly jumped as I felt two strong arms snake around my waist from behind.

"You're not going to send me away to play too, are you?" Jack said. "Especially since I'd rather play here." I felt his lips kissing my neck. "There hasn't been enough of this lately, has there? Not by half."

I turned in his arms, kissing him.

He was right. And oh, how I'd missed this.

I got so caught up in the sensations of the moment, I only dimly registered the sound of someone knocking on the beachside door.

"I should get that," I murmured.

"No, you shouldn't," Jack said, going back to kissing me.

When more knocking came, I said, "Well, someone should."

"Doesn't mean it has to be you."

More kissing until, at last, I extricated myself. "I'll be right back," I promised, laughing.

When I walked into the living area, I saw Denny standing in the doorway. He only had the door open as wide as his slender body, so I couldn't see who he was talking to, standing on the step below him.

But I did hear him ask, "Do you need us to bring anything?" This was followed almost immediately by, "Right, then," and he closed the door.

"Who was that?" I asked.

"Some bloke. Said he was your neighbor. Seems like a nice chap."

"What did he want?"

"Oh. Right. He invited us all to a small party at his place tomorrow, said it was in celebration of some holiday."

I could barely contain my surprise. "And you said yes?"

"Well, yeah. I mean, we have to get out sometime, don't we?"

• • •

Later on, after Jack and I had taken a trip upstairs to the master bedroom, and after we'd finally finished with the dishes, we were sitting on the porch, snuggled up close. We'd eaten so early that darkness was still a good ways off as we watched the boys play with their friends. As we sat there, a figure came around the side of the house. It was Denny.

We watched as he strode off in the sand in his blinding-white T-shirt and sailor pants. He didn't have on sunglasses or a hat as he made his slow way perpendicular to the water, the wind whipping his clothes. The beach was still crowded at that time of early evening, and people did stop whatever they were doing and stared as he passed, but no one approached him.

"What's he doing?" Jack asked as Denny slowed his pace and then slowed it yet more.

After two weeks cooped up, and having accepted Biff's invitation, apparently Denny was ready to be out and about.

"I think he's hoping to be noticed," I said, puzzled. "You'd think he'd want to get away from all that."

Or at least I would, based on what Denny had said.

"Not really," Jack said. "I think it must be like a drug for him at this point. Once you've had that, how can you ever want anything else?"

I turned to look at my husband. "Do you ever wish that life was yours?"

Jack seemed stunned by the question. "Why would I?" He gazed back at me. "I have you, don't I?"

WHENEVER WE'D GONE OVER TO BIFF AND MARSHA'S IN THE past, I'd dressed casually. But since Biff had told Denny this was supposed to be some sort of celebration, I took a little more care with my appearance that day. I even bothered to put on some makeup. When I finally came downstairs, Denny didn't tell me I looked fetching like he usually did. Jack was there, standing beside him, and when Jack whistled, Denny did raise his eyebrows in appreciation.

Normally when Jack and I went anywhere with the boys, the boys walked between us. But this time Denny did, a boy each on the other side of Jack and me. It felt oddly as though, with this his first social venture out and in the absence of his own bodyguards, he needed some sort of protection.

The day was the hottest we'd seen, and, despite having expected the party to be out of doors, as we approached the house, the only people outside were a man in chef's clothing manning a pig on a spit and other similarly garbed workers at grilling stations.

The railings surrounding the deck were festooned with red, white, and blue bunting, and the sounds coming from the house were loud. Biff had told Denny it would just be a small party.

I would have just walked right in, but Denny raised a fist to knock. Before he could make contact with the wood, however, the door was flung open and Biff was standing there. I got the strange sensation he might have been standing at a window, watching for our approach.

"Ah! You made it!" he said.

Biff kissed me on the cheek, and he and Jack did that hearty combined handshake with simultaneous clap on each other's shoulders that men so seem to enjoy.

Turning to the boys, Biff said, "The kids' party is down in the basement. You know the way."

Perhaps saving the best for last, Biff held out his hand to Denny. "You must be Denny. I don't believe I told you my name yesterday. I'm Biff."

As I said, Biff had told Denny it was to be a small party, and on our previous visits here, it had always been that way. It was either just the two couples and our kids, or maybe another couple too. At most, there might be a dozen people. But now, seeing the legions of adults behind Biff, it struck me that the only way this gathering could be deemed small would be if small were somehow a synonym for Gatsbyesque. Perhaps, after Denny had accepted the invitation, Biff just happened to call up a few more people to invite over? I bet Denny got that a lot.

"Thank you for having me," Denny said formally, shaking Biff's hand.

"Get you a drink?" Biff offered.

"That would be most refreshing, thanks," Denny said.

Biff was only gone for a moment, returning with an opened bottle of beer, which he handed to Denny.

Denny took a sip, gave an appreciative smile at the label. "Ah. The King of Beers, isn't it?"

Biff stared at Denny and then he burst out laughing.

"Wait 'til I tell Marsha—the King of Beers! Marsha's my wife. She's always ragging on me about—well, you'll see when you meet her."

And then we just stood there.

I don't know what I expected. For Biff to be so impressed with Denny that he'd glue himself to his side, showing Denny off to all his friends? Whatever the case, that's not what happened. Instead, Biff turned to Jack.

"Hey, Jack. Show you something out back?"

"Of course."

Biff and Jack peeled off, Biff turning around just long enough to call back to Denny, "Please, make yourself at home."

"Oh, I shall." Denny raised his Budweiser in salute.

And so it fell to me to tend to Denny.

Where were Matt and Walter when you needed them?

• • •

No matter how hard people tried to behave as though they weren't looking, it was impossible not to be aware of all the pairs of eyes, watching us. Denny seemed not to pay it any mind at all. I don't know how he did that, frankly. It was driving me crazy. I kept wondering if my panty lines were showing unattractively, kept trying to remember if I'd brushed my teeth. I read once that Queen Elizabeth never eats anything at those massive garden parties she throws for fear people will see her with spinach caught in her front teeth, and I could see where that would be so. I'd never been the focus of so much attention in my life, and, even though I knew it wasn't really meant for me, just being by Denny's side made me get hit with it.

"Ghastly stuff," Denny whispered out of the corner of his mouth, setting the beer bottle down on a side table. Then, a little louder: "Introduce me around, won't you?"

I felt his hand at the small of my back, steering me into the room. It was such a small and common gesture and yet such an intimate one too. It had been a long time since anyone other than Jack had touched the small of my back just so.

If I'd been asked in advance about what I thought Denny would be like in a large social gathering, I'd have said two things. I'd have said I expected him to be mobbed—after all, I'd seen the pictures of him in mags, seen the most famous one in which two fans had each grabbed an end of his long scarf, hoping for a souvenir, conveniently forgetting about his neck being in between and practically strangling him to death in the process; I knew that everywhere he went people wanted to touch him, talk to him, offer to have wild sex with him; I knew that, no matter how hard a time I'd given him about his entourage, he really did need those two bodyguards most of the time. And the other thing I'd have said? It would be that his conversational style would be completely self-absorbed, as it had been back at Easter when he couldn't stop nattering on and on about his accomplishments in Malaysia.

So what was the difference between expectation and reality?

As I said, this being Westport, people hung back. Even the women, most of whom looked like they were practically wetting themselves.

When I introduced him to Marsha first—she was, after all, our hostess—she coolly extended an elegant hand. "Jack's brother, right? How lovely to meet you. Here, let me get you both drinks. Mona, I know you're always white wine. And you." She turned to Denny. "I believe I saw you with a Budweiser?"

I half expected Denny to ask for something else, but he just smiled and said, "That would be grand."

When Marsha returned with our drinks, Denny took a sip of his beer and smiled. "Delightful, that," he said.

Marsha gave him a brisk nod, and then she focused her attention strictly on me, talking about the boys or anything else that came into her head. I noticed her smile looked incredibly strained, desperate almost, and realized she was torn: what she really wanted to be doing was staring at Denny—he was so close to her! she could touch him again! make sure he was really there!—but she didn't want to come off as being like any common fan. Such a dilemma.

At last, her talking led her to her favorite topic to gripe about: au pairs.

I let her go on for a bit, but then, worrying Denny must be getting bored, I thought to interject with something, only Denny beat me to it, speaking for the first time since he'd graciously thanked her for the Budweiser.

"Oh, it's just a terrible problem," he commiserated. "I can remember, when my three were younger, it was so hard finding anyone reliable who would stay for very long and certainly not twenty-four seven, which is what you really want in an au pair. For some reason, they all actually want to have their own lives too."

"Yes!" Marsha said, finally looking at him with a smile of relief. "*Thank* you!"

"But you know what I've learned over the years? If you don't mind my saying?"

"Please, do."

"It's that you really do get from anything what you put into it."

"I'm not sure I follow."

"Pay your workers a spectacular wage. Not a minimum one. Not even a good one. A *spectacular* one. Always be clear about exactly what you require of them, but treat them with politeness and respect. Beyond that, find out what the single most important motivation for them is. Perhaps it's education for a child back home in their native country? Maybe they worry that when they're too old or sick to work, they'll wind up living on the streets. Set up accounts, make those things happen."

When Denny had first started talking, Marsha's eyes had narrowed as though she thought he might be having her on. But as he continued, her expression changed, and in the end, she merely looked stunned.

"You know," she said, "I never thought of it like that."

"Not many do."

"But you're right. We do have the resources…"

"Obviously." Denny looked appreciatively at the well-appointed room.

"You know, I'm going to try what you suggested."

"Excellent. Let others exploit the masses." He pointed the neck of his beer bottle at her. "*You* be different."

In the brief time I'd known her, Marsha had never simpered before, but she was doing it now.

"Yes…well…thanks…don't let me monopolize you… would you care for another drink?"

He winked—I saw Marsha practically puddle at this simple gesture—and pointed his bottle at her again. "This one's still fresh, thanks."

I proceeded to introduce Denny, one by one, to everyone else I knew there. But after Marsha, instead of waiting for a conversational gambit, as he had with her, he took the offensive. He asked people what they did or about their children. He managed to find out what interested people most and then proceeded to talk about that very thing, knowledgeably. Investing, books, film, social and political issues, food, fashion—on all those topics and more, he offered advice and insight. The only things he didn't talk about were music or himself. And all that time, I just stayed by his side, watching him, listening.

Denny was so surprisingly good at talking to people.

He was more than just a nuisance now. He was actually interesting.

I never felt like an adult until I had kids. Jack and I had talked about this phenomenon and how, even after, we felt sometimes as though we were playing some version of emotional dress-up, kids wearing adult clothing. Denny had the capacity to come across like this too, but unlike us, there were times like now when he seemed not just adult, but *super* adult. And it wasn't simply a matter of sophistication: knowing how to order from a French menu, in *French*, or which fabrics were best for a particular article of clothing. It was as though he were constantly making decisions, living a life on a plane wholly different than the rest of us, no matter how old we might be in calendar years.

Which brought us to the oldest guest there: Biff's grandfather, Frank. I'd met Frank on just one other occasion and found him to be a rather clear talker for his years, which Biff put at close to a hundred. Frank was seated in a Queen Anne chair, his cane between his knees. After I had introduced them, rather than remain standing, Denny settled down on the floor across from Frank so that now the older gentleman had the height advantage.

"I know that name," Frank said, puzzling over it. "Denny Springer...Say! You're that singing guy, aren't you?"

It was the first time anyone there had acknowledged outright that Denny might be something more than just another guest.

"That's right," Denny said. "I'm that singing guy."

Frank leaned forward, lowering his voice.

"Is there any money in that?" he asked.

"There can be."

"I wasn't looking for generalities," Frank said testily. "I was asking about you."

"Well, I don't have as much as Paul. Do you know who Paul McCartney is?"

"Of course I know who Paul McCartney is! Do I look stupid? Uninformed, perhaps?"

"No, of course not. You look neither. As I was saying, I don't have as much as Paul McCartney. But then, no one does, right? I mean, some people think Paul's an idiot, but behind that moon face is a steel trap of a business mind. Outside of him though? I do OK. I suppose I have more money than anyone else."

*In the room?* I wondered. *In the world?*

"I hope you're investing it wisely," Frank said. "Real estate's the way to go."

"Oh, I am."

"That's good." Frank nodded briskly. Then: "Where are your holdings?"

"Oh, gosh." Denny sighed, totting it all up. "Let's see… Houses in London, France, St. Croix, and Los Angeles, then there's the apartment I keep in New York…"

"How big?"

"The whole floor of course. Well, you don't want neighbors too close if you can help it, do you?"

"No, you most certainly don't!" Frank laughed, showing teeth just this side of wooden. "That's good you've got all those holdings, wise to invest. After all, you can't be doing what you're doing now forever, right?"

"How's that?"

"All that rock-and-roll stuff, all that jumping around— you can't do that into your sixties or, worse, when you're my age, can you?"

I thought Frank had that part wrong. Why couldn't Denny go on being Denny forever? The idea that he might one day stop—it saddened me. Sure, if he went on past his prime, he ran the risk of becoming a laughingstock, but he'd already stayed current far longer than most bands, with each generation finding he had something to offer them. So why not go on with it forever? If he did it right…

I expected Denny to make the same arguments out loud that I was making in my own head, but instead:

"No," he said, sounding wistful. "I suppose that's exactly true." He was quiet for a moment, and then he shook his head as though brushing thoughts away, smiled up at Frank. "What can I get you to drink, Frank? Are you having Budweiser?"

There was such a gulf between this Denny—kind, solicitous, interested in other people—and the self-absorbed, Malaysia-nattering prat he'd been at his parents' house. But then I thought: perhaps Denny was only self-absorbed around family? After all, don't we all, in a way, reserve our worst selves for the people who love us most?

• • •

I felt an arm around my shoulders and looked to my right to see Jack standing between me and Denny, his arms around both our shoulders.

"How're my favorite wife and brother doing?" Jack asked jovially.

By definition, we had to be his least favorite too, but I saw little purpose in pointing that out.

Jack's eyes were bleary, and there was the smell of smoke about him.

"Jack," I said, "are you stoned?"

"Stoned?" He giggled. Then: "Well, maybe just a bit."

He leaned down as though to share with us a great secret.

"It's full dark out now," he said.

It was? I looked at the windows, saw he was right. Where had all the time gone?

"Let's go outside," Jack said. "The kids are coming too. Biff says we can do the fireworks now."

Fireworks? I looked across Jack at Denny and saw he was puzzled too. What fireworks?

• • •

We practically fell into the house, still laughing.

Well, Denny and I were doing most of the laughing. Jack only giggled a bit, while the boys mostly just looked confused.

"We won! We won!" I cried, doing my best American accent. And switching back to my own, a trifle sourly: "OK, we get it already. You won."

"But do you really need to set off fireworks too?" Denny added.

"Imagine," I said, "inviting a group of British people over to help celebrate the Fourth of July!"

"I should have realized what day it was," Denny said.

"Me too. But here, I find, I lose all track of time."

The boys were still confused, tired too, so I brought them up to bed. When I came back down, Denny and Jack were seated in the living area. Jack had an unlit joint that he was rolling back and forth between his fingers.

"Biff gave me this," he said, pleased. "A spliff from Biff. Do you fancy some?"

"You're not going to light that in here, are you?" I said.

Saying that, I remembered Edith at Easter telling Denny he couldn't smoke in her house. It occurred to me then that

I hadn't seen him smoke a single cigarette since his arrival here. Come to that, I hadn't been tempted either.

"Course not," Jack said. "We'll take it out on the porch."

Once we were outside, Jack pulled out a lighter, held the tip of the joint to it until it glowed, and took a deep drag. He closed his eyes as he released the smoke. After taking a second drag, he opened his eyes and extended the joint toward Denny and me.

"You go ahead if you want some," Denny said, gently pushing Jack's hand in my direction.

"You're not going to have any?" I asked.

"I never indulge," he said.

"Of course you do!"

"I can assure you, I would know if I did, and I don't."

"If no one else is going to..." Jack took another long toke.

"But how is that possible?" I insisted. "All those drug busts..."

"How do you know so much about me, Mona? Are you perhaps secretly"—and here he practically touched his head to my shoulder before looking up at me and saying in a mock dangerous voice—"*a fan*?"

"Of course not!" I pushed him off me. "Don't be absurd!"

I couldn't tell him that I'd gleaned most of my information on him from what I'd read in mags. Plus, if the mags had been wrong about the rampant drug use, what else might they have been wrong about?

"So you really never...?" I said.

"Oh, of course I've tried pot. But I didn't inhale."

Now I knew he had to be joking.

"Who are you supposed to be? Bill Clinton?"

"I can totally relate to Bill. We've discussed it. That

stuff's death to creativity and productivity, but you do have to try and fit in, at least initially."

The air around us was smoky, and Jack was leaning back in his chair, a silly smile on his face.

"*You've* met Bill Clinton?" I asked.

"Well, yeah. I suppose I've met just about everybody by now, haven't I?"

I realized it must be true. And not only had Denny met everyone, but at each meeting, *he* was the one of the two parties that the other party was impressed to meet. Imagine meeting presidents and princesses, artists and actors, and having each, down to the last man and woman, exude an air of: "I can't believe I'm meeting *you*!"

Fair play to him, sometimes even *I* had to admit: he had a good excuse for being such a prat.

"What's he like?" I asked. "Clinton, I mean."

"About what you'd expect. A bit paranoid at times—not that you can really blame him—but mostly he's just a lot of fun, extremely focused, exceedingly smart. I've never had a better game of Scrabble."

"Huh."

"And he plays a mean sax. I'm not sure he's quite as good as he thinks he is, but how many people ever are?"

"Huh." Then: "So all those drug busts? They were—"

"There you go again, Mona, revealing an unusual amount of knowledge about me."

I ignored this, instead pressing with: "Those were what then?"

"It was all for the image, especially when we were first starting out. You can't very well lead any kind of revolution, musical or otherwise, if people's mums are all like, 'Ooh, they're all so nice and sweet! I wish my daughter would date one!' can you?"

He had a point.

I couldn't seem to let it go. "So then Lex—he's a put-up job too?"

"God no." Denny snorted. "Lex is the genuine article. For over a quarter of a century I've tried to figure out how he gets so much done in his perpetual condition, and I still haven't figured it out."

Somehow, that was reassuring. At least one thing was as I'd thought it was.

"So you're, what, the straightest man in rock and roll?"

"Well, I wouldn't go that far. I do like red wine."

"Me too!"

I heard myself and was momentarily shocked. For a second there, I'd sounded just like I had on the first night I met Jack, when we were both all "You like the color blue best? Me too!" and "You like to breathe? Me too!"

I shot a glance at Jack to see what his reaction was to this, but he looked as though he might have dozed off, that smile still on his lips.

"Really?" Denny said. "But you were drinking white all night."

"That's because that's all the women around here ever drink. Well, except for when Budweiser Biff foists beers on us. But other than that? It's only ever white. I think they all think it's more slimming. Sometimes I'm tempted to say, 'It's not slimming when you drink the whole bottle!'"

Denny laughed appreciatively at this, making me feel more satisfyingly witty than my words had warranted.

"I prefer my red French and expensive," Denny said.

"I just prefer my red red," I said.

Denny laughed that appreciative laugh again. Then: "Where did I leave my phone?"

"It must be inside somewhere." I waved vaguely at the house.

He disappeared inside for a few moments.

"I should have realized," he said when he returned, looking mildly frustrated. "Between it being late, and what with this crazy American holiday thing going on…"

"Who were you trying to reach?"

"It doesn't matter right now. I made a note to myself for the morning, added it to the list."

"You make lists to stay on top of things?"

"All the time," he said. "Matt and Walter are great at keeping track of things for me, and I have a secretary who usually travels with me too, but they have other things to worry about, and I'm never convinced a thing will get done until I put it on the list."

"Me too!"

Gack, did I just say that again?

But Denny just laughed. "It's been a good day, night too. Thanks for this."

I was about to say I hadn't done anything, but just then, Jack let out a loud snore.

Jack had one ankle resting on the top of the other knee. Denny reached out and grabbed on to the raised foot, jiggling it gently until Jack's eyelids stuttered open.

"What?" Jack said dumbly.

"Do you want to go downstairs?" Denny said. "Maybe show me some of the songs you've been working on?"

Jack was instantly sober. "You're kidding, right?" he said

in a voice I took for eager. Then, more cautious, perhaps in more ways than one: "But you must be tired."

"Actually, I'm wide awake. And now, so are you. So what do you say?"

Now Jack looked nervous, rubbing the palms of his hands against his legs. "Well, if you really want—"

"I'll go get my guitar."

• • •

Jack and I were standing at the base of the stairs when Denny came back down with his guitar. Then, as the men headed toward the door to the basement, I just stayed there.

"Aren't you coming?" Denny said, turning back.

"I don't know. I don't think…"

Jack never let me hear what he was working on. With rare exception, I only ever got to hear his music when he played an infrequent club gig or once it was finally on an album.

I looked at Jack now but he just shrugged, noncommittal.

"Come on then." Denny smiled, holding the door open for me. "It's got to beat sitting on the stairs, right?"

Thankfully, Jack was currently too absorbed in his own thoughts to register what Denny had just said.

Once in the basement, as the men tuned their guitars, I found a seat in the corner, hoping to be as inconspicuous as possible.

Jack looked so nervous, and I was so nervous for him—I didn't want to add to that by being too obtrusive. As for Denny, he looked completely serene, as though he and Jack did this every day.

"What have you got?" Denny said.

"Three songs for the new album so far," Jack said, a stiff tone coming into his voice as though daring Denny to say that Jack's productivity thus far this summer had been paltry.

"Great," Denny said. "So what's the first one?"

"It's…" Jack started to play something, stopping after a few notes. "Sorry. It's…"

He started to sing, his voice stuttering the words out, the nerves back. But then he closed his eyes, keeping them shut as he played the song through, I can only guess in an attempt to convince himself that his brother wasn't sitting right there, close enough to touch, his knees just inches away.

The song Jack played was neither as polished nor as sophisticated as the one I'd heard Denny play, but it was still good.

When Jack finished, his voice having grown less wavery as he sang, he opened his eyes and looked at Denny defiantly, as though to say: "Well?"

"That was *good!*" Denny said.

I felt relief wash through my body as I released a breath I hadn't realized I'd been holding. Jack looked incredibly relieved too. And when I looked over at Denny, I realized that that made three of us because Denny's response hadn't been mere enthusiasm, there was also a huge measure of relief in there. I hoped Jack hadn't seen or heard that part.

But he was too busy being pleased to notice anything else.

"What about the second song?" Denny said.

"OK, then." Jack sounded more confident now, and

as he sang the next song, it showed in his voice. After he finished the first chorus and verse, Denny came in with his guitar on the second, playing rhythm to Jack's lead.

"That one was good too," Denny said, more casually this time.

"You really think so?" Jack said. "I mean, wow! *Thank* you!"

This struck me as being a little exclamatory—maybe *too* exclamatory—for Jack's normally low-key personality. But then I thought: maybe he was still high?

"And the third?" Denny prompted.

"Oh, yeah. Right."

This time, as Jack played, it was Denny who closed his eyes partway through, his expression one of someone listening closely.

"Well, what do you think?" Jack asked expectantly when he finished. "It's the most recent, but I think it might be the best."

I know what I thought: that it was a beautiful song. Really, all the songs Jack had played had been good. But this one was a love song, and, vain as it might sound, I always assumed all Jack's love songs were for me. After all, when he asked me to marry him, he did say he'd never been in love with anyone else before.

"Yes," Denny said after a long silence. "I can see why you like this one so much. The others are good, but this…?" Pause. "And yet…"

"And yet what?" Jack said when Denny failed to finish his sentence.

"It's only…"

"Only what?"

*Please*, I prayed silently, even though I've never been the praying sort. *Please don't break my husband's heart.*

"OK," Denny said, as though something had been dragged out of him. Then: "The lyrics are mostly good, but there are a few lines that could do with a tweak. Do you have the sheet handy?"

Silently, Jack handed one over.

"Right." Denny grabbed a pencil, pointed to two different parts on the page. "Here and here. It's good to give people what they want, but it's even better to give them what they don't know they want. And with lyrics, you don't want it to be so predictable that before the line is even over, the listener knows what the next line will be even if they've never heard the song before." He pointed with the pencil again. "Those are the two I'd fix."

He held the pencil out to Jack, who took it without looking at Denny.

Jack tapped the pencil against his lip a few times, then erased some things, scribbled over it, pushed the page back toward Denny. This time, Jack looked at Denny as he asked: "You mean like this?"

Denny studied the page briefly, nodded.

"*Exactly* like that. Now, the bridge could be a bit more dee-dee-dee-dee-*dee* than the dee-dee-dee-dee-*dum* you've got currently." Denny hummed as he played it on his guitar, demonstrating, and Jack joined in, matching what he heard.

"Good," Denny said. "Now this one word here. If you change the phrasing…Like, just as an example of what you might do…"

Denny sang what he meant. It was the same "it," with

him doing the same thing to it I'd heard him do with his own song that one time I'd been alone, listening from the stairs.

"Do you hear the difference?" Denny said. "It's counter-intuitive to what the listener will expect. It's like that word is a piece of heavy furniture, and I'm dragging it across a bumpy wooden floor, and when I slam on the final stress, rising up the scale—i-i-i-IT—it's like I've found the perfect spot for it. Do you see what I'm getting at here?"

Jack sang the hell out of it.

"Right," Denny said. "And, last, that Bono thing you're doing at the end of the final chorus—you've got to stop that."

"What Bono thing? I don't have any Bono thing!"

"Oh, yeah, you really do. And it has to stop. Imitation's fine for cover bands, but that's not for you. You want to sound like you, only exaggerated, you don't want to sound like anyone else." He paused before finishing simply, "You've got a good voice, Jack."

Was I the only one who felt like dancing for joy when Denny said that?

I thought Jack must be feeling pretty damn pleased with himself too. But then I wondered if he might be feeling hurt at what he would perhaps have perceived as Denny's harsh criticism. I was no artist, and yet I suspected the reason Jack had never shared his works-in-progress with me as he went was that on some level, he feared criticism, or being compared to some other ideal. And yet, having heard what Denny had to say, I couldn't fault Denny for any of it. He'd been clear and businesslike in everything he said. There was not a shred of malice, not like sometimes when people tell you something with an air of, "I'm doing this for your own benefit," when anyone can see the real subtext is, "I'm doing this for my own know-it-all benefit, so I can feel better about myself by making you feel like shit."

"Why don't you play the song through again with the changes," Denny suggested. "See what you think."

So Jack did that.

And it was better.

It had been good but now it was better.

Jack didn't necessarily look happy about this.

"What's wrong?" Denny asked with an uncharacteristic show of sensitivity.

"It's just that, it is *better* now, but that was all you, so it's not really *mine* anymore, is it?"

"You're kidding me, right?" Denny didn't wait for an answer. "You think songs just come out of me perfect, like Apollo from Zeus's head? OK, maybe sometimes they do. But mostly? I take something as far as I can, and then I toss it to Lex. Or sometimes I think something's fine the way it is, and then—hello!—one of the other guys starts playing around, and what I started turns into something else entirely, and that's OK too because it's all about making the music as good as it can be, and if that something is better, then of course I'm going to want to run with it." Pause. "This is still your song, Jack."

"And you actually think it's any good?"

"Are you kidding? That song's your single. It's your *A*-side. Why do you think I even bothered trying to make it better?"

"Huh."

Denny considered, looking torn. It was as though he was debating something in his head. Then:

"Tell you what: That 'it'? It's yours. I was going to use it for a song, but you keep it."

"I didn't know. Are you sure?"

"Course. Maybe I'll drag my 'it' upstairs or maybe just slam it against the wall. Don't worry. I'll come up with something."

I GROANED, BLINKING AT THE HARSH LIGHT, HAVING BEEN wakened by the sound of loud knocking coming from downstairs. At least, unlike the last time I'd been wakened by knocking, this time it was full day, so there was no need to be paranoid or grab a frying pan on my way to answer it. And answer it, I must, seeing as Jack was passed out beside me. Last night, I'd finally left the men around three a.m. They were still playing, and, no matter how good it sounded, I'd started to feel like a third wheel, and an exhausted third wheel at that.

"I'm coming!" I called, halfway down the stairs, as the knocking persisted.

On the counter, in the kitchen, there was a note. William's handwriting.

*You were all asleep, so I made Harry and me breakfast. See you around midday!*

I smiled. Sometimes my biggest little boy seemed so mature.

More knocking.

Oh. Right.

"Delivery for Mona Springer," the man said. He was holding a massive carton.

"I didn't order anything."

The man set the carton down inside the doorway. "No, but Denny Springer did." He handed me a bill. "Funny, I didn't know he had a new wife."

"I'm not his—" I started to object.

But the man was already walking away.

I shut the door, stared down at the box. What was this?

"Oh, good!" Denny's voice. "It's here." He pulled at some tape on the box, but it wouldn't come away. "Do you have a knife?"

I handed him a steak knife, and he squatted down, slitting the tape on the sides before pulling away the big strip in the center. Then he opened up the flaps and extracted a bottle of wine.

"Ah!" he said. "Chateau Latour Pauillac, 1990!"

"What's that?"

"Didn't I just say?" He looked at me like I might be dim. "It's a 1990 Chateau Latour Pauillac."

"Yes, I did get that part." Not that I knew what a Chateau Latour Whatever was, no matter what its year. "But what's it doing here?"

"I called around the liquor stores first thing when I got up this morning. I did say last night that I was making a note, didn't I?"

"Yes, but—"

"And you specified you preferred your wine red, French, and expensive."

Actually, he was the one who'd specified the latter two points. I'd said I was content with just the first.

"It wouldn't do for you to keep drinking that plonk your neighbor was pouring yesterday." He looked around the counters. "Do you have a corkscrew handy?"

"You want to drink it now?"

"I think we should try it, yes, make sure it's good."

"But it's not even noon!"

"So? We're not going to drink the whole *case*, Mona. And I'm not driving. Are you driving?"

It seemed easier to comply than argue, so I rooted around in a drawer until I found a corkscrew, handed that to him, and pulled down two dusty wineglasses from the cabinet.

With a few practiced gestures, he expertly extracted the cork, poured two glasses, and handed me the first before taking one for himself.

"Cheers!" He clinked his glass to mine, moved the glass toward his lips.

"Wait! Aren't we supposed to let it breathe for a while, or sniff it first and talk about the bouquet or something?"

"Nah." He shrugged. "I don't want to be pretentious. Well, actually, I just want to try it right away. We can always let the others breathe."

We clinked again, sipped simultaneously. I was thinking how good it tasted when he turned to the sink and spit the contents from his mouth all over the porcelain.

"I thought you said we weren't going to be pretentious about it," I objected. "Now we're doing the spitting thing?"

"I wasn't," he said, wiping at his lips with the back of one hand. Then he dumped the contents of his glass in the sink, followed by mine, and finally he started pouring out the whole bottle.

"Hey!" I said. "Are you insane? That must've cost a small fortune!"

"Small fortune. Large fortune. What's the difference?"

I picked up the bill from the counter, looked at it. "About seven hundred and seventy-four dollars a bottle!"

He stopped his pouring long enough to glance at the bill. "No. See? We got the case discount—ten percent off."

"That's not the point!"

"Then what is? All I know is, I didn't order this so you could drink an inferior version of a great wine. That bottle had gone off—not all the way, maybe, so as an unsophisticated palate would notice, but still. When it comes to my Latours, I want them perfect. Here, where's that corkscrew again?"

He repeated the process: extract, pour, divide the glasses, clink. My own clink was now nervous. This time, I only hoped I'd get to taste more than one sip before he dumped the rest of my glass.

I'd heard people say before that there's not much difference between an expensive bottle of wine and a cheap one, outside of cost, and I'd always smugly agreed. After all, I did know my cheap wines. But this?

I rolled the wine around in my mouth.

There was caramel. There was chocolate. There was licorice. There were even roasted fruits. And the individual parts were integrated into the whole of dark cherry.

And then...

Oh my God!

On the one side, there was every other beverage I'd ever

consumed in my life—the wines that tasted serviceable on first sip but by the third glass were a struggle to swallow, even causing a person to gag; the pleasant wines that paired well with whatever food was being eaten; the wines I'd *thought* were fine—and then there was this.

"Good, right?" Denny said with a smile and a firm nod.

I put my hand to my mouth. "I think my mouth just had an orgasm!"

He raised his eyebrows and saluted me by tilting his wineglass in my general direction. "Now, *there's* your wine."

• • •

It would be inaccurate to say we were drunk by the time the boys returned for lunch, but buzzed wouldn't be far off the mark. Jack had come downstairs when Denny and I were halfway through the bottle. We'd poured him a glass, he loved it, and we'd gone on to open a second. We even took the time to let that one breathe. Somehow, it never seemed wrong to have a beer early in the day. I mean, obviously, we never did that back home when we were working. But here? It went perfectly with the warm weather and felt more refreshing than alcoholic. But having red wine so early in the day, particularly red wine that cost over seven hundred dollars a bottle, never mind the ten percent case discount? It felt downright decadent.

"Are you OK, Mummy?" William asked now as we all sat down to lunch on the porch.

Denny had had a craving for something with lobster in it, so he'd called Matt and Walter, and they'd gone out with Jeeves in search of the perfect thing, coming back with pounds of a lobster salad, which I was serving up now.

"Why?" I said. "Do I look sick?"

"Only, you look like you sometimes do at night, just a bit funny."

Well, that was sobering.

When Denny moved to refill our glasses, I covered mine with both hands. "None for me just now, thanks."

I turned to the boys, who looked excited. Well, they almost always looked excited about one thing or another—sometimes I found myself envious of this, the youthful ability to find magic in the things in the world that were for me commonplace—but they looked particularly jazzed just then.

"So what's got you two going today?" I asked, stabbing a fat chunk of lobster and popping it into my mouth. I closed my eyes. Sublime.

"Only," William said, "Biff heard me telling Billy and Tommy that my birthday's coming up—"

"When's that going to be?" Denny asked.

*A normal uncle would know something like that*, I thought.

"In two weeks," William said, barely looking at Denny. They still hadn't warmed up to Denny and never called him "Uncle," only responding if he said something to them first. I got the impression they thought of him not as a real relative, but rather, as this strange person they bumped into from time to time. I don't think they disliked him or anything like that; I think they simply found his presence odd, didn't really know what to do with him, and just felt shy.

"He's going to be ten," I supplied, sure this was a fact

Denny was completely unaware of. "Harry turned eight before we left England."

"Eight! That's fantastic!" Denny said to Harry. And then to William, "Ten! Wow, that's a big deal!"

"Yes, I guess so," William said, that shyness on evidence. But when he turned to Jack and me, all that bubbling excitement was there again, so much so he was practically bouncing out of his chair. "Anyway, as I was saying, Biff heard me talking about my birthday and—get this!—*he* offered for me to have my party at *his place!*"

Perhaps it was the fault of wine early in the day, but I wasn't quite getting this.

"How do you mean?" I said.

"Just what I said," William said in that way children sometimes have, the way that makes you feel you must be thick. "My party. His house."

"But I thought we'd have it here, like we always do. Well, not here here—we've never had it here before—but like we do back home. You know, a family celebration."

Poor William. He looked stricken—he hated ever making anyone else feel bad—and I felt awful for having put that look on his face.

"Well, of course we'll still do that, Mum," he said, "I always love doing that, I'll want to have that party every year for for-*ever*, it wouldn't be my birthday without it." He was so good, it was heartbreaking. But even William couldn't keep from adding, "Only, I was just thinking..."

"That the house next door is much bigger?" I added helpfully.

"Well, *yeah*." He sounded relieved that I was finally catching on. "Don't get me wrong, this place is great—

great, I tell you! In fact, it's my favorite house in the world, outside of our house back home of course. But Biff's place being so big, I can invite *every* kid we've met, boys and girls—Biff said I could—and it will be the most amazing...!" He stopped himself. "Unless of course you'd rather I didn't because—"

"Wait," I said. "Biff said you could invite *every* kid?"

William nodded eagerly.

"That's too much," I said, and it was. I was well aware of the fact that relative to our summer neighbors, Jack and I were along the order of poor relations. I didn't like feeling that way, nor did I want to take advantage. "Think of the expense."

"That's exactly what you shouldn't be thinking about," Denny interjected.

"Pardon?"

"When a person has a lot of...*material wealth*, and that person wants to do something special for someone they're fond of, they don't want the person they're fond of to become obsessed with the expense. They just want to do it. If the situation were reversed, wouldn't you do the same?"

Well, when he put it like that...

"What do you think, Jack?" I asked.

"No objections from me." Jack waved his lobster fork. "The boy gets a party that will be—what're the words you used, William?—*the most amazing*. And someone else does most of the work and deals with other neighbors' complaints when the party gets too loud? Sign me up. Where can I get one of these parties for myself?"

"Mum?" William looked at me hopefully.

"*Well...*" I dragged out the word, narrowing my eyes at him. "Who gets to make the birthday cake?"

"You do! *Of course.* You do!" He held out his open palms, practically vibrating them. "How could I ever want anything else?"

"Well, OK then." I broke into a wide grin. "Actually, this all does sound pretty fab."

"I *know!*" William cried. "Only, you know, don't feel like you have to make a cake big enough for everyone because—"

"Stop!" Harry punched his brother in the arm playfully. "You're going to blow it!" Then he collapsed into giggles. "I was sure you were going to blow it. Every step of the way, I was sure."

William reddened but then he started giggling too. "I know! I'm the worst at asking for anything!"

"This is going to be so great," Harry said. "You know, William's the only one with a summer birthday, so this is just going to be huge. Huge!"

"I can see that," Jack said. "So, what were you thinking of for presents for this huge birthday?"

"Presents?" William practically screamed, turning to Harry. Then both boys screamed something unintelligible simultaneously as they did some kind of combination high-five/hand-clasp thing.

"I was so wrapped up in everything else," William said, "I forgot all about *presents.*"

"William, my lad," Jack said, "take no offense, and please don't send me the therapy bill years later for saying this, but you are a strange boy. So, what'll it be?"

"I think William would like a bicycle," Harry said.

"That's not really practical, is it?" Jack said. "He'd only get to ride it here. He'd have to leave it behind when we go back home at the end of the summer."

"True," Harry said. "But the older boys all have bikes to ride around on. I really think William would like one of those."

"It doesn't have to be a bike," William said quickly. "There are plenty of other things I wouldn't mind having. That is, if it's OK."

He proceeded to name them. It was a surprisingly long list, including small sporting equipment and various games—in particular a replacement for the Monopoly board game they liked playing with Matt and Walter in the evenings. All of the play money in that was hopelessly wrinkled, and the dog game piece was missing its head.

"I'm sure we'll come up with something good from that list," Jack said, stopping William when it began appearing he might go on with his list making all day.

"What about from me?" Denny asked William.

"From you?" William appeared puzzled by the question.

"Yeah. What can I get you for your birthday?"

"He did just provide a whole *list*," Harry pointed out.

"True," Denny said. "But that was for your parents, wasn't it? I'd like to give William something too. Is there anything else you want?"

"Well, I really think he could use a bike," Harry said.

William studied his empty plate for a long time. That's one of the weird things about having boys. They talk so much, getting excited about everything, a person would think they never have time to eat too. And yet, when you look at their plates, they're always miraculously empty.

At last, William took a deep breath. And then he shifted his gaze up, looking Denny directly in the eye.

"Could you sing 'Happy Birthday'?" William asked.

"Of course." Denny laughed. "That's what you do at a birthday party, right? Everyone sings 'Happy Birthday'?"

"Only, I meant just you, no one else."

"That's in two weeks," I said. "Your uncle might not even still be here then."

Would he be?

"OK. But if he *were* still here—" William turned from me and faced Denny squarely again. "If *you* were still here, could you do that? Only, there's this girl, Roberta—"

"William *likes* her!" Harry sang.

"Shut up or I won't let you play with my new Monopoly board!" And back to Denny: "The thing is, I do like her, but she doesn't notice me much. She likes one of the other boys, an older boy. I think she thinks I'm too young for her. But if you did that, if you sang 'Happy Birthday' to me solo, if you could make it somehow special like..." William trailed off. "I don't know what I mean."

"She'd see you in a new light?" Denny supplied.

"Yeah. Yeah, that's it! That's what I mean!"

"That's not going to happen, William," Jack said. "You can't just use your uncle like that, to gain social currency."

"Talk English, Dad," Harry said. "We don't know what social currency is when it's at home."

"But you both understand using people, right? And that it's wrong."

"What's the big deal, Jack?" Denny said easily. "I don't mind being used. Wouldn't be the first time." Denny turned to William. "When did you say this party was again?"

"In two weeks," William said, "on a Saturday." And then, as if any of us needed reminding at this point, he added, "It's my birthday."

"Yeah," Denny said, settling back in his seat. "I think I could maybe do something like that."

I WAS GRUMBLING TO MYSELF, PRACTICALLY SMASHING THE dishes as I loaded them into the washing machine.

What was wrong with that man? Who did he think he was?

After Denny told William that he could "maybe do something like that," meaning sing "Happy Birthday" at his party, William had erupted out of his seat in excitement.

"Are you serious? Is this for real? But wait. What if you're not still here?"

"Well, it would be hard for me to do it if I'm not here. But I will. Still be here, that is," Denny said, adding the magic word, "promise."

"Wow!"

Then Denny held both palms up, and, after only the briefest of hesitations, William slapped Denny's palms with his own, doing the same high-five/hand-clasp thing he and Harry had done earlier.

It was enough to make me sick.

"It's enough to make a person sick," I grumbled now, smashing around some more plates.

"Do you always talk to yourself when you're doing the dishes, Mona, or is this the Chateau Latour talking?"

Of course it was Denny.

I whirled on him.

"Don't you Chateau Latour me!"

"What's this all about?"

"You. You have a habit of promising people presents and then not delivering on your promises."

He looked surprised at the accusation. "What are you talking about? I always do what I say. At least, I always try to." His expression when he said this was completely innocent, which made it that much more galling. Did he just say whatever crap he wanted to, making it up as he went along, or did he actually believe the things that came out of his mouth?

"Jack's and my wedding," I said as though the implications should be obvious.

"Yours and Jack's wedding," he repeated. "OK." Then: "What about it?"

"You told Jack you would be his Best Man, but you never showed."

"That's going back a few years," Denny said.

It was. Twelve to be exact. Why was I bringing this up now?

"I believe I did send a telegram," Denny said in his own defense.

"You did," I allowed. "You said you couldn't shake the paparazzi. You said you didn't want to ruin Jack's big day."

Even after all these years, I could still remember that

184

telegram, remember what it was like seeing those words from Jack's brother for the first time, could practically quote it verbatim. OK, I could, and no practically about it.

"All that's true," Denny said. "Naturally, if I had it all to do over, I'd do it all differently today."

"You would?"

"Of course. I'd call, not telegram. There are mobile phones now."

Prat.

"You also said," and here I was directly quoting, "*present to follow.* The only problem is, no present ever followed."

"I'm sure I must have sent something."

"I'm equally sure you did not."

*Oh, why,* one half of my brain continued to wonder, *did I have to bring this up now?* Had I been nursing a grudge for so many years over something so trivial and somehow I hadn't been aware of this feeling in myself? I'd never been much of a material person. Did it really bother me so much, the lack of a present?

And what, I also started to wonder, was I really talking about here? Or maybe Denny was right and my behavior had something to do with the wine?

Denny frowned. "That doesn't sound like me at all. I'm usually very good at remembering things." He brightened as though remembering something. "I remembered the wine, didn't I?"

Earlier, when Denny saw how much I enjoyed it, he'd said, "Just let me know when the case is gone, and I'll order some more."

I'd thought he was mad. I wasn't going to kill that case

quickly! And order more just like that? At over nine thousand dollars a case?

"I'm not kidding, Mona," Denny had said.

I had taken another sip of my wine and thought: OK. A girl could get used to that.

"I never even asked for the bloody wine!" I half shouted now.

"But it's good wine, right?"

"*Yes.*" I was exasperated. "It is good wine."

"Then what? I'm sorry I never sent a wedding present. Would you like me to get you one now?"

I thought he might be being sarcastic—a part of me, the rational part, admitted to the other part of me that he'd have every right to be, that it would be a perfectly reasonable reaction on his part, that *I* was the one who was being unreasonable—but when I looked in his eyes, I saw that he wasn't being sarcastic at all. He was totally sincere.

"No," I said, somehow more peeved yet. "I don't want you to get me a wedding present now."

"Then what?" he asked again.

"You just promised William, *my son*, that you would sing on his birthday."

"That's right."

"But here's the thing, Denny. It's one thing to let down other adults, but William's just a boy, however much he might want to grow up in some ways. And you have an unfortunate habit of making promises and then not following through."

"But I will follow through on this. I gave him my word."

"See that you do." And then I got right up in his face.

"Because if you let him down, if you *hurt* him, I will never forgive you."

• • •

What could I do after all that? In the end, I had to take Denny's word for it, that he'd do what he said, that he'd do right by William. What other choice did I have?

The summer had somehow managed to divide itself into two-week chunks: the two weeks of peace before Denny's arrival; the two weeks when he was first there, crowding the house with everything that was him. Now came the two weeks after he'd sent his entourage away, coinciding with the run-up to William's party.

It was a busy time. It was a quiet time.

Busy, because Marsha and I were working together on planning William's big bash.

And quiet, because I was mostly alone.

Like other templates that had been set that summer, after the night of playing together in the basement, Jack and Denny continued with that practice. But after that first night, I didn't go down with them. I didn't ask, and they didn't say, but somehow I felt as though I'd be intruding now. They also sometimes had sessions during the day. In between, over meals, they'd discuss what they'd done, what they still wanted to do. And between jam sessions and meals spent discussing jam sessions, they'd go on excursions. They'd go out on Biff's boat or into town. A few times, they even went into New York City to small clubs Denny knew about and wanted Jack to see.

I took a lot of pictures that summer: pictures of the boys

on the beach; pictures of Jack with our new friends; even pictures of William and Harry playing Monopoly with Matt and Walter. But up until those two weeks, none of those pictures had included Denny. And now they did. My favorite one is of Jack and Denny together, just the two of them. They'd just come back from a day on the water, during which Jack had no doubt consumed a fair amount of Biff's Budweisers. In the picture, they're leaning into one another. Jack has an arm around Denny's shoulders, while Denny has an arm around Jack's waist, his other hand resting lightly against Jack's stomach. Even though it's a still shot, you can practically see the movement in their white T-shirts; I remember there was a strong breeze coming off the water that day. They're both looking off toward the same point at the side, and their laughing smiles are so wide, the picture almost feels like it must come with sound; I don't know what they're laughing at—I never learned what the joke was. And even though they're both so physically different you'd never peg them for brothers, for the first time I could see it, something in the lines around their eyes.

At long last, after a lifetime of being little more than brothers by blood and birth alone, Jack and Denny were finally bonding.

And how did I feel about this?

I was happy for Jack, of course. I'd wanted this for him, had a hand in orchestrating it, so why shouldn't I be happy?

But I was also sad too. As I said, I was alone a lot then. The first two weeks of the summer, it had been just me and Jack, and the boys of course. For the next two weeks, somehow it felt as though Denny and I had been thrown together, spending more time in one another's company than we ever had before, and that was OK too. But now it was them over there and me over here.

If I'm honest—and I do try to be in most things—I was jealous. But even that was OK. Years ago, before I met Jack and went to work with him at the travel agency, my boss at the bookstore used to like to say, "I may be a bitch, but I know it, so that's all right then." And that seemed just about right to me. It's not so bad being a negative thing if you see it clearly about yourself and don't try to pretend it's any different. So I'm not saying it's good that I felt that way, only that I did and I know it.

Anyway, I knew it wouldn't last forever. Eventually, Jack and I would get back to being just Jack and I, plus the boys, same as we'd always been. Because Denny would, eventually, go away, leaving behind a Denny-sized hole in our lives.

I only hoped it wasn't before William's party. After all, he'd promised.

I ROSE EXTRA EARLY THE DAY OF WILLIAM'S BIRTHDAY because I wanted everything to be ready when the boys came down.

I took all the ingredients out, arranging them in order on the counter. Then I got out mixing bowls and two pans, and preheated the oven.

"What are you doing?" a voice came from behind me just as I was whisking the eggs.

Denny.

"What does it look like I'm doing?" I said, not bothering to turn around.

"Dunno. Why do you think I asked? I supposed you're making something."

"I'm making a cake," I said.

"A cake?" His voice was so incredulous, you'd think I'd told him I was somehow taking a walk on the moon.

"Yes, a cake. From scratch."

I explained how the plan had changed. Originally, I'd

told William I wanted to bake the cake for his party. But then, when he came up with the list of guests he wanted, and Biff and Marsha added to that the guests they wanted, and the grand total came to a hundred—I'd had to keep reminding myself what Denny had said about them wanting to do it because they could—I realized how ridiculous my original idea was. There was no way I could make enough cake for a hundred. I'd be in the kitchen all day! So I compromised. We'd ordered bakery sheet cakes for the party, and I'd make my own for just the family to enjoy earlier in the day.

"How marvelous!" Denny said. "You know, I don't think I've seen someone bake an actual cake in over twenty years. Of course there were homemade cakes from Edith when I was growing up, but nothing since then. Do you mind if I watch?"

"Suit yourself." I shrugged.

"This is fascinating!" he said as I sifted the flour. "What are you doing now?"

"Still baking a cake. Did I mention no talking? I'm doing this all from memory and I don't want to louse it up."

"Oops. Sorry."

I was a few more steps into it when he spoke again.

"Can I do anything to help?"

I was about to tell him that I didn't need or want any help, tell him again that there was to be no talking, that he should go somewhere else if he felt the need to chatter, but something made me look at him, and when I did, there was such an expression of boyish eagerness on his face, I relented.

"Fine," I said. "Do you know how to break an egg?"

I kept one for myself, handing one to him. When he just stood there holding his, I cracked mine neatly against the side of the bowl, dropping the contents in before discarding the shell.

"The idea," I coached him, "is to get all the egg in but none of the shell. If you do get some shell in, you'll want to scoop it out. No one wants a crunchy cake."

I swear, he was concentrating so hard as he *slowly* cracked that egg, the tip of his tongue was sticking out of the corner of his mouth.

Well, cracking it so slowly, of course he got some flecks of shell in the bowl.

He looked distressed as he peered down at the concoction. "Did I…"

"It's fine," I said, briskly whisking it in.

"But you just said—"

"They're only tiny flecks. No one will notice."

"That's a relief. Still, I'd better get out of the way and let the expert continue. I don't want to spoil things."

I was about to do just that—let him get out of my way so I could get on with things myself—but there was one of those expressions on his face again, and this time it was wistful.

Oh, crap.

"Here," I said. I handed him a small saucepan and a bar of baking chocolate. "You put one in the other and melt it over a low heat—here, I'll set it for you—and then you constantly stir it with this wooden spoon so it doesn't burn as you completely melt it."

"Got it." Then: "So, what kind of cake are we making?"

"Chocolate on chocolate. I keep thinking the boys will

grow out of it, but it hasn't happened yet. It's not the most sophisticated thing in the world, but I don't mind."

We worked quietly for a time, side by side, with me telling him what to do whenever he completed one task and needed another, until at last it was time to pour the batter into the pans.

"This is the fun part," I said, handing him one pan once I'd filled them both.

"How so?" From the look on his face, I could tell he thought it was all fun. Really, after that first egg, the whole time he'd been almost giddy, like inside he was thinking, *I can't believe I'm baking a cake!* I couldn't believe it either.

I demonstrated by holding my pan over the stove and then dropping it.

"Why is that fun?" he asked.

"Because I get to make noise."

"What are we doing that for?" he asked, mimicking my motions as I raised and dropped my pan for a second time. We each did it several times.

"To get the air bubbles out," I explained. "We won't get them all—it'll never be perfect—but it will be better."

After I put the pans in the oven and set the timer, Denny wanted to know, "What do we do now?"

I handed him a stick of butter.

"Now," I said, "we make the frosting."

• • •

"I'm ten! I'm *ten! I'mtenI'mtenI'mten!!!*"

Apparently, William was up.

The shouting was accompanied by the sound of two

pairs of feet pounding down the stairs. Just in case that didn't waken Jack, I turned Harry right around and sent him back up the stairs.

"Tell your father if he's not down here in ten minutes," I said, "we're going to eat all the breakfast on him."

When Harry returned, the boys wanted to know what we were having.

"Birthday cake," I said.

The boys blinked at me like I'd gone mad.

"For *breakfast?*" William said.

"Without having to eat anything good for us *first?*" Harry added.

"Why not?" I said. "It's William's birthday, isn't it? We can make up for it at lunch or, better still, worry about going back to eating healthy tomorrow. But before we get to the cake, who wants some of this?"

I held up two spoons and produced the bowl with the leftover cake batter I'd set aside.

It didn't matter that William was now double digits, mature enough to have a crush on Roberta, some things were still reliably boyish about him. He leaped for one of the spoons I held high, and Harry did too, accompanied by shouts of, "I do! I do!"

As I handed them the spoons, I caught sight of Denny's face. I wasn't sure if the longing expression I saw there had more to do with the boys—perhaps he was remembering missing his own children's birthdays?—or if he just really did want that cake batter.

Whatever it was, it was enough to make me pull open the drawer and grab a third spoon.

"Here." I offered it to him. "There's enough for everybody."

●　●　●

Over our breakfast of birthday cake, we gave William his presents. There were a bunch of little things, and the inevitable clothing items, which William was gracious enough to thank us for. But the big item was the bicycle that Jack wheeled in.

"I can't believe it!" William cried, practically spinning in circles. "I know I asked, but I never imagined…Hey, why's it got two seats?"

"It's a bicycle built for two," Jack explained, "in case you want to ever take anyone else along for a ride."

"Like who?" William asked.

"Like one of your new friends," Jack suggested, "or maybe even your brother sometimes."

Jack, being Jack, had chosen this particular bike so Harry wouldn't feel left out. Jack always struck me as being sensitive to the particular needs of being a younger brother. But he also never wanted William's time in the sun to be compromised, so of course he quickly added, "But it's your bike, obviously, yours alone. You needn't take anyone if you don't want to."

"Are you kidding?" William said. "I think it's amazing! Hey, Harry, think of all the fun we'll have on this thing."

"Not in the house," I was forced to caution when both boys jumped on a moment later, looking as though they were about to take it on a spin around the small living area.

"Well, of course not, *Mum*." William, for the first time

LAUREN BARATZ-LOGSTED

in his life, rolled his eyes at me. Double digits for less than a day and we were already there? "We're just *sitting*, not *riding*."

Then Harry gave William his present, which was a soccer ball. He'd borrowed the money from me to buy it.

"Not in the house," I said a second time when William began attempting to bounce the ball off his head, and, his coordination never being the greatest, the ball went every which way.

Soon after, Matt and Walter came by, and they too had a present for William: a new Monopoly game.

"How about this, Mum?" William asked, with a voice that was equal parts sarcastic and sweet. But then his voice was all sweet as he laughed, "Can I play with this in the house?"

I told him I supposed that would be OK, grabbing him for a kiss on the forehead before letting him go. Where had the years gone? How was it possible that my baby was now ten?

The only one who didn't have a present for William to open was Denny. But that was OK, right? After all, Denny's big present was going to come that night, when he sang "Happy Birthday" to William. I had to admit, when Denny first said he'd do it, I'd been skeptical. OK, I'd been a downright bitch about it. But that's only because I'd been certain, or at least concerned, that Denny would let William down somehow. I thought that in the intervening two weeks between request and event, Denny might feel the need to take off, departing our lives as abruptly as he'd entered them. But that hadn't happened. Now the big day was here and Denny was still here too.

When I thought about it, I thought it was nothing short of amazing what Denny was doing. For anyone else to sing "Happy Birthday"? No big deal. But for Denny to do it, solo, at the birthday party of a ten-year-old he in so many ways barely knew? To do something so public when Denny had made it clear since arriving that he just wanted to lay low, avoid the public eye? Well, there had been his slow attention-grabbing stroll down the beach, but it wasn't like he'd sung while doing so. And he'd gone to that Fourth of July party with us and on a handful of outings with Jack and sometimes Biff. But again, there'd been no singing. No Denny being called upon to do the thing he was most famous for.

And yet he was going to do this.

Tonight.

For my son.

As the hour drew closer, if not for the awkwardness it would have presented, I could have kissed him.

So much in life begins with a simple knock on the door.

I remember reading once that all stories, no matter how different they seem, boil down to one of two basic plots: a man goes on a journey or a stranger comes to town. Either you go out seeking adventure or the adventure comes to you. Occasionally, like in *The Hobbit* and *The Lord of the Rings*, one incites the other.

In our case, when Denny had first knocked on our door that summer, both happened simultaneously. Denny began his journey, the purpose of which I was still unclear on. As for us, well, a stranger had come to town, hadn't he?

And now there came another knock, seemingly innocuous, disturbing the tapestry of the day.

When no one else jumped to see who it was at the back door, it fell to me.

It was six-thirty in the evening and we were planning to head next door any second. The party wasn't scheduled to start until seven, but since this wasn't a surprise party, William was determined to be there so he could greet his very first guests as they arrived. Unlike the Fourth of July party, I hadn't bothered getting all done up for this event. Yes, I was essentially one of the hosts, but it was a child's birthday party. So, even though the neighbors had also invited many adult friends, I couldn't see that the occasion called for more than shorts and a T-shirt.

"Yes?" I said, pulling open the door, uncertain who I would find there.

It was Jeeves.

"Oh!" I said. "When Matt and Walter came earlier, I should have figured you were around here somewhere. Did you need something to eat?"

"Is Boss ready?" he asked instead.

"Ready for what?"

"He told me to be ready to drive him at six-thirty."

"Well, that's kind of ridiculous!" I laughed, unable to keep the scoff out of my voice. "We're only going right next door."

"I only know what Boss asked me, ma'am."

"Den—" I yelled, turning and almost crashing into him. Never has the phrase felt more apt: speak of the devil.

And never, since arriving there, had he looked so much the rock star. He had on a white satin shirt with a boat neck, matching pants so low his hipbones seemed only to be holding them up with a prayer, and a crimson velvet scarf so long it would present a choking hazard were he to wear it while attempting to ride William's new bike. On his feet were boots that I expected came from some sort of incredibly expensive reptile, his hair was so perfect, if I

199

hadn't known any better, I'd have thought Lulu had been by to fix it for him, and he had on eyeliner and mascara.

"Isn't this a bit much?" I said, meaning the chauffeur ride for a few feet but also his getup. "We're only going next door."

"I need to go do an errand," Denny said, putting on dark sunglasses.

"We were supposed to leave any minute. What do you mean you have to do an errand?" I couldn't help it. Already the fishwife was entering my voice.

"It won't take very long," Denny said. Then he turned to Jeeves. "Will it?"

"I don't think any more than usual, Boss."

"What errand is so important that you have to do it now? Can't whatever this is wait?"

"No, I'm afraid it really can't. But I'll be back in time. I promised, didn't I?"

"Yes, but—"

"When were you planning to cut the cake?"

"Probably sometime between nine and ten. William wants it to be dark out so that it feels, you know, more sophisticated. But—"

"Another two and a half, three and a half hours?" He sailed past me, indicating Jeeves was to follow. "Oh, that's plenty of time, plenty of time."

"But—"

But my last "but" was met with the sound of a slamming car door. And what could I do?

He'd promised in advance, and now he'd promised he'd be back in time. I had to trust him. I had to believe him, didn't I?

• • •

Marsha'd had a huge tent set up on the beach. There was no threat of rain in the forecast, only fog, but she'd wanted it just in case. There were also tiki torches all over the place, which she planned to light as soon as it got dark.

We were the first to arrive, as planned, but a handful of kids soon followed, and William and Harry were off with them before I even had a chance to shout, "Have a good time!"

There would be food soon. I'd thought we should have the same thing for everybody—how do kids learn to have a more mature palate and how do they learn that everything doesn't need to be catered to their tastes if someone's always giving them a hot dog at every turn?—but Marsha didn't want to test out my theory, and she was tired of hot dogs herself. I didn't really have the right to complain though, so I didn't, not when she'd so willingly done all the work.

"What would you like to drink?" she offered now.

"What are my choices?"

She showed me where the bar had been set up: the inevitable white wine and beer, plus bottles of alcohol along with mixers. I was about to ask for a G&T for a change when she pointed to a large box in the sand.

"What's that?" I asked.

"It was delivered earlier today," she said, "with a note from Denny. It was very thoughtful of him, but I can't imagine who here would want to drink it. We all prefer white—less calories."

She extracted a bottle to show me what he'd sent.

It was the Chateau Latour.

"If you don't mind," I said, "I think I'll take a glass of that."

• • •

An hour later, I started to feel pleasantly buzzed, the pleasantness slightly compromised by the minutes ticking away. Biff had outdoor speakers, and he'd put on music that his boys liked. For the most part, it was the most infernal of pop music, the kinds of songs that catch your ear and make you play them over and over until you cannot stand to hear them anymore.

But the kids were happy. Many of them were even dancing in the sand down by the water, a bunch of squirming bodies, some with rhythm and some without. I squinted until I made out my two. It would've been nice if Roberta were dancing with William—it would've made his birthday complete; well, that and if his uncle would show up like he'd promised. Where was Denny? But Roberta was dancing with the more rhythmic girls while William and Harry were with the less rhythmic boys.

I felt lips against my ear.

"Dance with me?" my husband whispered.

Without waiting for an answer, he took me in his arms, slow dancing me around, even dipping me.

"I'm not sure it's that kind of song," I laughed. "Aren't we supposed to be flailing about like the kids?" I tried to demonstrate but he just held me closer.

"It can be whatever kind of song we choose to make it."

"What's gotten into you? Why the Mr. Romance act?"

"I don't know. I've got a pretty wife. I've had an incredibly good day. My boys are happy, so I'm happy. It doesn't really take much more than that with me, I guess."

And for a short time, or at least for the duration of the song, I was happy too.

But then I started to think about Denny.

• • •

Yet another hour later, it was dark out, and there was that fog that had been in the forecast, so now the tiki torches were lit, blazing up the beach.

William came running up to me, breathless from whatever he'd been doing.

"Is he here yet?" he asked.

"I haven't seen him," I said, trying to hide the anger I was feeling on William's behalf.

"Only," William said, "Billy and Tommy's mum was saying we were supposed to do the cake around now."

"Perhaps we should just go ahead then?" I suggested, trying to sound mild about it, when inside I was thinking, *What if Denny just doesn't bother ever coming back?*

"We can't do that!" William was aghast.

"But what if he doesn't—"

"It'll be fine," William said brightly. "He promised, so we'll just wait."

Before I could say anything else, he'd run back to his friends.

• • •

By eleven o'clock at night, I should have by all rights been supremely pleasantly buzzed, what with all the Chateau Latour I'd had to drink. But instead, the only buzzing I felt was intense anger.

That shit. That incredible weaselly shit.

What kind of a man promises something to a boy—his nephew, no less!—and then fails to come through?

"Mona? Are you all right?"

It was Jack.

"I'm fine," I said through gritted teeth.

"Well, you certainly don't look it."

"It's just...*your brother*..."

As soon as I said it, I heard myself, sounding exactly like my own mum anytime my dad pissed her off. He was no longer his name or "my husband"; he was someone else's responsibility.

"What's he done this time?"

"Did he not promise William he'd be here? So where is he, Jack?"

"How should I know?"

"It keeps getting later and later, and I've tried suggesting to William that we just go ahead and cut the cake, but he won't hear of it. I don't want to see him disappointed, but what if Denny never comes back?"

"He won't be disappointed, Mona. Look at him." He physically turned me in William's direction. "Do you see how happy he looks? He won't be disappointed, no matter what. Everyone's having a grand time. There's no need to worry."

Looking at William, I could see that Jack was right:

William was happy. But there was also a desperate anxiety to his laughter that, being his mother, I readily recognized.

And then, for the first time, seeing William's anxiety and looking all around me at the fog, I grew anxious too. What if instead of growing increasingly angry for the past few hours, I should have been growing concerned?

What if something bad had happened to Denny, an accident or something, and that was why he'd failed to return?

• • •

The chord was the first thing any of us heard.

That chord screeched out in the night, loud enough to be heard over the music coming from Biff's speakers and any conversations going on. If that chord had come from a human instead of an electric guitar, it would have been the equivalent of an attention-getting clearing of the throat, the loudest "Ahem!" imaginable.

As more chords followed, we made our way from the tiki-lit brightness of the sand in front of Biff's place in the direction of where the sounds were coming from, through the fog, to the beach in front of our own house.

And there they were.

It wasn't just Denny. Lex was there too, and Trey and 8.

Denny had brought the entire band.

"Now that everyone's here," Denny spoke into the microphone.

People went nuts clapping. They hadn't really done anything yet—just a few chords from Lex and a single line from Denny—and already people were going crazy. I could understand the feeling. I'd only ever seen the band perform once before, in Wales, but even then it hadn't been like this. They were so close now, on the same level with the audience, and with no bodyguards marking off the perimeters, I could literally reach out and touch them if I wanted to.

"We meant to be here sooner," Denny spoke over the crowd, quieting them. "Sometimes, though, events get in the way of intentions. But now we are here! And we'd like to play a few songs in honor of my nephew's—one of my two favorite nephews—birthday. Would that be OK with you, William?"

Denny located William in the crowd as he spoke this last, and I turned to look at William too. He was so excited as he nodded, I worried he might pee himself.

And then Denny was singing and the band was playing, some of their biggest hits from the last two decades, the handful of iconic songs that no matter what the age of the listener, everyone would recognize.

I know there were a hundred people there, and I had a vague sense of the others laughing and dancing and even singing along, yet my own attention was strictly held by two people: Denny and my eldest son, the former for what he was doing, the latter for the sheer joy on his face because of what Denny was doing.

At one point, I felt my hand being taken, and I looked to my side and saw Jack there. Immediately, I wondered how he felt. For, in that moment, it hit me harder than it ever had before: How do you compete? How can a new bicycle, even one built for two, rate against an impromptu concert, by The Greatest Rock-and-Roll Band In The World, in honor of your birthday?

Jack said something to me, but I couldn't hear him over the music and had to go up on tiptoe as he tried again.

"Still not a fan?" he asked me.

"What do you mean?"

"The first night I met you, you said you weren't a fan of his." He jerked his head at the band, at Denny.

That wasn't strictly true. It was Jack who'd said he wasn't a fan. I'd merely said I thought they were overrated. Of course I'd only said that because I thought it was what Jack wanted to hear.

I looked at Jack now, wondering what he wanted to hear from me this time.

But if I expected to see jealousy or resentment on his face, if I thought I'd see those things because that's exactly what I would be feeling if someone else had so roundly trumped me in one of my children's lives, that wasn't the case with Jack. Whatever he might be feeling for Denny on any other day, he was purely happy right now, purely happy that Denny was giving William this incredible moment.

"Still not a fan?" was the question Jack had asked me.

I looked away from my husband, to my son, and then to Denny.

"Well," I finally admitted, "maybe just a bit."

• • •

In all, they played a half-dozen songs before the police showed up.

Apparently, there was at least one neighbor who wasn't a fan.

"I'm sorry," the officer apologized to Denny profusely.

"My son's such a huge fan. Well, I am too. If it were up to me…"

"Just one more song," Denny said.

"I really—"

"It's a really short one," Denny said, "promise."

I could've told the officer a thing or two about Denny's promises—that sometimes they came late, if they came at all—but no one was asking me.

Lex leaned into Denny's mic like he sometimes did during regular shows and spoke to the officer in his growling smoker's voice, "Make it worth your while when we're finished, mate."

And then, before the officer could object further, the band was playing and Denny was singing again, and what Denny had promised was exactly true this time: the song was very short.

It was "Happy Birthday."

What William had asked for was for Denny to sing. And that would have been OK, although it might also have been corny. It was like what Denny had said to me earlier in the summer, though, about giving people what they didn't even know they wanted, didn't know they needed. William had never seen to ask for this—the whole band playing, just for him, in a crazy Jimi Hendrix does the "Star-Spangled Banner" version of "Happy Birthday." It wasn't just OK plus maybe corny; it was beyond cool—anyone looking at the faces of Roberta and the other kids, even the adults, could see that. William hadn't asked, no doubt, because he didn't know such a thing was possible. But Denny had known. Not only had he known what William hadn't known to want and needed, but, even more than that, Denny had delivered.

When they were done with William's song, Lex asked the officer if he could borrow a pen, and then he unplugged his guitar, signed it, and handed it over.

"For your kid," Lex said to the dumbfounded officer. Then: "Mind if I keep the pen, then? Never one of these around when I need one."

"Was that OK, Mona?" a voice said.

I blinked and there was Denny in front of me.

"I really tried to get here earlier," he went on, "but I didn't plan on the fog. I thought it would be a bit of a surprise, more of an event for William, to have the whole band here, so I flew them in. But because of the fog, the plane couldn't land on time, so...Was it OK?"

"Yes," I said, "it was OK."

"I can't believe it. I can't believe it! *I can't believe it!*"

And *that* would be William.

"Was it OK?" Denny asked him the same question he'd asked me.

"Was it *OK?*" William echoed exuberantly. "*OK?*" Then, with a quick look to the side—Roberta was there—he recovered his cool, tried on a nonchalant shrug. "Yeah, I mean, of course."

"Who's your friend?" Denny asked with a chin nod at Roberta.

William introduced them, but Roberta could only stare.

Poor Roberta. She'd gone completely deer-in-the-headlights.

Denny leaned into me, whispering low under his breath. "These are the ones that always worry me the most. I never know what to do. It's like they just died right where they're standing, and I wonder: 'What if it's for real? What if they're really dead?'"

"Try shaking her hand," I whispered back.

"Right, then." Denny held out his hand. "Friend of William's? Roberta, is it?"

Roberta grasped onto his hand with both of hers, and a sound came out of her that was only barely recognizable as being human, somewhere between a squeal and a scream, followed by, "Aieee!" After which, she dropped his hand like a hot coal, like she could barely stand to touch it anymore, running off into the night with William behind her.

"Definitely not dead," Denny concluded.

The band all joined him then.

"You all know Jack of course," he said.

Handshakes all around, with Lex throwing in a "Great to see you again, mate" for good measure.

"And this is Mona, my sister-in-law," Denny introduced me.

They behaved as though they'd never met me, and there was another round of shakes, which, I supposed, was just as well. I'd only ever met the band once before.

"Hello there," I said, feeling a bit strange about it. "Nice to meet you."

I was saved from any further awkwardness by the hurricane that was Marsha bearing down on us.

"What an honor!" Her hand was to her ample chest. "I'm so glad you could come to our little party! I wish Mona had said...Are you hungry? You must be hungry. Thirsty, maybe?"

It turned out that Denny and Trey and 8 were all hungry,

210

which was fine since there was a ton of food left. As for Lex, he found his dinner in an unopened bottle of Jack Daniels from the drinks table.

When Marsha offered to get him a glass, he practically giggled.

"You're a funny girl, aren't you?" he said.

From then on, mostly I just watched.

It was like being at a wedding, where etiquette dictates no one should leave before the bride and groom. Of course, the reason here had nothing to do with etiquette, but there was no way any of the other guests were going to leave before Denny and the band.

After about an hour, Denny approached Jack, who was standing beside me.

"Any chance we can use your basement?" Denny asked. "Lex's itching to play some more, but he gave away his guitar, and none of the rest of us are in the right mood for getting arrested, so..."

"Yeah." Now Jack looked flustered. "I mean, sure."

We said our goodbyes, William's to Roberta taking the longest, and then the band, my husband, my kids, and I made our way back to the house.

• • •

"So, here's everything," Jack said, still nervous, showing the band the setup in the basement.

"Oh, and Lex can use this." Jack chose the best from among his guitars, handing it to Lex.

Lex, cigarette in mouth, nodded down at the guitar appreciatively.

"So, right." Jack clapped his hands together. "Let me know if you need anything else."

He turned to go and I turned to follow.

"Aren't you going to stay?" Denny's voice called him back.

"I don't know." Jack looked down at me, a question in his eyes as he shrugged. "What do you think, Mona? Do you want to listen for a bit?"

"Listen?" Denny laughed. "I thought maybe you could sit in with us."

Jack looked at Denny sharply, as though to see if Denny were joking. But despite Denny's laughter, it was clear he wasn't.

"You're serious?" Jack still couldn't believe it.

"You play, don't you?" Denny said.

"Well, yeah..."

"You want this back then?" Lex offered Jack back his best guitar.

"No, thanks." Jack picked up his spare guitar. "You know," Jack told Denny, "what I do tends to be a bit more mellow than what you all do."

"So?" Denny said. "We'll do a little of both then."

And that's what they did.

They did some of the band's standards first, and Jack looked incredibly uncomfortable in the beginning, only occasionally jumping in with a lick.

"Why don't we try one of your new songs you showed me?" Denny suggested to Jack.

"Are you sure? I mean..."

When it became clear Denny was going to wait until Jack actually played something, Jack went ahead, bowing his head to his guitar. He played the first few notes of the song he and Denny had tweaked a few weeks back, singing the first line or two.

"So." He coughed. "It's kind of like that."

"Like this?" Lex played back the line and Jack nodded. "OK," Lex said, "let's go."

Jack began again and played the song through, only this time Lex shadowed his playing, shadowing so closely you could barely discern the fact that he was playing everything a half note behind Jack.

"S'not bad," Lex said. "Go again."

This time, the whole band came in on it, with Denny providing some backup hums. The resulting song was different than Jack's stripped-down version, not necessarily better but definitely more complete.

By the time they were finished, Jack looked both elated and stunned. In all his years working alone, I don't think it had occurred to him what it might be like to have a band backing him. He'd been so determined that his career, such as it was, be the anti-Denny experience.

"You got something there with that one," Lex said. "You should record that."

Jack beamed so widely. I don't think it even occurred to him to point out that that was what he'd planned on doing all along, that he didn't need Denny or the band's validation to do so. And yet it was clear that that's what Jack felt: validated.

"Why don't we do 'She's There'?" Denny suggested.

"What?" Jack said, clearly perplexed.

"It is your song, isn't it?" Denny said. "Second album, side B, next to last? I do think it's a bit buried there..." He shrugged.

It was my turn to be perplexed. As far as I knew, up until recently Denny hadn't even known Jack *had* recorded any albums. Now he was an expert? Then I figured maybe it was like the wine he'd ordered for me. While no one was looking, Denny'd gotten up to speed on Jack's music. It would appear Denny did a lot of things while no one was looking.

"Sure." Jack shrugged, clearly going for nonchalant. "We could do that."

They played Jack's song "She's There," then they did a few more standards, and finally just jammed for a bit, playing any old thing.

At some point, Jack and Denny had stopped playing and started talking instead, and Trey and 8 had drifted off to sleep in the corners, so that only Lex remained seated in a chair, guitar on his knee, playing, a cigarette dangling from his lips. That perpetual curtain of smoke so close to my eyes would have driven me mad, but Lex just stared through it, hardly even squinting. He was just strumming softly, so soft it took me a time to notice that suddenly all I was hearing was the low murmur of Jack and Denny's voices and that the guitar had stopped.

Denny got up from the floor and went over to Lex, who was in the same position but now fast asleep, the lit cigarette still burning down to ash.

"He does this all the time," Denny said, gently removing the cigarette from Lex's mouth and finding somewhere to put it out. "He'll be up again in fifteen minutes or an hour or ten, and he'll just start in playing, usually right where he left off. If he's in the middle of writing a song, it'll be even better when he wakes."

"I don't know how he does it," Jack said.

"Frankly, neither do I. But there." Denny pointed at Lex. "There's your rock star. 8 and Trey, even you and me—we're all just pikers by comparison."

"How do you mean?"

"Look, I'm not saying I don't love making the music—of course I do—and I'm not saying he doesn't love the life. No one loves it better. But if everything that goes along with it were stripped away tomorrow, Lex'd still be doing this. He wouldn't be doing it on the side. He wouldn't be doing it by any half measure or even sixteenth measure. He'd be doing it as hard as he is now, living in the gutter if no one would pay him to play. It's not just what he does. It's who he is. It's everything he is. For me it's part of a whole. But for him it is the whole."

"Well, what about you then? If all the rest of it were stripped away, what would you be doing?"

Denny looked surprised at the question. "I'd be in business, of course. After all, I'm good with people, aren't I?"

Jack stared at Denny and then they both burst out laughing.

There had been times, so many times that summer, when I'd wondered: really, why had Denny come? It couldn't possibly be for the reason he said, so that he could bond with Jack, a notion that would never have even occurred to him if I hadn't put it in his head. But now, after this entire amazing evening—amazing for William and for me, but more so for Jack than anyone else—I finally saw the truth in it.

Denny had come for Jack.

"Hey," Denny said, "here's something I've been working on. Let me know what you think."

He picked up an acoustic guitar and played a song I hadn't heard him play before, singing along with it.

"That's different from anything else I've heard you do," Jack said.

"And?"

"And I like it. But everything else you do is British or American, while that's…"

"That's what?"

"More Mediterranean somehow, like, I don't know. Morocco or something."

"Good ear. That's exactly right. I was there a few years back, always wanted to do something with the sounds I heard there. You ever been?"

"To Morocco?"

Denny nodded.

"No. We did a lot of traveling before the boys were born, but nothing really since, and for some reason, that's one place I've never been to."

Jack reddened. It must have occurred to him how foolish it sounded, telling Denny we'd done a lot of traveling when Denny had seen the entire world.

"Any interest in going?" Denny asked.

"Well, *yeah*. I mean, *Morocco*."

"What about you, Mona?"

It'd been so many hours since I'd been a part of the conversation, it took me a while to register that Denny had addressed that question to me.

"Well, *yeah*," I finally said, echoing Jack. "Who isn't interested?"

"That's what I figured." Denny strummed a few chords. "Everyone wants to see Morocco."

I WOKE TO A POUNDING ON THE BEDROOM DOOR THAT I'M
not entirely certain was louder than the pounding in my
head.

"You'd better get up unless you want to miss your plane!"
a voice called, followed by footsteps rapidly padding back
down the stairs.

I rolled over, groaning, and collapsed into the crook of
Jack's arm. "Who was that?"

"It was Denny," Jack groaned back. Then, more alertly:
"Did he say something about *a plane?*"

. . .

We were foggy-headed enough that even after we located
Denny in the dining area, it took a while to make sense of
what he was saying. Really, the only thing that finally did it
was when he waved two plane tickets in the air.

To Morocco.

"When did you get these?" I demanded while Jack, bleary eyed, made coffee.

"Yesterday," Denny said, "when I was at the airport to pick up Lex and the others. Why? Is there something wrong? Because if you'd prefer, you can take the private plane. It's only ever used by me or by all of us when we're using it together, so most of the time it just sits on the tarmac somewhere. Of course, I'd planned on it taking the others home today. But as I say, if you'd prefer—"

"I don't understand! What's this all for?"

Denny looked stunned at the question. "Why, it's an anniversary present."

"Our anniversary was in the spring!"

"Well, if it doesn't make any difference to you, it certainly doesn't matter to me."

I have to admit, the whole thing was confusing. *He* was confusing.

"You did say," he said, "that I never gave you and Jack a proper wedding present."

He hadn't even remembered about not coming through with a wedding present until I'd reminded him—he probably barely remembered missing the wedding itself—and now he wanted to make it up to me, twelve years later, with airplane tickets to a place I hadn't even known I wanted to see before he brought it up the night before?

"I wasn't hinting for you to do something like *this*!"

"I never said you were. I wanted to do it. So I did. I went ahead and booked the two of you for two weeks—"

"Just the two of us? For two weeks? We can't do that! Who would take care of the boys?" I was about to say, "*you?*" in my most scathing tone of voice, but something pulled me back from the implied insult, and instead I settled for a weak, "Lex?"

Denny snorted. "Not that he's not necessarily capable. You'd be surprised how good he can be with children—they tend to like him and he tends to like them—but even he'd be the first to admit that he's not exactly any parent's babysitting dream."

"Who then?" I asked, again avoiding the possibility of Denny doing it. Yes, he'd come through for William last night, eventually, but what if he got called away to do something—would he take the boys with him—or what if he just had the whim to do something on his own? Would he remember his temporary responsibilities, make other arrangements for them, or would he simply just go?

A part of me couldn't believe I was even bothering to engage in this debate, either externally or internally, since there was no way on earth I was going.

Denny shrugged. "What about Matt and Walter? Of course, I wouldn't take off for anywhere until after you safely returned, but would it make you feel any better about the whole thing if Matt and Walter stayed here too?"

Jack spoke up for the first time. "The boys do like Matt and Walter."

"Yes, I know but—"

Seeing a hopeful look on Jack's face, I stopped talking.

"When's the last time the two of you went anywhere on your own?" Denny asked.

I opened my mouth to answer, but Jack got there first.

"Before the boys were born."

"Then don't you think you owe it to yourselves?"

Jack grabbed onto my hand, swung it a bit.

"So," he said, "what do you think?"

"I don't know. What do you think?"

"I'd like to, but only if you want to."

"OK, then."

"OK."

"Right!" Denny clapped his hands together. "Now, get dressed and get going! Jeeves is waiting. I mean, *I* can get away with traveling in my pajamas, but I don't think *you two* can."

"But we need to pack!" I could be wrong, but I think I was starting to panic.

"Didn't you once say," Denny said, "that you and Jack used to get up and go with just your passports and one good credit card?"

• • •

In the end, the packing wasn't quite that bare bones, but close enough. We threw whatever we thought we might need into two suitcases—what was the weather going to be like in Morocco in mid-July? I had no idea!

"Mona?" Jack called upstairs. "Almost ready? The boys are awake."

"Almost!" I yelled back down.

I still needed reading material—things to read on the plane trips, things to read once we were there. I could never stand being anywhere without the next few good books to read in view. And what if there were no English-language bookstores convenient to where we'd be staying?

I grabbed the carryall bag I'd last used when we'd first

flown to America back in June—the only things still in it were a half-eaten roll of spearmints I'd told the boys would make sparks in our mouths if we ate them in the dark, but never got around to demonstrating, and a magazine I'd bought at the airport back in England but never got the chance to read. So I left the magazine and the spearmints where they were, piling on top of them several books I hadn't read yet and a couple of really good ones that I had, just in case.

"Mon—"

"Coming!"

•  •  •

And the rest, as they say, was whirlwind.

Jeeves taking the bags from us. The boys hugging and kissing us. Well, I had to pause the whirlwind for that.

"I know this is a bit of a surprise," I told Harry.

"If you'd rather we stay…" I told William.

I even meant that last. William was my sensitive boy. If he'd asked us to stay right then and there, I'd have said yes. I mean, this was all starting to sound like a dream trip, but I didn't want to traumatize my son. There'd be time for more trips when the boys were grown.

"Are you *kidding*?" William said.

"We'll have a great time with Matt and Walter," Harry said, adding, with a glance at Denny, "and him."

"Exactly!" William said. "So *go*! Have *fun*!"

"When did you get to be so mature?" I said, ruffling his hair. I was pleased he let me do it. I had the feeling a time would come, soon, when I wouldn't get away with that anymore.

"Well," he laughed, "I am double digits now you know."

And then the whirlwind was back on again, Denny hustling us out the door into the car, Jeeves starting the engine, the boys jumping up and down as they waved.

We'd actually started to pull away, and Jeeves was raising the windows, when I heard Denny's voice yelling, "Wait!"

He ran back into the house, returning a few minutes later with a carrying case, which he handed through the window to me.

"Here," he said, "take my phone. It'll make it easier for you to call and check in at the house, as you'll no doubt want to do on a regular basis—you know, to make sure the boys are OK."

"But don't you need it yourself?" I tried to hand it back but he waved me away.

"No, thanks. Just, you know, if anyone calls looking for me, maybe don't say where I am?"

# PART III

## *Morocco*

Morocco!

Morocco.

When I thought to write down my story, just for myself and to be burned immediately upon completion, I figured I'd want to write about the two weeks spent in Morocco in detail. But, as fabulous as the trip was in so many ways—the five-star hotel Denny put us up at, the amazing architecture, the exquisite food, the sheer adventure of it all—as it turns out, there are really just three things worth noting: one involved my husband, one involved my oldest son, and one involved Denny.

# Jack

Although we'd never been anywhere in Africa before, being travel agents and having sent many clients to Morocco, we knew all about the do's and don'ts. We knew how to bargain, how one should never accept the first price on anything, and that we should never tell a vendor where we were staying or what we paid for other items. We knew not to offer a price unless we were prepared to pay it, and we knew to show appreciation for the craftsmanship behind what was on display. We knew not to go off with anyone who offered to show us around, however kind the person might seem. We knew not to buy geodes (probably fake) or trilobite fossils (also probably fake).

We knew to keep a spare roll of toilet paper with us at all times, *just in case*, because it was possible, even in a hotel or restaurant, to find such an amenity lacking.

I specifically, as a woman, knew not to walk around outside the hotel without Jack unless I wanted to be subjected to constant catcalls or hisses, and I knew to dress conservatively, with no excess of skin showing anywhere. While a *hijab*, or headscarf, wasn't required, it wasn't a bad idea in terms of showing respect or to avoid unwanted attention.

We also knew it was probably best not to purchase any illicit drugs, but we chose to ignore that one.

• • •

We stumbled into the hotel room, laughing, stoned on hashish.

When we'd initially boarded the plane back in New York, I'd been somewhat nervous, although I hadn't confessed as much to Jack. What I was nervous about was this: It'd been over ten years since Jack and I had spent much more than just an evening out for dinner without being accompanied first by one and later both of our sons. Who were we without the buffer of the kids? Would we be able to talk to one another about things outside of them? Or would it just be awkward, revealing that without them, all we could do was miss something that was no longer there, like experiencing pain in phantom limbs; that without them, we were nothing anymore, no longer our own thing, a prelude to what life would be like once the boys were fully grown and gone.

But as it turned out, I needn't have worried. It wasn't that we didn't miss the boys or daily wonder what they were doing, but rather than pining for what lay on the other side of the Atlantic, Jack and I were ourselves, like two kids who'd escaped Sunday School early—free to go or do whatever we wanted because no one was expecting us anywhere.

And, also, free to buy hashish.

I slumped on the brocade sofa, and Jack slumped lower beside me, his head on my shoulder, giggling. That's a strange word to describe the sounds coming out of a grown man, but it's exactly what he was doing. So was I.

"What's so funny?" I asked. My own laughter was dying down, I could no longer remember what had set me off in the first place, and I was hoping that hearing what he was laughing at would get me going again.

"You still have your *hijab* on," he said, practically unable to gasp out the words, "but we're in our own room, and there's no one else here!"

"Well, that is silly of me," I admitted. I raised my hand to my head and started to push the scarf back, but Jack gripped his own hand around my wrist, stopping me.

"Leave it," he said in a husky voice, no longer laughing now. "Do you mind just leaving it?"

"Why?" I asked.

For an answer, he kissed me.

It wasn't the kind of kiss characteristic of the long married with young children hoping to get in a quickie before being interrupted by the demands of those children. It was the soft but growing in intensity leisurely kiss of a new couple with nothing more in mind than how to extend the current pleasure as long as possible, just barely able to contain the exquisite pain of waiting for the next step to come.

I could have drowned in that kiss, was drowning in it.

Abruptly, Jack pulled away. I tried to chase his lips with mine, but he stretched back just out of reach.

"Wow," I said. "You got all that from the headscarf?"

He nodded. Then he stood up, took my hands in his to raise me to my feet, and backed me up toward the bed.

"I know I shouldn't," he said. I felt the edge of the bed against the backs of my knees, causing me reflexively to sit down. "You know I'm not one for the subjugation of women." He pulled my shirt up over my head, then undid the clasp on my bra. "And I'd never expect you to wear a headscarf in our real life, back home." He gently pressed my shoulders down until I was flat on the bed, and then he undid my pants, pulled them off, slid down my underwear. "But I can see the appeal." He lowered himself on top of me, still fully clothed. "And I cannot tell you how sexy it is, seeing you like that when we're in public here, knowing I'm the only man who knows completely what you look like without that scarf."

He lowered his head to my neck, kissing what he knew was for me the sweet spot, the spot that when kissed, would make the rest of my body sigh with longing.

So, of course, I started laughing hysterically.

"You're kidding, right?" he said. "I say this incredibly—or what I *think* is an incredibly—sexy thing to you, and you *laugh*?"

"I can't help it. It's just so ridiculous!" I pealed off again.

"Thank you so very much." Then: "What is?"

"You say it's so sexy to see me out in public like this, but we're here, no one else is around, so how can that still be sexy?"

"Huh." Jack looked stumped. "Dunno. It just is. Although I must say, it's getting less so by the minute."

"Don't be like that! It's just that, what if I wanted to subjugate you?"

"I thought I established, that was not my int—"

"Maybe I'd like to have a version of you walking around such that the picture the rest of the world got wasn't the same as what I did?" I teased.

"Ohhhh." Jack's eyes lit up as he rose from the bed. "Now I know what you're after."

"Wait," I said, rising up on my elbows. "Where are you going?"

"Won't be a tick." He went over to the bags containing our purchases from the day, riffled through with his back to me until he found what he wanted, then, concealing it, he made for the bathroom. "Perhaps two ticks," he shot over his shoulder before closing the door.

I scooted up so my back was against the headboard, got partially under the covers, and waited for him to return.

And waited.

And waited.

Had he fallen asleep in there?

Just when I thought I might drift off myself, I heard the door click open and there was my husband.

"Is this what you had in mind?" he asked, hand on naked, cocked hip.

He was entirely naked, except for his head, on which he'd arranged a vivid red scarf I'd bought at the market earlier in the day. The scarf was tied in a little bow under his chin.

I stifled a giggle as he made his way over to me, watched as he peeled back the covers. Then he straddled me, kissing his way down my body. As he approached the cleft between my legs, the stifled giggle burst into full-out laughter.

"You think this is funny?" he said. "Here I am, obviously willing to subjugate myself for you, and all you can do is laugh some more?"

"It's just that...it's just that...it's like being gone down on by Little Red Riding Hood!"

"Well, I never," Jack mock harrumphed. At least I hoped it was mock. "I'll show you Little Red Riding Hood."

He jackknifed my legs apart and got on with showing me.

I wouldn't have believed before that moment that it was possible to laugh all the way through an orgasm, but that's what happened that night.

• • •

Later, we lay side by side, gazing at one another. I didn't say then, but I was thinking, how lucky I was. When I'd laughed at Jack earlier, he could have gotten seriously offended, and then he might have acted hurt or even angry to mask the hurt, from both himself and me. But instead, being Jack, he'd gone with it, turning the moment into one of pure joy, which was happily followed by incredibly energetic sex.

Jack's scarf was still tied under his chin, but our exertions had knocked it off his head, so now he looked more like a cowboy; a tired, naked cowboy.

"You know," he said, "no matter how many years it's been, sometimes there are still moments I can't believe I'm here, with you. I feel that way when I wake up in the morning and when I go to sleep at night."

I said I felt the same.

But as Jack drifted off to sleep, I couldn't help but think of his brother, nearly a world away now. I wondered if there were times, still, when he awoke in the morning and, for a moment, he forgot who he was. And then he would remember. He'd remember who he was and what he'd accomplished. He'd remember anew that, more than most people, he wasn't like anyone else in the world.

I thought that, yes, it must be like that.

# William

Even though Denny had given me his mobile phone so I could call Westport to check in whenever I liked, I'd been determinedly not doing that. After all, Jack and I were supposed to be on our second honeymoon, right? After all, Denny had Denny's number—obviously—so, surely he'd call if anything were amiss, right? And if we weren't calling them, it meant we were enjoying ourselves, like we were supposed to, and if they weren't calling us, it didn't mean the boys didn't miss us, but rather that everyone was just happy and healthy—right?

"Just call," Jack said on the eighth day. "You know you want to."

"And you want me to too."

"Well, *yeah*."

It was eleven p.m. Morocco time, making it seven p.m. back in Westport, the perfect time to call since that's when the boys always ate dinner.

But just because it's a perfect time for something, theoretically, doesn't mean things will work out as you planned.

"That's funny," I said. "No one's answering."

"Perhaps they went out?" Jack said.

"Your brother?" I snorted. "You know he's been staying close to the house. I wonder if something could be wrong..."

"Or perhaps they went out."

An hour later—midnight us, eight p.m. them—it was the same thing.

"I really think there might be something wrong," I said.

"Or else they went out," Jack said.

Easy for him to say.

At one a.m. us, nine p.m. them, Jack suggested we go to bed.

"You could try again tomorrow." He yawned. "I'm sure everything is fine."

"Or else," I said, "something's really wrong."

It was nearly two a.m. us and ten p.m. them when someone finally answered the phone.

"Mummy!" Harry said.

It was *so* good to hear his voice.

And then of course I couldn't stop myself from immediately demanding, "Is something the matter there?"

"What? No!" And then, in that non sequitur way children have, he added, "We had chicken fingers for lunch! Well, they weren't really fingers—that's just what they're called—but it was real chicken, organic, and so were the bread crumbs they were dredged in, and do you know what?"

"No, what?"

"It was even *better* than McDonald's!"

"That's great. Where'd you get those?"

"Right here! In our own kitchen! Super Mario made them!"

"Super Who?"

"Didn't you hear me the first time? I *said*, 'Super Mario'!"

"Who's he when he's at home?"

"Uncle Denny's chef, but here too."

Denny was "Uncle Denny" now? When we left, Denny was still just "him."

"After you and Dad left," Harry continued, "almost immediately, Uncle Denny rang Super Mario and told him to come straightaway on the next flight. Then he, Uncle Denny, explained to us that he didn't know how to cook anything himself except for the birthday cake he'd seen you make, and he said that didn't count as proper food, not three meals a day. Uncle Denny's big on proper foods—it has to all be organic—and he said it wouldn't be wholesome for us to be eating out or getting takeaway all the time. Uncle Denny said once Super Mario was here, he'd make whatever we liked—anything at all—only healthy, so today we asked for chicken fingers, and there they were! And do you know what else?"

"No, tell me. What else?"

"Super Mario is really big and he always wears a chef's outfit. He's super! Like a real chef!"

I couldn't help it. Harry's enthusiasm was so infectious, I was laughing.

"I would expect so," I said. "I'm glad you're all eating well. Was that where you were before, by any chance? Because I called earlier, several times, and no one answered. Perhaps you were all having a late picnic outside and didn't hear the phone?"

"No, we were *at* the hospital, as they say around here, with William."

"You were—"

"You'll want to talk to him, I know." There came the sound of the phone being dropped, but even without Harry's mouth being close to the mouthpiece, I could still hear his foghorn shout of, "*Wil-lie!*"

Willie? Did Harry just call his brother Willie? And what was all this about being at the hospital?

"Mum!" William's voice came on the line. "It's so good to hear from you!"

"And it's great to talk to you too. But did I just hear your brother call you Willie?"

"Oh, that. It's my new name. Roberta says it makes me sound older, more mature, and when I told Uncle Denny"—there was that 'Uncle Denny' again—"he said he had to agree. He said there'd be less confusion between Harry and me and the Royal Family."

"I suppose..." Really? Willie sounded more mature to them than William?

"So you and Dad'll have to get used to it too."

"We'll try but we may need some time. You've always been William to me. But never mind that now. What was that nonsense your brother was saying, about you being in hospital?"

"I wasn't *in* hospital. I was *at the* hospital. But, oh yeah, I broke my arm!"

He *what*?

"You're kidding, right?" Surely, he wouldn't sound so gleeful, not if he'd broken his arm and been *at the* hospital that very night.

"Not in the slightest!" Still, he sounded gleeful. "I broke it while out riding my bike. Harry wasn't on it with me or he might've gotten hurt too, so that part was good."

It was so like William to think of Harry.

"I'm so sorry I wasn't there," I said. My heart was beating faster in my chest. I couldn't believe that William had been hurt and I hadn't been there to do anything about it. If possible, I would have clicked my heels together if it would've put me instantly by William's side.

"S'OK, Mum, because Uncle Denny *was*—there, I mean. He took me to the hospital. Well, Jeeves did the driving, but everyone went, including Super Mario. Did Harry tell you about him? And when we got there, to the emergency room, and the doctor saw us, I hadn't cried up to that point—I was trying to be brave—but when the doctor said the arm was broken, which I hadn't really thought it was before, not completely, something about it made me start to cry, which I know isn't a very double-digits thing to do."

"It's OK," I said. "It's not bad to cry when you need to."

"That's what Uncle Denny said too. He went into the examination room with me. I think the nurses wanted to make a fuss over him, the doctor too, but he just paid attention to me. When the doctor said he was going to set my arm in the cast, for some reason that made me cry harder, and Uncle Denny asked what it was—you know, was I scared? And I told him, of course I was crying because I was scared! And you know what?"

"No, William. Tell me: what?"

"Uncle Denny was *amazing*!"

"What did he do?" I asked. "Sing?"

William laughed. "That's a good one, Mum. Did he sing? No, he didn't sing! He told me stories. The whole time the doctor was working on me, Uncle Denny told me story after story. Did you know he could do that?"

Well, he did write lyrics quickly—everyone who read the mags knew that—but I sensed that wasn't the sort of storytelling William was getting at.

"No," I said. "No, I didn't. What kind of stories did he tell you?"

I pictured Denny regaling William with stories of his time spent in Malaysia. Perhaps he'd share some stories about doing drugs? Oh, wait. It was only the mags that said Denny did drugs, but Denny had told me he didn't, and everything in his behavior since he'd come to stay had borne that out.

"He told me stories of all the times that *he's been scared*! He said he's scared of flying even though he has to do it practically all the time. And on a day when he's giving a performance? Even after all these years? That's all there is, all day long, the not knowing until it's done if it's everything you'd planned and hoped and dreamed it would be. Oh, and big hairy spiders. Did you know that there are places he refuses to tour, like the American Southwest, just in case he might see one there? Anyway, he told me so many stories about him being scared that I stopped crying and stopped noticing anything the doctor was doing, and before I knew it, I was done and we were going. The cast is *so cool*! Everyone here at the house has signed it, and I'm going to get my friends to sign it tomorrow too. I'll bet Roberta will sign it *To Willie*. You'll remember that's my name now, right, Mum?"

"I'm still working on it."

"OK, good, because I've got to go, Mum! We're teaching Uncle Denny to play Monopoly. Can you *believe* he's never played before? He said he'd only do it if we let him be the Hat, so of course, we did."

"May I speak with him?" I hurried to ask before William could hang up the phone.

"Sure thing. Love you, Mum! See you…whenever!"

Clank went the phone.

As I waited for Denny to come on the line, I was mostly just astonished—that William had broken his arm when I wasn't there, but also at what William had sounded like. Harry had always been my bold talker, while William had lacked confidence. But the boy I'd just spoken with on the phone, the double-digits boy, had plenty of confidence and was talkative to spare. More than that, he sounded genuinely happy.

"Mona!" Denny's voice came over the line.

"Hello, Uncle Denny."

He laughed. Then: "It must be after two in the morning where you are! Is everything all right?"

"Everything's fine here. I just wanted to check in with

the boys, make sure everyone was fine there too. Imagine my surprise to learn that there's a new chef *and* William broke his arm."

"You object to the chef? If so, I can send him back."

"No, I don't object to the chef!"

"That's good, because he makes the best eggs Benedict in the world."

"Where is he sleeping?"

"The basement. It's a bit of an issue if I want to work late, but not much. He plays a mean ukulele when he's in the mood."

"Can we move on from the chef to William's arm?"

"I'm sorry. I thought you expressed surprise at the chef *and* William. Actually, it's Willie now, if you hadn't heard."

"I did, and I also heard you heartily approve."

"Hardly." He snorted. "It's ghastly, isn't it? But if it impresses the bird he likes…"

"You lied to him, didn't you?" I said softly.

"Excuse me?"

"When you told William those stories about all the things you're scared of. You told him big hairy spiders were one of them, that you wouldn't even tour in places that might have them, but that isn't true. You've been to the Amazon"—the mags had said—"and, I don't know, I'm sure you've been to lots of other places that do."

"Well, not everyone knows that, do they? And I wanted to come up with something anyone could relate to, and the kinds of things that do scare me probably wouldn't mean very much to a ten-year-old boy, so."

I digested that. It wasn't just that he'd told stories to

keep William's mind off his own fears, it was that he'd been so thoughtful in the way he'd done it.

"So," I said, "what are you really scared of?"

There was a long pause before he answered: "Being less."

And now it was my turn to pause as I digested that too.

"I should come home," I said abruptly.

"Please don't," he said, just as abruptly. "I mean, of course you can if you want to—it's your house, at least for the summer; your kids—but honestly, everyone's fine. William, especially, is fine."

"But isn't it a bit much for you? Watching them, particularly now that William has a broken arm? Wouldn't you rather get back to…your life?"

"Mona, if you're worried I'm going to scarper off and leave the boys in the lurch, that's not going to happen. I'll stay at least until you come home."

*At least until…*

"That wasn't what I—"

"Look, I have to go soon. They're getting restless. They're supposed to be teaching me how to play Monopoly. I'm the Hat. I made them promise I could be."

"So I heard."

"Harry tried to make me be the Thimble. Can you imagine—me? The Thimble? Well, you do have to have standards. Otherwise, they'll walk all over you."

I had to laugh at that. It was the kind of thing Jack might say or even me.

A thought occurred to me then.

"Did you ever get to spend much time with your own kids? Like this?"

There was silence. Then: "No. That was something I somehow missed."

I saw it then: the reason why Denny had come. He didn't come for Jack. Or maybe he did, but he also came for this, the time spent with my boys, the second chance at being a father.

"You're doing a great job," I said then. "I can tell the boys are loving having you there."

He didn't say thank you. Instead, he said a cautious, "Right, then," as though expecting there to be a "but." But there wasn't.

"See you at the end of the week then," I said. "Enjoy being the Hat."

So that, William breaking his arm, was the second thing that happened.

# Denny

The third thing that happened, happened on the plane ride back from our trip—and what a trip it had been!

For a long time, years even, I'd had a niggling worry in my mind that once the boys were grown and Jack and I were alone again, we'd discover that there was simply no *there* there for us anymore, that with the connective tissue gone, we were just two people bouncing up against one another from time to time. But the trip had shown me, shown us both, that we were more than just the parents of two boys. We were still us.

Funny, I hadn't known we positively needed this time away, but Denny had.

At any rate, it was on the plane ride back from that wonderful trip that the third significant thing happened.

No sooner had the plane cleared the runway than Jack let out a huge yawn. Then he folded his arms across his chest, tilted his head to one side, and shut his eyes.

"You're going to sleep already?" I asked.

He opened one eye. "You're not? Aren't you tired?"

"I am actually," I said. And I was. One of the great joys of our time in Morocco was rediscovering "we can have sex whenever we want to without fear of interruption unless we ourselves choose to call room service." On our last night, we'd turned it into a marathon session. We hadn't fallen asleep until we'd watched, arms around each other, as the sun came up, and then we'd only slept an hour—we had this plane to catch. So yes, I was tired, and luxuriously sore in ways I hadn't felt in a long time. "But I don't think I could sleep right now if I tried," I told Jack now. "I suppose I'm too keyed up about seeing the boys again."

"I'm excited about seeing them too, but I'll be even more excited if I'm not completely exhausted. And it'll be easier to get back to work if I rest now, since I certainly won't be able to later."

The whole point in coming to Connecticut for the summer had been for Jack to work on his music, to come up with enough songs to finally put out a fourth album. Jack's career may not have been big by Denny's standards—whose is?—but he did have a small independent label that believed in him and was eager to have something new to put out. As keen as Jack had been to accept Denny's offer of the trip to Morocco, when we first arrived there, he'd felt guilty about leaving his musical ambitions behind for two whole weeks. But then, during the trip, we'd seen and heard so many great things, causing Jack to make notes on any stray paper he could find, and I knew he was just as eager to return to the beach house so he could get back to work.

"Do you want me to wake you when food service comes around?" I asked.

"Only if they're serving lobster." He closed the eye. Then: "It was really great, wasn't it?"

"Which part?"

"All of it, every second, but especially just being us again. Know what I mean?"

"I love you, Jack."

"Love you too."

And then he was asleep, a huge smile on his face. It wasn't until he started to snore lightly that it occurred to me how rare it was—not the snoring; that was common enough. Rather, the part where I said, "I love you," first. It had almost always been Jack who would say it, with me then responding in kind. We were like a call-and-response in church, with me only able to participate if someone else led the way.

I kissed him gently on the forehead, knowing I wouldn't wake him now, and said it again even though he couldn't hear me: "I love you, Jack."

Then I rooted around in my carry-on bag for reading material, and so that was when I finally got the chance to read the magazine that I'd bought at the airport nearly two months ago, when we'd first flown from London to the U.S.

• • •

In the past, the mags had always been my guilty pleasures. I'd read them only when Jack wasn't around or when he was sleeping, like now.

I looked in the Table of Contents to see what page the article on Denny was on and was about to flip through to it, but then I thought: *Wait. I don't have to do this!*

Yes, when I was a young teen, I read about Denny and the band obsessively. Well, of course I did. I was a fan and he was a Rock God, and for a time, even more than that. Then on my wedding day, I'd discovered he was to be my brother-in-law. But in the ensuing years, we hadn't gotten to know each other the way in-laws do, not the way I had with Burt and Edith or Jack had with my own parents. No, in the dozen years after my wedding, I'd seen him scarcely as many times and always with other people around, so we'd hardly spoken really, and he remained a stranger and a Rock God, albeit one who happened to be my husband's brother. But now? After this summer? Why, we'd spent weeks together, living under the same roof. We'd shared meals, we'd talked—we'd even laughed. Who could forget the cake we'd baked together? And look how wonderful Denny had been with William! It would not be outside the realm of reason to say that Denny and I were now friends, that I knew him. I was no longer an outsider trying to look in. I was on the inside now. So what did I need to be doing reading about him in the mags like some lowly fan?

Laughing at myself, laughing at how silly that would be, I began at the beginning of the mag and read every single thing from cover to cover—from the Letters to the Editor at the front to the book reviews at the back; I even looked at all the adverts in between—studiously going around the article on Denny, not even letting myself look at the pictures. It was only after I'd read the very last page, with its ad for menstrual pain reliever, and looked over at Jack, saw he was still sleeping, that I thought: *Well, the mag is right here...* And anyway, wasn't it even more silly to deliberately not read the article than it would be to just read it and get it over with?

• • •

*THE NEW MRS. DENNY SPRINGER? HARDLY!*

Talk about your attention-grabbing headlines! And how ridiculous. Of course there wasn't a new Mrs. Denny Springer on the horizon. Denny would never have come to stay with us all these weeks if there were. Even the headline itself couldn't keep up the pretense; the denial was right there. Still, I did glance at the accompanying picture before reading the rest of the text. I supposed the person depicted was pretty enough, but in a rather skanky sort of way. And she did look frightfully young. But then I'd found as I moved into my thirties that a lot of people looked young to me now, and anyway, it was impossible to assess her true age, what with all the raccoon eye makeup. Denny's previous wives had all looked like models, while this person looked more like the sort you might see waiting for the Tube in a sketchy part of town. So what was this really all about? I read on.

*A fair amount of print is devoted to speculation on that evergreen subject: who WILL the next Mrs. Denny Springer be??? (OK, we confess: we create a lot of that print. But we're curious! Aren't you?) And yet of all the candidates, there has never been one quite so unlikely…or so young.*

*Fifteen-year-old Tiffany Glynn first met the forty-two-year-old rocker, frontman for The Greatest Rock-and-Roll Band In The World, following the band's concert two weeks ago in Leeds. (In case you're worrying that your eyes are deceiving you or that there's been some kind of misprint, we need to point out that that is not a mistake, and we did in fact say FIFTEEN.)*

*"I just hung out at the backstage door afterward," young Tiffany said. "I guess you could say I got lucky."*

*We're sure some would agree, although perhaps not all. After meeting her idol, Tiffany somehow found herself back at his hotel room, where events occurred that are too salacious to detail in the pages of this magazine.*

*"He was really good," Tiffany did share with us without prompting, "for a geezer."*

*Normally we wouldn't print the name of an underaged girl (Did you hear that, Denny? UNDERAGED!), but it was in fact young Tiffany and her mother, Amber Glynn, age thirty-one, who brought the story to our attention.*

*"I'm proud of her, aren't I," said the elder Glynn. "When I was her age, I had a thing for Denny—still do! My parents were positively horrified. Denny was*

*the kind of guy they warned me away from...which only made him more attractive! But I never got my chance. So you could say Tiffany is living my dream!"*

*Look, we're all for a little salacious scandal. (You know we are. And the bigger the little salacious scandal, the better!) But even we have to draw the line somewhere.*

*And apparently, we're not the only ones. Word has it that even some of Denny's most trusted insiders are appalled by this latest turn of events. Even Trudi Lundquist, longtime president of Denny's biggest fan club, was so disturbed by the news, she's resigned her presidency. In fact, we think she puts it best when she says:*

*"It was funny in the beginning, when he was younger. But those were different times, weren't they? Back then, you'd hear stories about rock stars picking up thirteen-year-old girls in L.A., having sex with them, and then leaving them on the opposite coast in New York, with no way to get home. We all thought it was all fun and games—cool even. But the old days aren't these days, are they? And the idea of a forty-two-year-old man with a fifteen-year-old schoolgirl? That's not funny or cool. And it doesn't matter if Tiffany and her mum think it is. It's just wrong."*

*We couldn't agree more.*

*As for the aging rocker himself?*

*He's not saying. When we tried to reach him for comment, all that came back were the sounds of crickets chirping.*

Was this, in the end, why Denny had come?

By the time we deplaned, I'd convinced myself that the article had to be wrong. It *had* to be.

The Denny I knew wouldn't sleep with a fifteen-year-old. Perhaps he might have once, when he was younger, when he was closer to still being a teenager himself. But surely not now. This girl was only five years older than William, only a few years older than Roberta from the beach. It couldn't be true.

And hadn't I learned, after taking them as my bibles for so many years, that the mags could be wrong about things having to do with Denny? They'd certainly been wrong about his partying habits. To hear them tell it, his life was one big orgy of drinking and drugs. But he'd told me it wasn't like that, and, having spent several continuous weeks in his company, I fully believed it. The man didn't even smoke weed. Why, he was practically a teetotaler. OK, an expensive-wine-drinking teetotaler, but still. He was in every way much more...*mellow* than the mags made him out to be. So they were wrong about that and they were wrong about this.

"Are you OK?" Jack asked as we walked through the arrivals door.

"I'm fine," I said. "Why?"

"I don't know. You just look like your mood changed somewhere while we were in the air."

"I'm fine," I said again, thinking of the magazine, which I'd shoved back down far into the bottom of my bag.

There was Jeeves, waiting for us.

"Boss sent me," he said.

"How thoughtful of him," I said.

And it was: thoughtful. I could see where after my initial push-and-pull with him, Denny had been exceptionally thoughtful all summer long. So surely, he was not the sort of man who...

I shook it off.

When we got home, I figured, I'd get this all sorted out.

• • •

"*William!*" I cried as soon as I saw him step outside as we pulled up in the stretch limo. Behind him were Harry and Denny.

I know it was a bit mother-hennish of me, but I couldn't help myself as I enveloped him in a big hug. I still couldn't believe I hadn't been there when he broke his arm, and now here he was with that arm in a cast and a sling.

"I'm so sorry I wasn't here!" I said into his hair. "Are you OK?"

"S'alright, Mum," he said, wriggling out of my embrace.

"Uncle Denny took care of everything. And it's Willie now, don't forget, not William."

"I'll try," I said, ruffling his hair as I drew away, and then Jack moved in for his own hug from our eldest.

"What did you get us?"

That, of course, was Harry.

"How about a hug first?" I said.

"All right." Then, when I'd barely had a chance to enfold him: "So. What'd you bring us?"

I laughed. "Come on. Let's go inside first."

But before we could do that, I had to get past Denny, who was moving toward me now, arms slightly extended. When he was inches away, too close for comfort, I thrust out my hand for a shake. We'd never been the hug-each-other-kiss-on-the-cheek sort of in-laws before, and I certainly wasn't about to start now.

"Nice to see you again," Denny said stiffly, taking my hand. "Welcome home."

. . .

Inside, I opened my carryall and pulled out the identical souvenirs I'd bought for the boys.

"What's this?" Harry said, fingering the maroon felt and the black tassel.

"It's called a fez," I said. "The men in Morocco wear them."

"Cool," Harry said, trying his on right away. "Do I look Moroccan?"

"What about me?" William tried to put his on with one hand but immediately ran into trouble. I moved to help him, but Harry beat me to it. "You should see me try to take a shower with this thing," William said, shaking the cast. "Well, no, you shouldn't, Mum. But really, it's very funny."

"Who're all the other fezes for?" Harry asked, indicating the items I was still holding.

"I also got them for Matt and Walter," I said, "plus Jeeves, and of course Super Mario if he's still around. It was so nice of him to come cook for you while I was gone." I paused. "And I also got a fez for you," I said, extending one toward Denny.

It had seemed silly even while I was purchasing it, the idea of getting something like this for The Man Who Has Everything. But then, it would have felt mean spirited not to get something for him when I'd gotten something for everyone else. After all, he'd done so much to take care of the boys, not to mention the fact that he'd paid for the whole trip himself.

"Here," I said, in a voice that could have been more gracious.

I don't know what I expected—that he'd laugh at the paltry offering or perhaps raise a sardonic eyebrow? Whatever the case, he immediately tried it on.

"What do you think, Willie?" Denny turned his head to show off several angles.

"S'great," William said.

"Cool!" Harry added.

"I think so too," Denny said. "In fact, I'm going to wear it on my next tour."

I hardly believed he'd remember, or even do it if he did

remember, but I had to grudgingly admit: it was nice of him to say so.

"OK, boys." Denny clapped his hands together. "Time to wash up. Your parents must be starving after their long flight—I know I always am—and Super Mario should be serving up dinner soon."

It was only then I noticed, for the first time, the heavenly combination of aromas in the air.

"Wait," I said. "Is Super Mario extraordinarily thin? Because I swear I didn't see anyone in the kitchen when we passed through there."

"Super Mario extraordinarily thin?" William echoed, breaking into giggles.

"More like…" Harry giggled too as he blew out his cheeks and made a gesture with both hands indicating the shape of an enormous pregnant belly.

"He was probably just in the bathroom," Denny said.

• • •

The foods served at dinner that night were all my favorites: a frisée salad with cranberries and sugared walnuts, balsamic vinaigrette on the side; she-crab soup ("I asked Super Mario if he couldn't make it *he-crab* soup, since I was sure that would be better," said Harry, "but he said there was no such thing"); broiled lobster with drawn butter and fresh corn on the cob; green beans amandine; there was even a chocolate mousse for dessert.

Someone had dug out a pristine white linen tablecloth I hadn't seen before—the dining table had been bare all summer—along with matching napkins, and there were even lit candlesticks on the table.

"What about Matt and Walter?" I said when we first sat down. I hadn't seen them yet.

"The boys ate already," William said.

"Then Uncle Denny sent them out to the movies," Harry added.

"Ah, I see," I said, tucking in to my salad.

I wouldn't have thought I'd be hungry again so soon—I'd eaten on the plane while Jack slept—but Denny was right: I was. And if I was hungry, Jack was ravenous.

"This is incredible," I said, lifting my soupspoon, knowing the courses to come because Harry had informed me. "And all my favorites. Jack, did you call ahead and tell them?"

"No." Jack looked surprised. "I didn't even know you liked she-crab soup so much."

But if Jack hadn't known, and the boys certainly wouldn't, then how...

I looked over at my brother-in-law only to find him studying my face, and that's when it hit me: It was all Denny. He'd been paying attention all summer, making mental note of it whenever I expressed pleasure with a particular food item. Then he'd stored all that info away, to be used when the moment arose. It was incredibly thoughtful—right from sending us on the trip in the first place to the table settings and the perfectly prepared meal. Of course, I'd been thoughtful too, but in a different definition of the word.

"Is it OK?" he asked now, just a bit anxiously.

I tasted the soup.

"It's perfect," I admitted.

And, of course, accompanying it all was that special red wine, the most expensive to be had.

But having looked at him once, I found I couldn't again, nor could I bring myself to speak. I was too busy dwelling on that ticking time bomb in my carryall, trying to convince myself things weren't as they seemed.

My lack of speaking drew no notice, however, because Jack took up the slack, detailing for the boys everything we'd seen and done during our time away—well, except for all the extraordinary sex.

No sooner were the dessert plates cleared away than:

"Who wants to play Monopoly?" William asked.

"With Matt and Walter gone, we could use more players," Harry added.

"How about giving your parents the night off?" Denny said, not unkindly. "You know, whenever I come home from being away, first I want a good meal and then I want a good sleep."

The boys looked at him with a lack of understanding. Surely, they were no doubt thinking, this wasn't true. Surely, when a person came home after a long absence, they'd first want to do all the things they hadn't been able to do while away, like, say, play a rousing game of Monopoly?

But finally the boys just shrugged.

"S'OK," William said. "But then can we go next door for a sleepover? Only, they asked us—"

"But Uncle Denny said we should spend time with you your first night back," Harry finished.

"Go on," I said. "But first, give us a kiss."

They both rushed in, hugging me at the same time, and I

wished I could freeze the moment: all the love in the world right there in my arms. Soon, they'd think themselves too old for this.

And then they were gone, banging up the stairs to get their things and then banging out the door.

"So?" I looked across at my husband, ignoring the Denny between us. "Sleep?"

Oh, how I wanted him to say yes. As much as I'd wanted to confront Denny, I wanted to avoid any confrontation that much more.

"You go on," Jack said, suddenly looking excited. "I thought I might go downstairs, get a little work done. All those different sounds we heard in Morocco..."

"It's like that," Denny said.

"Do you want to come?" Jack offered, eager to get started. And yet somehow, for the first time, it struck me—was there something slightly...*insincere* about Jack's offer?

"Maybe in a bit," Denny said. "I thought I might go for a walk on the beach first. All that food."

Jack turned to me. "Do you mind?"

Well, of course I minded. Hadn't he seen how much tension there had been during that dinner, however wonderful the food? Couldn't he see how much tension lay between me and Denny still?

But no. Apparently, he couldn't see, and I couldn't tell him.

"Of course not," I said, forcing a smile, feeling the quick kiss on my cheek, listening as his steps took him away. Then came the sound of the basement door opening and closing.

"So." Denny removed the fez, which he'd worn all

through dinner, carefully laid it on the table. "Why don't you tell me—what seems to be the problem?"

. . .

On the beach, it had gone full dark, but there was still a strong moon overhead as we walked.

"Look," Denny broke the silence, "if this is about William's arm, I don't blame you in the slightest for being upset that it happened on my lookout. I was upset myself, still am. But surely you can see that it wasn't my fault. Once a boy has learned to ride a bike, you can't keep him from falling, not unless you walk beside him the whole time. And you can't do that once he knows how, can you?"

"It's not about the arm," I said.

"What then?" Denny was perplexed. "Because I can't think of anything else that I—"

"It's *this*," I said, producing the two-month-old mag from the bottom of my carryall, which I'd grabbed before leaving the house. I thrust it at him.

"Well, this is nice," he said, taking it from me, barely looking at the cover. "Of course, after getting me the fez, you really didn't need to get me a second souvenir. But it is always good to have spare reading material, although I do tend to prefer Proust, possibly a little Martin Amis if I'm feeling like something a bit more modern—"

"Turn it to page eighty-seven."

He looked a question at me and, when I didn't say anything more, commenced riffling the pages.

But I no longer had any patience for this.

"Here." I snatched the mag from him, went straight to

the required page, and turned it around so he'd be able to see it right-side up. I jabbed a finger at the article with its picture of Tiffany Glynn. Then I thrust the magazine close to his face so that, never mind the dark, he couldn't possibly miss it. "This."

He looked down, saw what I was pointing at. "Oh." Then back up at me: "*Oh.*"

I hadn't said anything to Jack yet—because what if I was wrong?—but in that moment, the recognition on Denny's face, I briefly pictured how such a conversation would go.

Me: Your forty-two-year-old brother slept with a minor.

Jack: How minor?

Me: Minor. Isn't that bad enough?

In fact, I hoped never to have such a conversation with my husband. But the look on Denny's face now—whatever else there was in that sordid article, there was some truth in it too.

"How could you?" I demanded.

"Look at her!" Denny countered. "Does she look fifteen to you?"

I had to admit, she didn't. Still…

"Didn't you think to ask?"

"No, I didn't *ask*. If you're offered a huge, juicy steak, do you ask how old it is? I don't think so. Not unless there's some indication it's going bad." He waved a hand. "Ah, you wouldn't understand."

"I suppose I wouldn't."

"Too right."

"No, I meant, I don't suppose I'd understand how you can be such an enormous prat."

"Prat? That's a bit much, don't you think?"

"No, I don't think."

"You don't know what it's like."

"Why don't you enlighten me then?"

"Everywhere I go, there's not a woman I can't have."

"Ho! Is this you trying to get me to feel sorry for you?"

But it was as though he hadn't heard me.

"Even at that first party you took me to, all those women there—do you think there's one that wasn't thinking about it? Even your friend Marsha, with all her au pair problems—did you know she invited me to the lav with her to discuss it further?"

"She did not!" Marsha loved Biff. She wouldn't—

But then I saw it clearly. Of course she would. She did.

"Of course I said no," he said, "politely of course. But I've been leery of her ever since, made sure *not* to accept any invitations out while you were gone. Because if there's one thing I've learned: never underestimate the determination of a fan."

"I'm not talking about Marsha!" I jabbed the mag again. "*She was fifteen!*"

"And I already told you: I thought that she was older! As a matter of fact—"

"No. *You* said you never asked."

"Because I *assumed!* Look, one thing we need to get straight here: *I* didn't go after her. *She* came after me."

"And that's supposed to make it all right?" And now, suddenly, I was no longer angry. Rather, I was incredibly sad when I said, "She was only fifteen. *Fifteen.* Is that some kind of regular thing for you?"

"You don't know what it's like," he said again.

"Actually," I said, "I know *exactly* what it's like." Pause. "But then, you know that, don't you?"

"What are you talking about, Mona?"

"I'm talking about *me*."

Finally, the moment of acknowledgment, brewing all summer, had arrived.

REMEMBER WHEN I SAID GIRLS HAD BEEN KNOWN TO WALK on broken glass to get to Denny?

That was not a figure of speech.

• • •

The train from Paddington Station in London to Cardiff Central in Wales took just a little over two hours, and we remained giddy the whole time.

Stella had told her parents we were spending the weekend at Bria's. Bria told her parents they were spending the weekend at mine. I told my parents we would be at Stella's until Sunday. It would all work out so long as no one's parents called anyone else's house to check up. Since that had never happened in the past, we weren't too worried, although we'd never tried pulling off the ruse for quite so long before. Still, as we sped toward our appointment with fate, we were no longer concerned with what our parents might think. By the time they twigged to anything, if they ever did, it'd be too late. And besides, we had a concert to get to.

• • •

We'd never been to see the band before, although God knows we'd tried. But every time we had, either our parents said no because of the location, or tickets sold out before we could get to the front of the line. This, though? At the Coal Exchange? The arena only held a thousand people, max. Denny and the band hadn't played anywhere this small since their first months together so many years ago. But they'd decided to do a small-arena tour as part of some "Get Back/Give Back to the People" thing or some such, and I'd won the tickets by being the nineteenth caller to a call-in radio program. The prize was actually four tickets, but I didn't have a third friend I loved half so much as I loved Stel and Bri, didn't want the evening compromised by feeling the polite need to make sure one who wasn't part of our regular group was having just as good a time as we were. So I did a crazy thing. Having failed to invite someone to be our fourth, I didn't try to profit by selling the ticket, I didn't even bother to just give it away. Instead, I kept it. Unlike the tickets we'd be using, which might get torn or stamped at the door, this one would remain pristine forever. Who knows? I thought. If I were ever asked to put something in a time capsule, this would be my contribution.

• • •

Once upon a time, with Cardiff being the leading coal port in the world, the Coal Exchange had been what its name implied—a place where screaming men struck deals and traded in coal—with as many as ten thousand people passing through each day. Some said the world's first million-pound check was written in that building. But none of that mattered to us as we sat there in awe, scarcely able to believe our good fortune.

"Can you believe this?" Stella screamed, her eyes wide as saucers as she handed me a joint that was coming down the row.

"I know!" I shouted back. Then I took a hit, handed the joint off to Bria.

"This is insane!" Bria's eyes were dilating before she'd even taken a hit.

"I know!" I shouted back.

And I did know. Those other times I'd wanted to see the band and it hadn't worked out—none of that could've compared to this night. This small arena, the closeness, the sheer intimacy of everything. With so few people, you really could close your eyes, if you dared to, and imagine that every single song had been written *for* you, that every single word was directed *at* you. And me being right in the very center, as I almost never was. I felt special, chosen in a way.

The night was beyond perfect. It was magical.

On such a night, anything could happen.

• • •

Borne along by the sea of a small tide of humanity, we spilled out of the concert hall, giggling.

After a few more rounds of "Can you believe this?" and "I know!" Bria, ever practical, said, "So? Back to the hotel?"

*Hotel* was a rather euphemistic word to describe the below-rate flophouse we'd secured a room in for our weekend stay, but it'd been all we could afford with our whatever-we-saved-from-babysitting bank balances.

"I don't know," I said. "Why don't we go round back and find the stage door? The band's got to come out sometime. Maybe we could catch a glimpse?"

Turned out, we weren't the only ones with that idea. From the looks of it, the entire small sea from inside the hall was now out back, waiting. Still, I thought, weren't the odds greatly improved? After all, following most concerts, I'd be competing with tens of thousands of people, while here it was just a singular thousand. My chances of being up close were never going to be this good again, and I was still feeling special, chosen.

When the band finally did come out, however, they were so quickly hustled into the back of a waiting van, if I'd have blinked, I would have missed that flash of Denny's shaggy hair.

"That's that then," Stella said as the van sped off.

"Not necessarily," I said.

"So?" Bria suggested again. "Back to the hotel?"

"Excuse me." I placed a hand on the arm of the guy closest to me. "Are you from around here?"

"No, sorry." Then he gave me a salacious grin and added, "But I could be."

I ignored him, as I had Bria, proceeding to pose my

question to various strangers until one answered in the affirmative but without making any sexual suggestions.

"Can you tell me," I asked, "what's the most expensive hotel that's also the closest to here?"

"That'd be the Angel, over on Castle Street. Do you need directions?"

"Yes," I said enthusiastically. "Please!"

"So," Bria said, "not the hotel?"

• • •

In the end, peculiarly enough, the thing that worked in my favor was that I was *not* dressed like a fan.

"We can't just go in there," Stella said as we stood outside the Angel Hotel.

"We're not guests," Bria added. "They'll toss us out."

"Course we can," I said, "course they won't. Just convince yourselves we're guests with reservations who checked in earlier in the day, then just act the part. If we look like we belong, we'll belong."

I don't know where my bravado came from as I led us under the exterior arched portico and into the hotel, sailing through the marbled lobby with its soaring crystal chandelier on toward the lift. Their giggles in my wake nearly betrayed us, but I kept my head held high, all the while repeating the mantra in my head *I belong here, I belong here, I belong here*—as I instinctively pressed the button for the penthouse. That bravado. I think it stemmed from the feeling of being chosen I'd derived from winning the concert tickets, the feeling of being special I'd had sitting in the arena. I'd been chosen, made to feel special, once. It could, *would*, happen again.

They almost blew it again with all their giggling when we stepped off the elevator and I knocked on the penthouse door.

"What if we've got the wrong room?" Stella said.

"What if they're not even here?" Bria added. "Probably just get some rich nabob trysting with his secretary."

I shushed them, knocking more loudly.

"What do you lot want?" said the burly bouncer who answered, his arm muscles straining impossibly large against the tightness of his T-shirt sleeves as he held the door only partially open.

"Room service," I said boldly.

No sooner were the words out of my mouth than I stole a glimpse at the room beyond him. And there, in a room already crowded with all kinds of people, many of them women, *they* were: Denny and Lex, leaning into one another and laughing. So close. Even 8 and Trey were there. If I couldn't yet touch them, I could now see where a person might be able to.

"Room service." The bouncer snorted. "Like I haven't heard that one before. But OK. Here's the room. What sort of service?"

As I tried to frame a winning reply, the bouncer snorted again.

"Ah, never mind that. We'll take you." He grabbed onto my arm, pulling me forward. "But not you two." He chin nodded at Stella and Bria.

"Wait!" I said. "But they're with me!"

"Not anymore." He eyed their clothing scathingly.

Before the concert, outside the hall, we'd each bought tour T-shirts of the band. Immediately, Stella and Bria had pulled theirs on over their heads, but I'd just stuffed mine in my shoulder bag. What did I need with wearing a badge of belonging when I already had the special ticket to get in? I'd save that T-shirt, I thought, along with that pristine unused ticket, to be used in my time capsule.

And now that sartorial decision had paid off.

The bouncer spoke more to my friends' chests than to their faces, as their chests were where the band's name was emblazoned. "We don't need any more *fans* in here," he scoffed. "We've got enough of those already, don't we. Besides, you both look too young." His eyes narrowed at me in my sky-high platform shoes, skintight jeans, and midriff-baring baby T. "You're sixteen, aren't you?" I figured that must be part of his job, making sure that anyone who entered had passed the age of consent.

Something about being on the tall side—I'd always found people took me as being older than I was, while shorter females, like Bria, were often treated as being younger than their age.

I was, in fact, fifteen.

"Only just," I qualified, as if the qualification would somehow erase the lie or, better yet, make it truth.

"Good enough." He tugged my arm again.

"I'm not going to leave—" I started to defend my friends. No matter how much I wanted this, it was all of us or none, right?

But apparently they neither needed nor wanted my defending.

"You've got to be joking." Stella gave me a shove and I

stumbled into the room. "You're not going to *not* do *this* because of *us*."

"But what will you—"

"So," Bria said, waving, "see you back at the hotel!"

The bouncer slammed the door shut behind me.

• • •

"You'll want to take your shoes off." The bouncer indicated my platforms. "Don't want to mess up the carpets."

"Oh!" I said, feeling guilty. "Right!" But as I bent to undo the straps of my shoes, adding them to the lineup of those in the entryway, I was on an eye level to appreciate that the carpets were getting pretty messed up already. It hadn't taken us *that* long to find the hotel after the concert had let out, but already the floor was getting trashed with dropped cigarette ashes, spilled drinks, and even some broken glass. It didn't seem like whatever dents or marks my shoes might make could ever compare with that mess, so why bother. But then I thought: Maybe Denny, being so slight—and now that I was in the same room as him (oh my God), I could see how much smaller he was in person than when he loomed everywhere else—preferred to keep those surrounding him closer to his height?

Now that I was in that room, I actually had to actively tell myself not to hyperventilate, which I was very much in danger of doing. But I couldn't do that. Act too much the part of the fan, and Bouncer Boy would bounce me right out.

And yet, I was so aware of Denny, I couldn't stand it. A part of me was actually tempted to run back out the door.

No matter what I'd thought before about being special, I wasn't meant to be here. People should never meet their idols. And mere mortals should not come into the presence of Zeus.

And yet, there I was.

"Could I get a drink, please?" I asked. If I hadn't wanted to be just another concertgoer hours earlier, wearing a uniform band T-shirt, I wanted desperately to look like I belonged now. And since everywhere I looked, people had drinks in their hands...

"Do I look like your maid?" Bouncer Boy sneered. "And besides, didn't you say *you* were room service?" Looking a bit disgusted with me finally, like I'd let him down somehow, he chin nodded at a bar set up in the corner. "Help yourself."

I studied the drink options available: various whiskeys, beer, even soda. I'd done my share of moderate drinking before—Stella's basement, of course—but the buzz from the concert had long faded, at least the pot-induced one, and I wanted to keep my wits about me. Plus, I was in the process of formulating a plan. I decided I wanted to say hi to Denny, just that, and have him say hi to me back. Not such a massive aspiration, right? I figured, I was in the room—it had to be doable. But I also figured that if I just went up to him, it'd be lame. Everyone else was talking so naturally, like most of them knew each other—or at least knew one other person there—but I didn't know anybody. And if I tried to approach him now, what if he looked at me like, "Who the fuck are you?" And maybe Bouncer Boy would even toss me out before I got the chance to say anything. So my plan was, I'd wait everyone else out. Let everyone else get progressively more stoned and drunk, fall asleep even, while I waited here with my one beer and—

"Hey, new girl!" Denny's voice came from across the room. It was only when I looked at him, looking at me as he said, "Yeah, you," that I realized he was talking to me.

Denny Springer, one of the most famous people on the planet, the most famous person in my world, was rattling an empty glass in my direction.

"Can you bring me another ice water?" he yelled over the crowd. "With extra ice?"

I think my eyes must have bugged nearly right out of my head.

Ice? Denny Springer was asking *me* for some ice?

As I pulled myself out of my trance, I practically tripped over myself, all thumbs, as I sought out a jug of water, sniffed to make sure it wasn't a jug of vodka or gin or rum or something else deceptively clear, filled the glass, realized I'd forgotten the ice, dumped the whole thing, manically searched for the ice, located it, dropped some in the glass, *then* filled it with water.

I had one job to do, and I was determined to get it right.

*Don't drop this, don't drop this, do not drop this*, I exhorted myself as I carried the glass across the room, carefully negotiating the path cleared for me by the others like Philippe Petit walking on a high wire between the towers of Notre-Dame Cathedral.

I was halfway to my destination when I felt something sharp dig into my right heel. Involuntarily, I winced, wincing again when I took two more steps only to feel whatever I'd stepped on poke more deeply into my heel. Determined not to stop—I would not fail at this!—I forced the wince off my face, forced a smile, as I stepped ever onward. At last, when I was standing right in front of him, I held the glass forward to where he was sitting on the couch.

He hadn't even been looking at me—he'd been continuing his conversation with Lex—but when he saw the glass, he looked up long enough to acknowledge with a radiant smile: "Thanks."

He took a sip, moved to set it down on the table. And then, seeing the carpet behind me, he frowned.

"What's that...?" he said. Then up at me: "New Girl, what did you do to your foot?"

Before I knew what was happening, he was rising from his seat and then pressing me down into the place he'd just vacated.

"Oh, crap," he said, raising my foot, looking at the deep gash in the heel, the shard of glass protruding from it. "I don't know why Lawrence makes everyone take their shoes off," he muttered. "It's not like I don't have to pay to replace the carpets anyway every single place we go. Does that hurt?" Then: "Lawrence!" he shouted. "I need the first aid kit here!" And to everyone else: "Give her space. Or better yet: get out." And to me: "Do you need to go to hospital?"

I couldn't speak to answer. All I could do was stare as he cradled my foot, heedless of the blood dripping onto his own clothes. Then he was fiddling with a first aid kit. Lawrence must have brought it, but I hadn't even seen him. If I'd registered anything at all, it was the equivalent of arms coming in from offscreen to deliver something before disappearing, and I only distantly heard the sounds of other people hastily departing. All I had ears for was Denny Springer, making soothing noises as he worked on my foot. All I had eyes for was Denny Springer—Denny Springer!—first cleaning my foot with antibiotic cream and then bandaging it up.

"New Girl." He snapped his fingers in front of my face. "Don't go all deer-in-the-headlights on me now. I said, 'Do you need to go to hospital?'"

Dumbly, I shook my head.

"Not much for talking, are you?" he said.

I shook my head again.

He looked at me a bit more closely, narrowing his eyes as though I'd tried to pull a trick on him.

"You are pretty," he observed.

It was as though his words were coming at me on tape delay, and by the time they penetrated my brain, he was smiling, holding my hand as he raised me to my feet.

There had to be someone else he was smiling at, someone else he was touching. It couldn't possibly be me.

"Well," he said easily, letting go of my hand, "if you don't need to go to hospital, do you want to just go?"

Of course. The party was over—because I'd killed it— and now my heel was bandaged, everyone was gone, and it was time for me to...

With no one else there, it was easy for me to find my discarded shoes. But as I bent to pick them up, I heard Denny's voice calling to me from a different part of the room, and I looked up to see him standing in a doorway.

"New Girl. I said, 'Do you want to go?'" He tilted his head toward the room behind him and then, with one hand on the knob, gestured for me to enter. "If you'd like," he added.

No longer feeling the pain in my foot, I don't think I

hardly limped at all as I crossed the room again, now empty except for one other person.

• • •

Here's one of those things that people generally don't know about Denny Springer: what he looks like with his pants off. There may be rumors, it may get debated in the mags, but there are no pictures. And, true, some of the hundreds—thousands? thousands upon thousands?—of women he's slept with have been known to talk, but it's just their word against his, and he's not saying.

Back then, in 1977, there had been plenty of talk about Denny Springer's cock. Hell, there'd been talk for as long as he'd been famous. People would look at that impossibly huge bulge in those impossibly tight jeans and say: "Can't be real." Nothing could be that big. Some people even claimed to know that he stuffed his pants with balled-up socks. A stuffed plush toy was another nasty rumor.

But there now was Denny Springer, standing before me, removing his own T-shirt, stripping off his own pants, under which he wore no underwear.

I know it's rude to stare but...

"It's OK to stare." He laughed. "I call it my embarrassment of riches." Then: "Just don't try to take any pictures."

And then he was pulling my baby T over *my* head—Denny Springer!—and lying me down on the bed so he could pull off my jeans. I'd had to lie down to put them on before going to the concert, and this was the only way they'd come off. And then his hand was between my legs and he was looking puzzled—"Gee, that's very tight"—

and then he was smiling as he pointed toward his own lips—"This mouth was made for two things, and only one of them is singing"—and then his mouth was on me, between my legs, and it was *insane* to have his mouth there because no one's mouth had ever been there before—no one's mouth had ever even kissed my lips before!—and the things that he was doing truly were amazing. There was just one problem as he entered me, which was not without its own challenges.

Sleeping with Denny Springer. Of all the times in my life, I wanted to live in the moment. But I just couldn't do it. The more I tried, the more outside my body I felt— watching my body with Denny's rather than living inside of it. I kept trying to catch *it*, the moment, like racing after a horse's reins as it gallops away, but I couldn't, so even as I was living it, the moment was passing me by, part of my past.

He was twenty-four, divorced. I was fifteen, never been kissed. Still hadn't.

There was one moment, when he was on top of me, he looked in my eyes and—I don't know—it was like I was being seen for the first time.

But then, that moment too fled past.

"You OK, New Girl?" he asked a few minutes after he'd finished.

Still having spoken not a word, I nodded.

"Right, then." He yawned, rolled over. "Traveling day early tomorrow. I need to get some shuteye, but you're welcome to stay a bit if you'd like."

"My name is Mona."

"How's that?"

"My name. It's Mona."

"Right, then. 'Night, Mona. Sweet dreams."

When his breathing took on the even rhythms of sleep, I quietly put my things back on and left.

Out in the hallway, still holding my shoes, I felt an uncontrollable smile break across my face.

I'd just slept with Denny Springer!

If anyone had asked me to right then, in that moment, I would not have traded that fact for anything in the world.

IF I'D KNOWN IN 1977 THAT SIX YEARS LATER I'D MEET AND marry Denny's brother, I'd have done things differently, chosen differently that night in Cardiff. Of course I would have. But you don't get to see the future. None of us do.

• • •

On my wedding day, for the first time in a long time, I was glad I'd never told Stella and Bria about that night in Cardiff.

I'd deliberately wiped the massive smile off my face before entering our room in the flophouse of a hotel we were staying at, and when they eagerly asked for details of what had gone down in the Angel Hotel penthouse, I'd played it off nonchalant.

"Oh, you know." I yawned. "Just a bunch of people sitting around and getting stoned, talking rubbishy things."

"But what did *you* do?" Stella asked.

"Did you get to talk to *him*?" Bria added breathlessly.

"I got to bring him a glass of ice water," I said.

"*Ice water*?" Stella was incredulous.

"And I said hi," I said.

From Bria: "You brought him a glass of *ice water*...and you got to say *hi*?"

I nodded. The first was true of course, but the second was a falsehood—I never had gotten a chance to say hi.

"Well," Stella snorted, "I don't think that quite ranks against my chewed-up guitar pick."

"Oh, come on!" Bria objected in my defense, hitting Stella over the head with a pillow, the case on which looked like it could use a good washing. "She got to be in the room *with them*...for hours!" Then she added: "Of course, *ice water* and *hi* are not exactly the dramatic interlude I'd been imagining..."

"No, you're both right." I yawned again. "It really was no big deal, hardly worth talking about."

Of course, they noticed I was limping slightly and asked, so I couldn't help telling them about cutting my foot on some glass, and then I really couldn't help telling them about Denny bandaging said foot...

"*Denny Springer bandaged your foot???*" they shrieked in unison.

Honestly, it was plenty gratifying. I didn't need or want more than that, not then.

So, when it happened—Cardiff—I'd kept the best of it to myself, not wanting to share it. It was mine. In a way that nothing ever had been before in my life up to that point, it was all mine. As time went on, though, I did want to share—for the glamour, for the social cachet, to have my one moment in the spotlight, be *seen* by someone other than me; and Denny, of course. But by then, the moment had passed. They'd never believe me. They'd think I was making it up to compete with Stella's chewed-up guitar pick from Lex or Bria's cousin meeting Denny in a bar in Rome. But it was just as well they never knew the truth. My wedding day was chaotic enough, what with the Best Man being a last-minute no-show coupled with the revelation of who that Best Man was. If they knew the truth, they'd have freaked out. ("Oh my God! You slept with Jack's brother! *What are you going to do???")* As it was, they were freaked out enough. ("Oh my God! *Denny Springer is Jack's brother!!!")* Like I said, as far as freak-outs go, that was plenty.

There was plenty for all of us to adjust to.

No need to go all the way.

• • •

When's the right time to tell a man you've slept with his brother?

In the days when Jack and I were newly a couple, first sleeping together, first getting to know one another, we fell into the same trap many other couples do early on—we traded stories of earlier relationships. As if *that* ever did the world any good. And, as with many before us, the talk inevitably turned to tales of losing our virginity. It was Jack's idea.

Jack's own story involved an older woman.

"Babysitter?" I asked.

"Hardly! The only reason she was with me was because I

told her I knew someone well who it turned out she was very interested in. It seemed like a good idea at the time, but," he shrugged, "you could say it left a bad taste in my mouth. I couldn't escape the feeling that the one she wanted to be with was him, not me. I can tell you one thing: I never did *that* again." It wouldn't be until later, after I learned who Jack's brother was, that I'd put it together: that the man the older woman had really wanted to be with was Denny Springer, and Jack knew it. "So, how about you?"

I was tempted to tell him the truth. After all, it did make quite a story, didn't it? And wouldn't we both laugh about the fact that my first-time story involved someone who had the same last name as Jack? Almost like we were destined to be together. But, then, I knew that Jack wasn't a fan of The Greatest Rock-and-Roll Band In The World and its lead singer. So maybe, instead of being something for us to laugh over, bond over, it would put him off me.

In the end, I lied. I told him about my second time instead.

It seemed like such a small, inconsequential lie at the time.

And, in the years since, I've never been sorry I told it.

· · ·

There were only two people in the world who knew about that night in Cardiff, only two people who knew that Denny and I had once slept together.

And now, after eighteen years, we were finally discussing it, the secret that we two shared.

I'd always been grateful to Denny, in the years since my

wedding day, that he'd never once let slip, either by word or deed, what had happened. It had been quite the balancing act on my part, and his, never more so than it had been this summer, when we'd been thrown into such close proximity for such a protracted period of time. But now, at long last, there was at least the opportunity to acknowledge that it had, in fact, happened.

"So," Denny said wonderingly, "William is mine?"

"Of course he's not, you prat!" God, what was wrong with this man? "Can't you do simple maths?"

"Well, that's a relief." He ignored my insult, both of them. "I mean, he's a great lad, but if he had been mine, that would have been quite the sticky wicket, no?"

It was all I could do not to roll my eyes. Like *that* was the biggest problem here, *not* that I'd once slept with my husband's brother.

THERE'S JUST ONE PROBLEM.

It didn't happen like that.

Oh, everything about Cardiff was true—as well as what I did or didn't tell Stella, Bria, and, most importantly, Jack—but the aftermath? The discussion? The moment of acknowledgment? None of that ever came.

Because when I said to Denny, "I'm talking about *me*," and then I waited for the recognition in his eyes, it simply never came. There was merely a vacant look, followed by, "What are you talking about, Mona?"

A tidal wave of sadness washed over me then, a wave so tall that it engulfed me and I could scarcely breathe. For eighteen years I'd kept the secret, the one I shared with Denny—the one I'd *thought* I shared with Denny—and now it was just me.

"She was actually nineteen," Denny said when I failed to speak.

"What?" It was like trying to swim out of a fog.

"That girl, Tiffany Whosit."

"Glynn," I corrected reflexively. "And what are you saying?"

"What I started, what I *tried*, to tell you before. After the story broke, my attorneys looked into it, in case there might be a lawsuit coming our way. Turned out, the girl had lied when she told the reporter she was only fifteen. Her mother's older too."

"But it says—"

"I know what the article *says*, but it's true, Mona. My attorneys even have the birth certificate to prove it. I'm sure in a later issue of that...*thing* you have, there would have been a correction—they'd have to do that—although no doubt it would be in the back, where almost no one would notice it. Not that it would do much good. Once something like that is out there, people tend to remember the original accusation, *not* what follows."

There was some resentment in his tone, but not as much as one might expect.

"But the age," I said. "Why would someone lie about such a thing?"

"Why does anyone ever lie about anything?" And now he sounded weary. "Sometimes people lie for what they think are good reasons. Sometimes their reasons are bad. And sometimes, people just lie."

I supposed that was true.

"Look, I can see that you're upset," he said when, again, I failed to speak. "You're thoroughly disgusted with me, so I'll just go. But, if it's all the same to you, perhaps I should wait a few days? Only, I wouldn't want the boys to interpret my rushing off right after your return as meaning that I'd only stayed with them out of some sense of duty, that I hadn't enjoyed my time with them, when really I had."

I swallowed hard, nodded.

"You're still upset," he observed.

"It's just," I started. "It's just…"

"It's just what, Mona?"

I couldn't tell him. Not now. So, instead I went with:

"It's just that this summer was supposed to be about you and Jack finally getting to know one another."

And then he did a strange thing. He placed his fingers gently under my chin, a touch so faint I could barely feel it.

"Ah, that's sweet, Mona," he said. "But don't you know yet? You can't 'get to know' other people. It's just not possible."

"Of course it is," I insisted.

"Anyway," Denny said, "I'd think you'd need both parties to be on board to achieve something like that."

"What do you mean?"

"Well, look at Brother Jack. He's hardly been receptive, has he? Oh, sure, he's been pleasant enough, and we've had a few nice moments together, but for the most part, I don't think he's much bothered if I'm here or not. And if he'd had his choice? He'd have voted for not."

"How can you say that?" I said. "Maybe it was true at the beginning. I can't deny that Jack was a bit chilly at first. But can you blame him? You'd barely paid him any mind for twenty years! But what about after you started playing together in the basement? The jam sessions, the excursions on Biff's boat, the trips into the city?"

"That was just him trying to please you, because it was

what you so obviously wanted. I suppose we were both trying to please you."

"No, it's been more than that," I insisted. "It's been good you've had this time together. Jack's grateful. I'm sure of it."

"And I'm grateful too. It has been good. Thank you, Mona, for all of it."

I'd ask Jack about it later, whether he was glad or not that Denny had come, but I was sure he was. I was sure that I was right.

I saw then another truth I hadn't seen before. I hadn't done it for Jack—I'd done it for myself. Because as much as I'd said I wanted Jack and Denny to get to know each other—and I had—really, I'd wanted to know Denny. In my stunned state, I confessed something to the effect.

"That's a bit hard, though, don't you think?" Denny said with a wry smile. "I'm what I am and what people think I am, and sometimes neither and sometimes both. But isn't that true of everyone? Aren't you and Jack unknowable too? I'm just more unknowable than most."

He must have seen something of what I was feeling on my face because he said, "Aw, don't look so sad, Mona. Tell you what: how about if I tell you something about myself, something no one else knows?"

I nodded.

"OK, then. Did I ever tell you about the day I left home? No, of course I didn't. I was eighteen."

I did know that part.

"I told them I was moving to the big city with Lex. Edith, of course, just about had a cow. 'But you *can't* do that! You're supposed to go to university, *Dennis*! Oxford! What about *Oxford*?'"

I had to laugh. His impersonation of Edith in full-on hysteria mode was spot on.

"'How can you give this all up?' she said. 'How can I not?' I said. 'I've got to take a chance on myself or I'll never know.'"

That part was never in the mags.

"'Just let him go,' Burt said."

His Burt was good too.

"'But he's supposed to be a *maths* professor!' Edith shrieked. 'And he'll be back as soon as he's hungry,' Burt told her. And then, while they proceeded to fight, Jack, thirteen at the time, pulled me aside and hissed, 'They're always fighting over you. Why don't you just leave now?' So I did." He paused. "And I didn't go back until I was number one in the whole fucking world."

He smiled as he spoke the last, but there was a brittle edge to that smile.

I was aghast, for more reasons than one.

"But you can't blame them for that! Lots of people say they're going to be musicians, that they're going to be famous. And yet so few ever succeed. You can't blame them for looking at you at eighteen and not somehow seeing that one day you'd be"—I gestured impatiently at him with my hand—"*this*. No one could have foreseen *that*."

"Oh, but I do blame them. You know, you never quite get over that: the feeling that the people who should love you best just don't believe you've got what it takes to achieve your dreams."

I thought about that.

"So how about you?" he said.

"How about me what?"

"I've shared something about me that no one else knows. Would you care to tell me something about you?"

But there was only one thing about me that no else knew, and I wasn't about to tell him that.

"No? I didn't think so. But don't you see? Yes, I told you a story, but it's just one. So now you know a tiny thing, an unglimpsed corner of my universe, but it's just one moment. Every day for forty-two years I've amassed moments, and you can't possibly know what it's like to be me—you can't know me—unless you've lived those moments in my skin. Like I said, everyone is unknowable, Mona. I'm just more loudly unknowable."

Then Denny said he was heading back to the house to try again with Jack, see if Jack wanted some company while he worked, and he asked if I wanted to come too. But I shook my head.

"Hi!" I called after his departing figure.

"What?" he said, turning.

"I said, 'Hi.'"

I'd wanted to say that to him eighteen years ago. For eighteen years, I'd waited, wanting desperately to be seen.

"Oh. Right." He was deeply puzzled by me. Well, who could blame him? "Hi, Mona."

And then he walked on.

When he was gone, I thought about the few small things I did know: that Denny's life was defined by who he was, while Jack's was defined by who he was not.

And me? What was I defined by?

A moment only I knew about or remembered.

WHEN'S THE RIGHT TIME TO TELL A MAN, "I'VE SLEPT WITH your brother"? Was there a moment I could have confessed such a thing to Jack? On our wedding day? On our wedding night? Perhaps once the shock had worn off? Now? Would now be a good time?

When's the right time to tell a man you once slept with his brother?

There's only one right answer to that question:

It's never.

. . .

In the end, Denny stayed on for another week. During that time, he was the perfect guest. He played Monopoly each night with the boys—he was always the Hat; he hung out with Jack whenever opportunity arose, or when Jack would let him; he stayed away from the dayroom whenever there was even a hint I might want to use it. Here and everywhere, Denny tried at all times to be all things to all people. It must be exhausting, I thought, being him.

It occurred to me that when Denny first came, I'd expected outrageous behavior from him, and, even though nothing he'd done had been particularly outrageous—more inconvenient, really—I'd reacted at the time as though it had been. I suppose I'd been working out my own history. Now I found myself feeling more patient with him, more inclined to react with light rather than heat. And, realizing that I never wanted Jack to know what had happened before we met, for the first time it occurred to me to feel relieved that Denny didn't remember me. Now, it could finally be a moment in my life that was just about me. For so long, I'd wanted to be seen by others. Well, I hadn't gotten that. But I'd gotten something else. Finally, I could see myself.

Mostly, I just watched—watched all the men in my life—and thought. I wondered: just how well did I know any of them?

I'd see Jack smiling or laughing at something Denny had said, but when I looked close, I'd see a tightness there I hadn't noted before. And I realized it had always been there. I'd just never seen it.

If Denny's greatest fear was being less, perhaps my husband's greatest fear was not being enough.

I thought about what Denny had said about other people being unknowable and how all these years I'd thought the distance between the two brothers had been because of Jack's hurt over Denny leaving when, in reality, it had been Denny who'd been hurt by Jack telling him to go.

I wondered: just how well did I know my own husband?

After all, I'd been harboring a pretty big secret for the entire time I'd known Jack, one I would take to the grave. What secrets might Jack be harboring that I would never know?

I thought about what Denny had said, about us only ever being able to glimpse small moments of other people's lives and how we could never see the whole picture, and I saw that he was right.

But then I thought: Maybe it's not the knowing, because we'll never get to that. Maybe it's the trying.

What did I really know about Jack Springer?

That he was a good husband. That he was a great father.

In the end, it was enough.

• • •

On Denny's last day, I watched Jack and Denny hug good-bye before Denny climbed into the back of the limo, a hand out the window waving as the vehicle whisked him away from our lives to the plane that would fly him back to his.

Who knows? I thought, as I stood there waving, my husband on one side, my boys on the other. Maybe, at some point, Denny would invite Jack to come on tour with him or at least to play in the show, and maybe Jack would even say yes. And then Jack would know, at least for a moment, what it's like to be near the center of all that.

As for us, we'd stay on for the rest of the summer, as planned, and it would be good, so good—we really were so good together!

But it would never be the same.

I WISH TO THANK THE FOLLOWING PEOPLE:

- Jaime Levine, for wanting to work with me and then being amazing about everything
- Everyone at Diversion Books, for being so good to me and my book
- Jon Clinch, for being an amazing writing friend and early reader on this book
- The members of the Friday Night Writers Group who helped with this one: Lauren Catherine, Bob Gulian, Andrea Schicke Hirsch, and Greg Logsted
- Greg Logsted, because: you
- Jackie Logsted, because: you
- Readers everywhere

LAUREN BARATZ-LOGSTED IS THE AUTHOR OF OVER thirty books for adults, teens, and children. Her books have been published in fifteen countries. Lauren's always been fascinated by Mick Jagger, but the closest she's ever come to him is the nosebleed section at a concert.

Visit her at **www.laurenbaratzlogsted.com** or follow her **@LaurenBaratzL** on Twitter.